F HEADS AND DUCK SKIN

A Novel

LINDSEY SALATKA

swp

She Writes Press, a BookSparks imprint
A Division of SparkPointStudio, LLC.

Published 2021
Printed in the United States of America

Print ISBN: 978-1-64742-128-1
E-ISBN: 978-1-64742-129-8
Library of Congress Control Number: 2021901236

For information, address:
She Writes Press
1569 Solano Ave #546
Berkeley, CA 94707

She Writes Press is a division of SparkPoint Studio, LLC.

AUTHOR'S NOTE

While *Fish Heads and Duck Skin* is a work of fiction, I've drawn on the experiences I had while living in Shanghai with my family (from 2005 to 2009) for much of the material. At the time, life in Shanghai was both glorious and challenging. This book depicts many of the more challenging moments I lived through and witnessed. However, even on my most difficult days, I knew it was a privilege to live in China, study a language so much older and more complex than ours, and show our children another way to live, so (one hopes) they don't grow up believing there is only one "right" way to be, look, or feel. When we moved back to the US, I enrolled my three children in a Mandarin immersion school, and this remains one of the best choices I have ever made. I feel deeply indebted to the people I met on this journey and the experiences we shared celebrating the Chinese history, language, and culture, both in China and the US. I am honored to have lived there and to be here now sharing this story about how opening our hearts and minds can transform our perception, our understanding, and our world.

"Stop leaving and you will arrive.

Stop searching and you will see.

Stop running away and you will be found."

—Lao Tzu

July, 2005

"It's a bad idea, Piper. No, a terrible idea."

I looked around the swampy, football field–sized hut where we stood—inside the world-famous Shanghai Fabric Market. Fabric bolts, stacked in giant, colorful, Jenga-like towers, surrounded us, blocking any clear view of a restroom. I heard a man hock a loogie behind me, and I stiffened, willing away the exclamation that appeared like a cartoon thought bubble from my head: *Tuberculosis!* My eyes burned from the thick curtain of tobacco smoke; I felt like I was swimming open-eyed through ashtray water.

"The bathroom won't be very nice here; I bet you'll have to squat over a hole. I only need ten more minutes," I pleaded. "Come on, you're four years old, Piper—a big girl! I'll buy you an ice cream in ten minutes if you can just hold on."

"But I need to go now now now now now, Mommy!" Her lip quivered. As she clutched her crotch with one hand and her butt with the other, her ten-month-old baby sister, Lila, woke up in her stroller, observed Piper's distress, and dissolved into tears. Lila hated feeling left out.

I paused to problem-solve. Four months earlier, my American family, complete with husband, two kids, and myself, had relocated to Shanghai, a city famous for, among other things, its fabric markets. We had moved to "the Paris of the Orient," which had sounded potentially glamorous but so far had proven to be anything but. However, there was a possible upside: I'd overheard two expat women talking about an amazing market, even giving clear directions on how to find it. According to them, a person could purchase a new wardrobe at said market for the cost of a closet full of clothes from the Goodwill. Except made to order! After being measured by a professional tailor from top to toe! Finished in twenty-four to forty-eight hours! I had never given much thought to my wardrobe, but this sounded like something I couldn't afford to miss. Plus, I needed a win.

I had chosen one shirt for myself, and I had already found the tailor to make it for me. She had measured every part of my thorax and was madly scribbling diagrams and notes in characters I couldn't read on her tiny pad of see-through paper. I already had picked the fabric, too—a simple black linen. The shirt was going to cost me six bucks. If I walked away now, I wasn't sure I'd be able to navigate my way back through the harlequin, sauna-like maze—packed with people hollering at each other in close proximity—to this unmarked stall. It didn't help that I was directionally challenged.

Piper could just pee her pants. Wouldn't be the first time, or the last. I thought these things, I admit it. I was not in contention for Mother of the Year.

I looked at my girls. Four large blue leaking eyes blinked back at me.

"Number one or number two?" I asked.

"Two!" she cried.

I sighed. "Okay then, let's go find the bathroom." I turned and smiled at the tailor. "*Deng yi xia.*" Wait a minute. It was one of the few Mandarin phrases I knew. I pointed at Piper, crossed my legs and then pointed at my crotch. She nodded. My Mandarin was poor, but I was fluent at charades.

I pushed the stroller down the aisle and held Piper's hand as both girls whimpered. I turned right at the end of the row the tailor had vaguely gestured toward. In the far corner was a door-sized hole in the wall that looked like it had been knocked out with a sledgehammer. I knew I had found the bathroom—I could smell it from ten fabric stalls away.

It was worse than a roadside Porta-John in Arizona in July, the kind that hadn't been cleaned or emptied since the Village People were in the Top 40. A rectangular lean-to, about thirty yards long and with filthy plywood walls, each section green and slimy around the edges, had been scabbed onto the building. The "roof" was a patchwork of rusted tin siding. The space between the roof and the walls provided the only light. No bathroom stalls, no sinks, of course no toilet paper. There was only a long, deep cement trench jutting up about a foot out of the ground. The trench sat three feet in from the back wall and stretched the entire length of the room.

A short, dirty hose protruded from the shorter wall to the left of the trench at about knee height. Two women were squatting over the trench near the right wall, about ten feet apart. Without their unknowing demonstration and the ungodly smell, I would not have known the trench was a toilet.

The women stared at us as they squatted and chatted. I understood nothing but the smell.

I turned away and blinked, forcing myself to breathe through my mouth, eyes watering.

"Now do you think you can wait, Piper?" I quacked.

She shook her head and whimpered.

"Alright then." I sucked in air over my teeth. "Do you see what those two women are doing? Squatting over the trench like that? That's what you need to do. I'll stand up there with you and hold your hands. We'll do it together, okay?"

She nodded.

Lila turned up her scream as I stepped onto the lip of the trench. I didn't look at her; I knew that would just make it worse. I turned to pull Piper up. We faced each other, straddling the gully of stool.

"Wait, wait, wait a sec," I said, stepping down. "Let's take those pants off first and get them out of the way."

Piper stepped down next to me. "Should I take my shoes off too, Mommy?"

"Oh my God, NO!" I blurted and saw the panic light up her eyes. I paused. I needed to make this no big deal. "I mean, I think we should just leave your shoes on, because, you know, it's a little dirty in here, which is *fine*. Let's just get those pants and undies off. Then we'll step back up on that trench."

I crammed Piper's bottoms into the storage basket under the stroller and squeezed Lila's chubby hand. "I'll be right back, baby girl," I said in my soothing voice. She shrieked louder.

"Okay, Piper, let's do this!" I said, switching to my peppy voice. We remounted the trench and resumed our straddle. "Now squat down and get your bottom close to the trench. I'll hold your hands."

"Okay, Mommy."

"And when you're done, we'll stand up together and step down. I'll grab the wet wipes and hand sanitizer and clean you up. That should work."

We squatted.

"See? You can do this."

She stared at my face as she did her business. I smiled at her, projecting calm. Then I made a fateful error—I glanced down.

Why? Why did I look? For the same reason people rubberneck at car accidents, I guess, but I will always wonder. I knew what I would see. Best-case scenario (BCS), it would be foul and atrocious. But, of course, it was not BCS, it was WCS. There were layers of generations of excrement. A surrounding swamp. An overpowering smell. I felt my gag reflex kick in. I turned my head away from Piper so we wouldn't be face to face as I imitated a cat ejecting a furball.

And then it happened. We were both sweating. Her hand slipped.

"NO!" I screamed. I grabbed her other hand with both of mine and

4

pulled it straight up as hard as I could. Too late. Her foot sank into the mire as she lost her balance and swung her arm out. In her panic, she kicked and splashed a wave of sludge onto her other leg and my jeans.

"Oh my GOD!" I yelled. I picked her up and tossed her from the swamp to the ground in front of the trench. She rolled twice and then screamed, "Mommy!"

I spotted the cracked hose by the far wall. "Come here, Piper, hurry!"

I ran and she waddled toward the hose. I cranked open the spigot and doused her as she moved toward me, hard, like I was putting out a fire. "Turn to the side, honey!" I yelled over the hose. I sprayed her everywhere—her shirt, her head. "Close your mouth!" I yelled, but she couldn't—she was crying too hard.

Once I was sure I had removed every speck of poo from Piper, I turned the hose on myself.

I sprayed my pants with as much pressure as I could make with my sweaty, shaking thumb.

It was only when I felt I was as poop-free as I could get that I noticed the crowd of local women that had formed in the center of the bathroom. They were staring at me and my girls, smiling. Some were hollering and pointing. Everyone seemed to have an opinion about the ridiculous foreigners and their very bad day. I didn't want their opinions. I wanted their help, and I really wanted to cry, but my kids . . .

I dropped the hose and looked up at the rusted roof, swallowing the massive knot in my throat. It immediately bobbed back up again. I heard a woman laugh.

My eyes narrowed. In washed the fury. I looked back at the crowd and inhaled to full height. At five foot seven, I felt giant. I thought about my life in the US and how ready I'd been to walk away from it. How I had dropped everything—my booming career, beautiful home, great friends, cuddly cat—and left it all in the dust to move here and start from scratch. I had crossed the globe to build a life where I could be better at everything, a life where I could spend time with my kids without mentally writing emails, resuscitate my marriage (if that was even possible), and finally find myself, becoming the person I was put on Earth to be. I'd walked away from that life and every creature comfort I had worked so hard to provide for my family and myself, for this.

"What the heck are you looking at, you—" I hesitated, glanced at Piper, and then looked back at them. "YOU STUPID PEOPLE!"

No one responded, most likely because they didn't speak English.

"Mom!" Piper protested, sniffling, hose water still trickling down her face. "They don't understand you. And also, you shouldn't say stupid, it's mean."

I looked at Piper, so sweet, so unjaded, so wet. I looked at Lila, eyes like saucers, too shocked to continue crying. I took a ragged inhale, looked back at the women, and squeezed Piper's hand. I wanted to stop myself, but for the life of me, I couldn't.

"You know what, sweetie? You're exactly right. Stupid is a mean word, but more importantly, in this situation, it's the wrong word." I took a step forward. "Hey ladies! Never mind what I said before. You people aren't stupid, you're ASSHOLES! Well how do you like this, you assholes?" I reached down, grabbed the hose, and pointed it at the women closest to me. I spun that spigot hard to the left until it would twist no more and then I stood there with my two hands holding a hose that for some reason had lost pressure and could barely spray far enough to lightly mist the front row.

The women saw my intent. As I frantically tried to create pressure, grabbing the water line and bending it in my hand, they ran from the room, all in a fuss.

When the room was empty of bystanders, I dropped the hose. I looked at the dirt floor and then the tin ceiling, and I laughed. I laughed and laughed, loud and crazy-like.

And then I cried.

2.

Six months earlier

I switched on my phone as wheels struck runway. I needed to push back a conference call with a client, but my phone rang before I could dial.

"Hi, uh, I'm looking for Mrs. Martin?"

"This is Tina; who's speaking?"

"Oh, hi Mrs. Martin, this is Miss Amy? Piper's pre-K teacher?" She cleared her throat nervously.

"Hi Miss Amy! Sorry, I thought you were a customer. Is everything okay? Is Piper sick?"

"No, Mrs. Martin—"

"You can call me Tina."

"Oh, thanks. Uh, the reason I'm calling is everything is not exactly okay. As I'm sure you know, we've had a few issues with Piper on the playground lately. We have a parent/teacher conference scheduled with you for next Tuesday."

"Oh, right. I think my husband set that up."

"Well, Mrs. Emory asked me to call and confirm that both you *and* your husband will attend so we can talk about the corrective actions we'd like to implement. We'll need both of you to sign the contract."

"Contract? Is this a new policy for all the parents?"

"No, Mrs. Martin, this is for Piper, and it's specifically regarding the biting issues we've been seeing in greater frequency."

"Oh, I'm sorry. I didn't realize that was still happening."

"Yes, it is. It happened again today, in fact; we'll go over it on Tuesday. I just wanted to confirm you'll both be here, and that 4 p.m. is—CLICK—venient time for you since you've never been able to make a confer—CLICK—portant that we see you in person."

My shoulders dropped. "Yes, 4 p.m. works. I'll be there, Daniel and I both will. Thanks for the call, Miss Amy. See you Tuesday."

I hung up and connected to the new call.

"This is Tina."

"Tina, it's Greg."

"Greg! I was just about to call you."

"I'm still waiting for that proposal, Tina."

"And I'll have it to you tonight, you have my word."

"Tonight? I thought you said by 2 p.m.?"

"I did, and I'm sorry, but I'm just stepping off a plane and I need final approval on a few details. I'll have it to you as soon as my boss signs off. I'm scheduled to call him in fifteen minutes. He'll sign off, don't worry."

"I needed that proposal *yesterday*, Tina. Also, my new director, Jeff, is about to leave for the rest of the week, but he'll be here next Tuesday mid-afternoon to go over the implementation of the first steps of our roll-out. You need to be here in case he has questions."

"Of course I'll be there. What time on Tuesday?"

"2 p.m."

"Perfect. I'll bring coffee."

"Great. Jeff prefers a latte."

"I know what Jeff likes, I've got a file on him—CLICK—I'm sorry, Greg, I've got another call coming in. I'll get you the proposal ASAP and—"

8

The guy in the window seat tapped my shoulder and pointed to the aisle.

"Oh sorry! I'm getting up."

"What was that?" Greg asked.

"Nothing, Greg." I grabbed my briefcase and stood up, stepping into the aisle. "Can I reach you at this number later?"

"After four you can call me at——"

"Hold on." I sidestepped into the area where all the strollers and wheelchairs awaited their occupants. I grabbed a receipt and pen out of the side of my briefcase.

"Go ahead, Greg," I said. My other line cut in. "Never mind. I'll call you back at this number before four, okay? I'll have the hospital page you if you don't answer."

I answered the other call as I reached the concourse and hung a left.

"Hello?"

"Mrs. Martin?"

"Yes?"

"This is a courtesy call to remind you of your Pap smear appointment with Dr. Lee at 4:30 p.m. tomor——"

"No way, not a chance." I stepped onto the moving walkway heading toward baggage claim.

"I'm sorry?"

"I mean, I'm sorry, but I need to reschedule."

"I see. Well, looking at the next few weeks, Dr. Lee has a cancellation next Tuesday."

"Ha ha, no."

"I'm sorry?"

"Tuesday won't work. Let me find a time and I'll——CLICK—— Seriously? This is bananas. I'm sorry, I'm going to have to call you back. Hello?"

"Tina! It's Melanie."

"Melanie! I love you, but this isn't a good time."

"But this is when you told me to call you."

I stepped onto the escalator overlooking baggage claim and scanned the marquee for my flight number. "I did? Did I say why?"

"You said you wanted to see if I had openings for both haircut and highlight on Tuesday afternoon, which I do."

"Did I say Tuesday? That's crazy! Tuesday has become a cosmic joke, Melanie. Can we do it Sunday instead, like early early Sunday?"

"I don't work Sundays."

"Of course you don't! But what if I said I could make it worth your while?"

"Meaning what?"

"Meaning I'll pay you double."

"Double? Seriously?"

"Yes." I glanced at my reflection in the mirrored wall facing the escalator. "Oh geez."

"What? Is Sunday bad now? Because I'm suddenly wide open."

"No, no, Sunday works, but if you can also get someone there to organize my eyebrows so I look less like a blonde Frieda Kahlo, I'll also pay *that* person double. And, if you know someone who can legally perform a Pap smear, the numbers will really start to get obscene."

"But our salon chairs don't come with stirrups."

"Of course they don't. Forget that part."

"How's 8:00 a.m.?"

"Six would be better."

"Six in the morning?"

"I promised I'd be better about family time. Please? Pretty beautiful please?"

"Yes, okay, 6:00 a.m. this Sunday. I'll see you then."

I hung up and looked at my watch—twelve minutes until I called my boss. I would have to call him from my car, which he hated, but oh well. I stepped off the escalator and eyed the carousel with my flight number. Why isn't this turnstile moving yet? I thought. Someone, anyone, please unleash the baggage!

I squished myself into the line of fellow rumpled travelers and waited for the luggage to rotate in my direction. I waited and waited and waited. It felt like the arrival of the bags on the pleated steel oval in front of me was taking as long as the flight from Dallas to San Diego had.

I let my head fall onto the back of my neck and exhaled loudly. "Seriously?" I said to no one. I stormed over to a man wearing blue coveralls who was whistling and swinging his legs while sitting on the wall next to the conveyor belt where the bags were not appearing. This guy apparently had all the time in the world.

"Excuse me, sir, do you know what's taking so long?"

"I do not," he said, still kicking his legs like a little kid even though his temples were gray.

"Is there someone you can call to make sure our bags are on their way?"

"The bags are coming. They have nowhere else to be."

"Maybe the plane took off back to Dallas without having the bags unloaded."

"That wouldn't happen."

"Uh, I believe the bags from two flights that arrived after ours are already spinning on turnstile number two."

He craned his neck to see behind me. "I believe you're right."

"Thing is, I'm in a rush. I have to call my boss in," I looked at my watch, "two minutes, and I should've been—"

"Well, you can go make that call and come back later if you want, but I wouldn't suggest it, because the guy who checks tags at the exit didn't show up for work today."

I tapped my toes in annoyance. "Is there a customer support desk?"

"Yes." He pointed to a cluttered desk in an unlit glass cube manned by a guy with a Justin Bieber haircut and adolescent acne. The line to speak to him curled around the corner, ending near a cluster of new restaurants, all serving a variation of fried bar food.

His eyes followed mine. "You could go get a snack," he offered.

"I appreciate the suggestion, but I'm in a hurry."

"Why'd you check your bag then?"

I threw up my hands. "Because I was awarded a massive trophy at an awards banquet last night—an outlandish piece of metallic abstract art. And while it's very nice, and I'm sure it was quite expensive, it apparently resembles a weapon of mass destruction. But I didn't know that until I got to the security line, and by then it was too late to ship the trophy and still make my flight."

"Congratulations on your award." He smiled at me.

"What? Oh. Thank you." I looked at him like he'd been sent from outer space. He was far too friendly to be from this area. Maybe he was on drugs. Or a serial killer.

"You know, sometimes in life we must wait," he said.

I raised my eyebrows and shook my head, chuckling. "That's not what they said when they upgraded my mileage rewards status."

"He that can have patience can have what he will." He smiled and stretched his arms over his head.

"That is very enlightened of you, but I should tell you that I'm in sales, and in sales we have this thing called a quota. The more we sell, the higher our quota is. If I hit my quota, they give me a bigger one. And if I blow my quota out of the water, like I did last year? I get a sizable bonus, a metallic weapon, a President's Circle trip to the Dominican Republic, and *triple the quota* the following year. There's never a moment to rest and celebrate, not even in Casa de Frigging Campo! Every day I must inch closer to closing business if I'm to reach the almighty quota."

"I see." He nodded, looking faintly amused.

"Which is why quotas and patience cannot coexist."

"Patience is not the ability to wait but the ability to keep a good attitude while waiting," he said.

"Why, thank you, Aristotle." I looked away and put down my briefcase.

"With time and patience, the mulberry leaf becomes a silk gown. That one's a Chinese proverb."

I smiled, then inhaled sharply. "Oh crap, I'm late for my call!"

I hustled to the far end of the shoeshine stand and wedged my phone between my ear and shoulder.

"Tina, you're late."

"I'm really sorry, Chuck, I—"

"No excuses right now, Brian just quit! Took his bonus and went to sell heart valves. We're in a world of hurt. He had the second-largest quota on the team after you, and now we've got no one to cover Ohio. We can't have his deals fall out of the pipeline! Ohio alone could affect our stock price. He has a huge meeting in Cleveland next week, so you'll need to be there."

"But I have my own territory."

"And it just grew. Congratulations."

"I'm taking over Ohio?"

"Of course not, that would be crazy. You'll only manage Ohio temporarily, until we find the right candidate to take it over permanently."

"But wouldn't it make more sense geographically for Brenda to manage Ohio?"

"Brenda isn't you. Plus, she's a single mom."

"But I'm a mom too, just not single. Not yet, anyway."

"I can't believe you're not jumping on this—it's an amazing career opportunity! If you close half of what he started, you'll hit a massive bonus. You know that exotic Asian holiday you've been talking about for the last few years? This will get you there. President's Club next year is in Bali! Please, Tina, *pretty please*. I need you."

"Sounds familiar."

"What?"

"Nothing." I sighed and turned back to the turnstile. It was finally moving. The philosopher in blue was humming loudly and

maneuvering bags into some sort of unclear order. "Look, I need some time. Why don't you send me the new numbers in writing, and I'll talk to Daniel."

"I wish I could give you time, Tina, but there's no time to give. Think it over tonight, but I need your answer by tomorrow morning, first thing."

"Seriously?"

"Yes! My forecast is due to our CFO tomorrow night. There's a lot riding on this territory."

"I got that. Look, my suitcase just appeared. Send me the numbers and a list of what Brian was working on. When's the meeting in Cleveland?"

"Tuesday."

"Tuesday? Of course it is. Excuse me," I said to the woman in front of me as I wiggled past her to fetch my bag. "Tuesday is not good for me, Bill."

"Make it good. I promise, it'll be worth your while. You'll see."

3.

"**W**hy is there a gargantuan pink structure on my side of the garage?" I whined in every shade of grumpy. I was excited to be home with the people I loved, but I could feel a wave of exhaustion rolling towards me like a tsunami. My eyes stung and my arms felt physically heavy, as though the sleeves of my maroon suit jacket were weighted. My head was sweating, but the rest of me felt cold. I slouched in the entrance to the living room, still clutching my briefcase and the handle of my silver rolling suitcase.

Daniel sat on the couch, watching *SportsCenter*. "Oh, you mean the fairy house?" he asked, shooting me a quick smile in the reflection of the TV.

I slid my suitcase against the wall and set my briefcase next to it. "I don't know if that's what I mean."

"Mommy!" Piper ran in, squealing, and wrapped herself around one of my legs. She was wearing her favorite cheetah costume; her thick hair straggled down her back. Her bangs, self-cut five months earlier, still had a solid six weeks before the longest parts would touch her eyebrows. "While you were in Dallas, Daddy built me a fairy house! I love it so much!"

"I think it's great that your dad built you a fairy house, but I didn't expect it to be in my parking space, and I almost crashed into it." I frowned at Daniel. "Why can't the fairies live in the backyard next to the swing set?"

"Because fairies don't like rain," Piper said, matching my frown and jamming her hands on her hips.

"Neither do I, so it's great we live in San Diego!"

"No, the fairies don't like even a drop of rain," she insisted. "They turn into beetles if they are hit by *one drop* of rain."

"But I turn into a beetle if my car gets dirty. See?" I hitched up my maroon skirt, dropped onto my hands and knees and looked up at her, curling my lip.

"Beetles don't make faces like that," she said.

"The fairy house isn't staying in the garage," Daniel said. "I'm going to move it to the backyard later."

"'Later' as in today," I interrupted from my beetle position on the carpet, "or 'later' as in a year from now?"

Daniel looked at me with a quizzical expression. "Sheesh, what's with you today? I'm going to move it to the backyard as soon as the paint's dry. Is that okay? Or should I go blow on it right now so I can move it in a time more in line with your self-imposed schedule?"

I sighed. "I'm sorry." I stood up slowly and ran my shaking hands through my sweaty hair. Piper squealed and ran down the hall, looking to be chased. I looked after her and sighed. "Can we start again?" I looked back at Daniel. "Rewind the last ten minutes and take a do-over?"

"Yeah, sure," he said, looking down.

"Okay, thanks." I walked to the couch, leaned down, and kissed him loudly on the cheek. "Hi honey, I'm home!"

He clicked off the TV and stood up. "Hello, lovely wife." He hugged me and then ruffled my hair. "How was your sales meeting?"

I shrugged and pulled away. "It was a typical sales meeting. Up early, out late. I'm not sure if I actually ever slept; it's already a blur."

"Correct me if I'm wrong, but didn't you get Salesperson of the Year?"

"Yeah."

"And isn't that a three-peat?"

"Yeah."

"Well if kicking ass makes you sleepy, it's no wonder."

I shrugged. "I guess that's one way to look at it." I plunked myself on the couch in the same spot Daniel had just occupied. It was still warm, but I shivered from a chill that ran through my shoulders. I squeezed the bridge of my nose, lessening the pressure building in my temples, then put my hand on my forehead as though I could feel if my own head were hot.

"You okay?" he asked.

I looked up at him. "I'm not sure; I feel a little woozy. There was a guy sitting behind me on the plane who must have sneezed fifty times."

"I hope they arrested him," he said. "Turned his ass in to the germ police."

"My thoughts exactly." I dropped my head back and closed my eyes.

Daniel walked toward the kitchen and called over his shoulder, "Maybe you're just hungry. Did you eat on the plane?"

"Nope."

"Good, I made tacos. They'll definitely cure all your maladies."

I started to moan and then stopped myself. "Tacos? I mean, don't get me wrong, I truly, madly, deeply love tacos, but I've just had five straight nights of Tex-Mex."

"Well you're in luck then, because I made SoCal tacos—no relation to Tex-Mex."

I looked at him and blinked.

He started chopping something. "Did you sleep on the flight? In between sneezes, that is?"

"I can't sleep on planes. Remember?"

"Oh, yeah. That sucks."

I yawned. "Where's Lila?"

"Sleeping. Why don't you take a nap before dinner?"

"I can't, I'm behind on four proposals and I need to look at some numbers. In fact, I need to do that right now." I scrambled to my feet and walked over to grab my briefcase. "If you need me, I'll be in the office."

He looked at me and sighed. "Okay."

I dragged myself up the stairs, arms heavy and head light. At the top of the stairs, I stopped to calculate the total number of hours I'd slept in the last week, then tried to think of the last time I hadn't felt exhausted. I was too tired to recall.

I plopped myself into my black leather desk chair. I spun my mouse and the screen came to life, lighting up what looked like the top fifty of tens of thousands of emails. As my inbox screamed, *I NEED YOU NOW,* I forgot about sleep.

I clicked on the top email and lost myself in the deluge. In between responses, forwards, and deletes, my mind swirled with questions: *How will this proposal impact my quota? Is my time better spent closing business in Ohio? How can I train teams in two places simultaneously? I'll need to ask for more support. Who do I trust to support me? Who will do the job the way I would do it? How will I tell Daniel about Ohio?*

As I considered the last question, Daniel knocked on the office door jamb. "Hey, Lila's up and the girls are both ready to eat. Can you come down for dinner now?"

It's not a good time to talk about Ohio. It will never be a good time to talk about Ohio.

"Oh, uh, yeah, let me finish this one thing and I'll be right down."

"Hey." He sat in his desk chair and pulled it next to mine so our armrests touched, but we didn't. "Is everything alright? I mean, besides being tired and hungry, are you okay? You seem really tense."

"I am tense," I said, squeezing the bridge of my nose again. "I feel like there's a steam roller on my chest and a geyser about to burst forth from right here." I tapped between my eyebrows.

"Why?"

"Because it's the beginning of the year and I have a new, ginormous quota and a million things to line up so I start strong."

He snorted and looked away.

"What?"

"At the end of the year you say you need to 'end strong,' and in the middle of the year, you need to 'keep up the momentum,' and at the start and end of every quarter . . ."

"Well, what do you want me to do? Not care? Not try?" I pushed my chair back. "I could be un-tense and sit around building fairy houses, but someone has to support us." I rubbed my face with both hands, wishing I could retract that statement and erase the look of pain that had just flashed in his eyes. Still, the resentment gained strength and maintained control. "Someone has to be tense," I mumbled.

Daniel took a deep breath. "That's great, Tina. I can see you're still mad at me for getting laid off."

"I'm not still mad, I'm just wondering why it's taking so long."

"Because an engineering job that fits my specs is really hard to come by right now! You know I'm doing everything I can. This is going to take time and patience on your part."

I spun my chair toward him. "Why does everyone think *I* need to be patient when I'm never afforded the same luxury? No one is concerned with what *I* want—not you, not the kids, not the job."

He stood up. "What exactly *do* you want, Tina? If I got a job tomorrow, would you be less angry? Would you dislike me less? And would you spend more time with your kids? I don't think so. Your sole point of focus is your career, and, let's face it, you'll never quit that job—you love it too much, and you won't admit it, but you love to hate it, too." He walked to the door and turned around. "Maybe it's a pattern: you love to hate things, and I am one of those things."

"But that's not true!" I cried. "I don't have a hate pattern. I don't hate you or anything! Well, maybe a few things, but that's not it.

19

I'm just stuck. I don't know who I am anymore, but I can't make a change because our whole existence depends on me and my work, and I don't know how to do it half-way. I pay the bills, and I'm proud of my success, but my career does not define me, and this job is not what I was put on this earth to do. I am not Tina, the Seller of Things. I am Tina, the Something Else! But if I tried to pursue the Something Else we'd be screwed!"

"So you want me to get a job faster—a job that may not even use my engineering degree or my MBA—so you can quit your career and decide what color your parachute is?"

"I don't know if that's what I'm telling you," I said as I buried my face in my hands. "I don't know what I want anymore."

He was quiet for a moment, and then he said softly, "Maybe you should skip dinner; I think it's identical to Tex-Mex."

When I heard his steps retreating in the hall, I moaned and dropped my head onto my desk. *Why can't I do this right?* I thought. Why can't I do anything right?

I woke up three hours later with a piercing neck-ache. I stood and walked into the hall. All the lights in the house were off; all creatures fast asleep. I slapped my hand on the banister. I felt hot tears of self-hatred fill my eyes at the thought that I'd missed yet another dinner.

I walked into the girls' rooms and leaned over and kissed each of them before tiptoeing into my room. Daniel had cocooned himself in a duvet cover and was asleep on the couch in the adjacent sitting area—this had been happening with greater frequency lately. I squeezed my eyes tightly and exhaled, then padded out and down the stairs. I filled the largest clean glass with tap water and drank it in one gulp. Then I opened the drawer beneath the mini-desk in the kitchen. A glue gun and a Ziplock sandwich bag of replacement sticks were wedged in the back left corner.

In the garage, I found two clear plastic bins filled with plastic yellow daisies, pink roses, and purple forget-me-nots—remnants from a long-ago craft project gone wrong—next to the Christmas ornaments. I plugged the glue gun into an extension cord.

An hour later, I wiped the sweat from my forehead. The perimeter of the fairy house roof was now exploding in yellow, pink, and purple blooms. It only needed one more thing. I pulled a small cylinder of silver glitter from a container on a higher shelf and sprinkled a path from the door of the fairy house to the garage window. I wrote a note and taped it to the glass. It said, "Thank you for our new home, Piper and Lila. We love it and we love you. Love, the Fairies."

If only fairy dust fixed everything.

Daniel and I met during the second semester of our freshman year at the University of Arizona. It was a case of love at first essay test when, in US History 101, he leaned over to mooch a pencil and I said, "Sure, if you give me the other blue book in your two-pack." The rest, as they say, is history. His oldest brother used that line in his speech at our wedding. Looking back, it seems possible, however, that a modest surplus of supplies and a lukewarm appreciation for well-intended cheesy lines were where our commonalities ended.

My parents were predictably unpredictable, largely due to their shared resistance to the surprisingly difficult chore of raising accidental progeny. It was no surprise to anyone when they divorced before I turned two. I hadn't spoken to my dad since my sophomore year in high school when he no-showed at Thanksgiving. He had a new wife by then, but I assumed his second marriage would go the way of the dodo as well since the ditz he was married to was sitting next to me at Thanksgiving when he called during the pie course to say he wasn't *quite* going to make it. Second wife's uncensored diatribe against dear old Dad complemented the undercooked blob of canned pumpkin pie—my contribution to the feast. That holiday was a disappointment in every way—most of my childhood holidays were.

My mom's favorite pastimes were reliving her youth and making regrettable decisions. She had dated not one, but two of my grade school basketball coaches, not one, but two of whom had been married at the time. Mama liked her hooch a little too much. Her dad—my grandpa—had tried many times to intervene on my behalf without success. He was the only dependable adult in my childhood, so when I was eighteen and my grandpa died, I steered clear of my mom and my dad as much as possible.

Daniel's family hailed from Ohio, and was, in contrast, stalwart, Christian, and stern. With five boys, all exactly 2.5 years apart, they participated in activities like church, *on Wednesdays*, and vacationing at the same lake for the same week, *every summer*. His mom had had the same sensible hairstyle, *for decades*. They had organized, chronological photo albums to prove all of this. Photo albums! I couldn't relate.

In reaction to his buttoned-up, stay-the-course, grace before dinner and same-bedtime-every-night home situation, Daniel pursued a path with less structure. He didn't concern himself with routines or expectations. He did what he wanted to do and aimed to please no one but himself. He was even-keeled and well-adjusted. Kind and friendly. His resting expression was a smile, and not a dopey one. I've always envied his ability to fall asleep in a nano-second and his stress-free countenance. I can't even fake that calm demeanor.

Why? Because my personality pendulum had swung the opposite way. In the interest of being nothing like my parents, I was rigid, strict and calculated. No one could ever accuse me of not trying my best, of not working hard, of not showing up. My routine was rigorous and rarely broken; my expectations for myself were high and multitudinous. I set the curve in every class. I was at the gym every day at 6 a.m. My diet was limited and almost completely fat-free. I worked twenty hours a week at the bookstore to maintain my academic scholarship, and I wrote a weekly column for our campus newspaper, the *Daily Wildcat*. I was relentless and high-strung. I pushed myself at everything I did, until I met Daniel.

I never had to try with Daniel because our relationship felt easy and natural. Initially I must have been drawn to him as my polar opposite: his non-volatility, his happy-to-be-here attitude with zero angst. He was not gifted with freakish tendencies at birth and then left to his own devices to manifest them to toxic levels. After eighteen years of being me, Daniel was foreign and refreshing, like how a PB&J on Wonder bread might taste like a delicacy after a lifetime of rancid egg salad on a stale Triscuit. I never considered looking for someone more like me, someone who shared my tenacious drive. He provided a much-needed break from the voice in my head that incessantly whipped me into a frenzy.

I majored in journalism and received many awards for my craft. Before Daniel, writing had been the only thing to occasionally silence the internal critic. I loved to write, and since my earliest memories of latch-keydom, I had been maniacal about it. Stories and plays, poems and letters, and, when hormones kicked in, notebooks upon notebooks of pre-teen rants. Writing calmed my jiggy ways and quelled my inner vex.

Daniel studied engineering. Since early childhood he had been obsessed with robots, saying they were the "next big thing" and "someday we'll all have one," which everyone knew was as absurd as a pocket-sized portable phone. I thought he read too much sci-fi, but I also found him to be adorable and funny. Even his cockamamie dreams were charming. What he saw in me was more of a puzzle. I was cute but not pretty, slightly taller than him, with the body of an adolescent boy. Sometimes I was quiet but other times, often in the middle of the night, a deluge of plans and ideas streamed from my head. I became impatient and moody when something or someone altered my routine.

Daniel was good-looking enough to entertain other options in the female department. Once I asked him why he liked me.

He shrugged and said, "You sparkle." I still don't know what that means. The laws of attraction are strange and mysterious.

Early in our final semester, Daniel was accepted into a master's program in engineering at San Diego State University. The day after graduation, we headed west as a unit. We moved in together to save money while he went to school and I looked for a job.

We were both broke during undergrad, but in San Diego, money was tighter than ever. Rent, even in a dumpy apartment located in a busy, smelly alley, was significantly higher than in Tucson. I needed a j-o-b, right away, and no one was hiring journalists. I decided to walk my resume into every journalistic establishment in San Diego County until I found a position.

When I was almost out of both journalistic establishments and resumes, the fate eagle landed. After dropping my resume at the front desk of the *San Diego Business Journal*, I rode from floor 12 to the underground parking lot in the world's slowest elevator with Jeff, an extra tan, extra friendly guy with extra white teeth. Jeff acted as the sales manager for a new magazine with the same parent company as the *Business Journal*. He told me all about the advertising sales position he needed to fill as we crawled from floor to floor down the elevator shaft. He liked my pointed, persistent questions. He noted that I was perfect for sales, but because I had no experience and the magazine was a fledgling, he could only pay a small monthly draw and commission. However, if I worked hard, I could easily make triple the income of the already-hired staff writers in my first year. Triple the income? I envisioned myself buying food that was not ramen or Taco Bell. Purchasing running shoes that hadn't been previously worn. A new used car! I would never need anything from my parents ever again.

This was on a Thursday. Jeff said I could start in four days, on Monday. Did I want to give it a crack? Yes! Wait. No, I was a journalist, a writer, and writers write. So no. Hold on, yes! I was plagued by indecision.

Daniel didn't want to influence my decision. "Do what makes you happy," he said. I was too full of doubt and fear and determination and occasional hunger pangs to care about being happy—it's possible that I didn't even know what happiness meant. I only knew I didn't want to be poor anymore. I wanted to be the opposite of poor so I would never need help from anyone ever again. I thought about our bare fridge and the strange odor emitted by Daniel's car, which smelled expensive.

I took the job and didn't look back. Not until much later anyway.

5.

"**A** speculum is a medieval torture device," I whined. "And I'm pretty sure it's about to come out my nose."

Jennifer, a.k.a. Dr. Sanders, a.k.a. my OB/Gyn and BFF since grade school, glanced up at my face and then back at my crotch. "Actually, a speculum is a diagnostic tool used to—"

"No, no. Just stop." I shook my head, rustling the paper mat below me. "I know they make you say that, but we women know that—"

"I'm also a woman," she said as she rolled her stool over to the counter to grab the sample container and rolled back between my legs.

"Right, well, if it were truly a diagnostic tool, they'd have improved upon it in the last century. Changed the lines at least, like they do to cars every few years to enhance aerodynamics. *Something*. No, I'm certain it's an archaic tool used to keep women down. Immobile. Helpless."

"Once again, I'm a woman, and I couldn't do my job without it." She pushed her glasses higher onto her nose with her forearm.

I ignored her. "It's basically a car jack with a satellite dish on the end of it, used to identify signs of alien life in hoo-has every-where, and it was most definitely designed by a man. A real asshole of a man, probably in ancient Mesopotamia." I peered at the ceiling tiles, noticing the hole missing in the corner of the tile straight above my head. It looked like someone had taken a messy bite out of it.

"Relax and stop talking." She adjusted the beam of light.

"Relax? Please. I think you're getting me back for that time in sixth grade when I called you out at recess for not wearing deodorant."

"I'm not getting you back."

"But everyone laughed at you, and you ran away crying."

"Well, the truth hurt, but I forgave you the next day. And besides, if it weren't for you, I might still have BO today."

"Just admit it, I'm a shitty friend, and that's why you're torturing me," I said.

"We're both shitty friends because we work all the time and have families and life's very busy. But we love each other and always will." She pressed into my abdomen, one hand inside, one hand outside.

"Why are you trying to get your fingers to touch through my skin?"

"Be serious for once."

"I use humor to deflect agony," I said, shredding the side of the drape.

"You know what would really be remarkable? If I didn't already know that. We're done," she said, pulling off her gloves with a suck and a smack, then liberating her ears from the straps holding on her mask. "Now, tell me how you're doing while I wash my hands. Quick, before the nurse knocks."

"I'm okay. No, that's a lie. I'm a disaster," I said, and without warning, I started bawling. My tears blind-sided us both.

"Whoa, whoa, whoa. What's going on, Tina?"

"I hate my life," I sobbed.

"Did something happen that I don't know about? Did Daniel cheat?"

"What? No!"

"Did you cheat?"

"No!"

"Are the kids okay?"

"They're fine!"

"Did you get fired?"

"Of course not, I got promoted," I said and cried harder.

Jennifer sat heavily on her stool, brows furrowed. She leaned toward the sink, pulled three tissues from a box, and held them out to me.

"Thank you," I whimpered.

She waited for me to quiet down and then said softly, "I can't help you, or even comfort you, if I don't know what happened."

"Nothing happened, I swear."

"So Daniel's fine, the job's great, kids are healthy, home's still standing?"

"Yes, yes, go ahead and say it. I'm despicable," I wailed.

"You'll never be despicable," she said. "However, if nothing's changed, it may be time to watch my gratitude DVD again."

"No, Jennifer. It's not . . . no," I said firmly.

She frowned at me as I stood and tugged on my underwear, sniffling.

"I've watched umpteen series of DVDs, listened to endless sets of self-help books on cassette, and even completed the bonus work-books. I've moved my cheese, been highly effective, discovered my strengths and then workshopped the snot out of them. I probably pay for Brenda's entire car lease on her new 5 Series."

"Wait, who's Brenda?"

"The therapist I've gone to since I had Piper!"

"Oh. That's right."

"Nothing's changed except that I become more aware every day that when my kids cry? Like this?" I waved my hands at myself. "They don't ask for me. I don't comfort them, Jen, *they barely know me*. And after all we went through to conceive . . ."

"I remember." Jennifer sighed.

"And Daniel is, I don't know. He's someone I don't understand at all. And Jen," I leaned toward her and whispered, "I'm starting to think I never will!"

"Because he's from Mars and——"

"I know Jen, I read that book, too! But the problem is, Daniel and I are on two different journeys, and the roads are veering even farther apart. There is so much distance between us that I'm not sure we'll ever be connected again." I wiped my eyes and took a deep breath. "I've been working at my company for ten years—two years longer than we've been married—and the work just grows and grows, and I don't want it to grow anymore because it's taken over everything, but I can't make it shrink because I'll get fired. And then where will we be?"

"You could always get a different job?"

"No, I can't! Our monthly expenses are too big now for me to make any dramatic changes. I could never quit my job and, you know, go build homes in Ecuador with my family. I have to *feed* my family! And pay for daycare and preschool and ballet and piano and soccer and baby singing time and all the rest of it!"

"Do you want to go to Ecuador?"

"No! Forget I said Ecuador. I just want a lighter burden. Life feels too heavy; there's too much pressure bearing down from every direction." I blew my nose and squinted at her. "Hey, wait a sec, why don't you feel heavy?"

"What do you mean?"

I balled up my tissues and lined them up on the crease of the exam table. "I mean, we're in the same boat. You work your ass off supporting your kids and paying your house payment. Jeff must make one-tenth of what you bring home."

"Well his job's a lot more flexible."

"So why don't you feel the weight of the world? You don't seem miserable. *Why aren't you miserable, Jennifer?*"

She thought for a moment. "Because I have a good life?"

"But so do I!"

She shrugged. "I love what I do."

I looked at her like she was crazy. "Seriously? You love this?" I pointed at the small square of an instrument table with both hands. "And these?" I waved at the stirrups.

She gave me a look that I disregarded. "My work entails more than vaginal exams."

"I know that, you delivered my babies."

"I'm guessing you wouldn't love my job, Tina, but I've always wanted to be doing exactly what I'm doing, looking after the health and well-being of women. Nurturing and fostering life is a privilege to me. Do I love it every day? No. Do I occasionally run the numbers for early retirement? Absolutely. But on the macro, I love what I do."

"That's so great." I started sobbing again. "I'm really happy for you." I walked over to the sink and pulled out four more tissues.

"You sound ecstatic."

"I am ecstatic! I just can't relate."

"You love parts of your job, admit it!"

"Of course I do! The money, the trips, the other rewards, the recognition . . . but the work itself is bleeding me dry."

"I remember how much you loved writing," Jennifer recalled.

I snorted. "I also loved playing trombone in the eighth grade honor band." I sniffed. "But I couldn't have supported a family with either of those things, so I jumped the track and started in sales. The irony is, if I'd sucked at sales, I'd probably have gone back to writing and be living my dream right now, like you're doing, except a lower rent dream—more of a Stouffer's/Ikea-type dream. My lifestyle would've never become so grandiose and expensive. I'd have never ended up trapped in this career." I dropped my face into my hands and took a deep breath, then another. "Sometimes I want to disappear," I said softly.

"Tina! What're you saying?" She strode up and put her hands on my shoulders. "Do you really mean that?"

"No," I said into my hands. "I don't know. I'd never hurt myself, if that's what it sounded like. I'm too big a chicken."

She squeezed my shoulders and then let go, gently pulling my hands away from my face to hold onto them. I stared at my toes, curled them, wondered where my flats were.

"That's where you're wrong, Tina. You're not too chicken, you're too *brave*. You've planted yourself firmly in this struggle, because that's exactly how brave you are. Even this—questioning your life and your choices—this is incredibly brave. Tina, look at me."

I blinked, sniffed, and lifted my head, lips quaking even as I willed them not to.

"The next level of your bravery is recognizing that this place you're in, where you feel so terrible? It's all part of the journey. My path was more direct, or at least it has been so far. But yours? Who knows where it will take you? Of all people, Tina, you aren't stuck, not here, not anywhere. You just *feel* stuck because you're banking into an unfamiliar turn that feels a lot like a corner."

"I'm pretty sure it's a corner," I said, letting go of her hands and wiping my eyes.

"It's not a corner."

"Then it's a ridiculously long turn, and I wish the exit sign would light up because it's getting tedious."

Jennifer smiled at me. "There's the one-liner I've been waiting for." She hugged me and said into my ear, "You're brave and your time is coming, do you believe me?"

"I want to."

"You *must* believe me. Please, be patient. Things will get better, we just don't know how yet."

I squeezed my eyes shut, then opened them again. "Yeah, okay." I nodded.

She grabbed my chart and started jotting notes while still looking at me. "Say it then: 'I'm brave.'"

I groaned. "I'm brave, mostly."

"*No.* Say, 'I'm brave, always.'"

I inhaled. "I'm brave, always."

"This feels like a corner, but it's only a blind turn. Say it."

I looked at her and wiped a fresh tear. "This feels like a corner, but it's only a blind turn."

"This is all part of my journey," she said, nodding at me.

"This is all part of my journey," I said, nodding back.

"We can stop chanting now."

"We can stop chanting now."

Jennifer looked at me and rolled her eyes. She put down the file and stood up.

"I'm sorry I vented to you," I said.

"Please don't apologize. Come on, we've known each other too long."

"But I can never repay your kindness."

"Actually," she clicked her pen quickly several times in a row, signaling the arrival of a great idea, "you can."

I cocked my head. "Really?"

"Yes, I need you desperately, in fact. Kyra's hosting an all-women's career event at her house next Thursday night."

"Wait, your brother's wife, Kyra?"

"Yes! And everyone is required to bring a friend. I have missed the last three of these event-things and Kyra is counting. If I don't go to this one, I'll lose my seat at Thanksgiving. And I don't have a clue how to cook a turkey! *Please* come with me. I need you to, *please.*"

"But I thought Kyra was a stay-at-home mom?"

"She was! I mean, she is! Look, I don't know what she does all day, I just know I need to show up for this thing or I'm eating Thanksgiving at some dodgy Chinese restaurant."

"You can always come skiing with us," I said. "I won a week at a ski-in-ski-out chalet in Vail. We went last year, too. I'm telling you, the place is phenom—"

"Tina!"

"Alright, fine, I'll go," I grumbled.

"Thank you!"

I paused and turned my head to look at her out of the side of my eyes. "Wait a sec. Is this one of those event-things where people try to sell you a bunch of overpriced crap you don't need?"

"I'm not going to lie. Yes."

"But I hate those things! Talk about a trap, those events are terrible! Please, Jennifer, you can ask me to do anything else, just not this."

"Tina, *I need you*. I wouldn't ask if I didn't."

I moaned. "Ugh. Fine."

There was a knock on the door and Jennifer opened it. The nurse handed her a new chart and said something under her breath.

"Okay, yes," Jennifer said to the nurse before turning to me. "I gotta run, but I owe you forever. I'll pick you up at 6 p.m. next Thursday. That's nine days from now. Put it in your calendar. Don't forget!"

6.

"**P**lease pay careful attention to where my rectus abdominis intersects with my external obliques," Emilio, the fitness trainer, instructed in a South American purr. He stood in the center of a large grassy expanse adjacent to Kyra's infinity pool wearing minute purple shorts. His dark hair was secured in a low ponytail except for a few rogue pieces near his temples which waved playfully around his face, tickling his prominent jawline. He was about 6'3" or whatever the perfect height of a man is.

He arranged his arms into side steeples, fingers grazing his navel, and contracted his stomach muscles, turning slightly to and fro so we could identify the area he was referring to. He looked like a museum piece—an evenly tan, talking, flexing statue. Forty women were fanned in a semi-circle around him, not blinking. Water burbled from a large spherical stone water feature behind him.

He dropped into an effortless handstand, first with his legs straight up, then splitting them until they were horizontal. His knees remained at his sides as he slowly brought his feet back to center, about a foot above his groin.

The crowd emitted a low ooooooh sound punctuated by some stray coughs. Women in black halter dresses circled silently with trays of champagne flutes.

"The lower oblique is an area where we often lose the reins

once we have children, ladies," he said, casually upside down. "This will be one of the first areas we address in our sessions."

"Who knew there was such a thing as a lower oblique?" I whispered into Jennifer's ear. "I thought it was a universal soft and squishy place."

"I knew there was such a thing. I'm instructing myself not to look at his lower oblique, but my eyes refuse to obey," Jennifer whispered back.

"You mean because his lower obliques extend into the front of his tiny pants?"

Jennifer snort-coughed as Kyra suddenly appeared like a floating magical fairy between us, resting her arms lightly on our shoulders. "Bless you," Kyra said and produced a dazzling smile. "May I borrow you two for a moment?"

"Right now?" Jennifer looked at her, startled. "That's just mean."

Kyra threw her head back and made soft musical sounds. "I won't tell my brother you said that." She winked and grabbed our hands. "Don't worry, you can come back; Emilio will be posing on the grass for the next two hours."

We walked past the four perfectly adorned tables on her patio and into her kitchen, where every surface gleamed with polished onyx and stainless steel. The back wall looked like the control panel of a spacecraft—flecks in the onyx panels were twinkling like distant stars, control lights blinked, screens communicated coded messages, and hidden latches led to secret compartments. The appliances, while certainly running, were not humming, grinding, or mimicking the sound of an airplane about to take off. I made a mental note to call my contractor the next day to modernize my weak excuse for a canteen.

"This is where the magic will happen later," Kyra said, smiling.

"You hired a magician?" I asked. Jennifer frowned.

"No, better. I'm doing a cooking demonstration. It starts at seven. You won't want to miss it." She looked at her watch, tapping the crystal. "Oh geez, tick tock, I better show you around so you can make it back in time. Follow me." She hustled through an archway and then another archway, stopping at a sitting area with a large low dark wood table covered in scarves and infant-sized handbags. "I'm not sure what Jennifer told you about tonight, Tina, but we run this party twice a year so our neighborhood mom-preneurs, including myself, have the opportunity to show their wares to our community of women in the interest of SIS."

I squinted at Kyra and then at Jennifer. "Am I, wait, who's SIS?"

Kyra held up three fingers and ticked them off one at a time. "SIS means to Spread the Word, Inspire Others, and Sell A Bunch of Stuff. It's our SISterhood, get it? We're all SISters here." Kyra grinned. "And we're always looking to grow our network, with people just like you." She cocked her head and raised her eyebrows. "We can talk about that part later. In the meantime, enjoy a stuffed mushroom!" She plucked a pewter oval filled with glistening orbs on toothpicks from the corner of the table and held it out to me.

"I'm really full, I—" She pushed the platter closer. "Yeah, okay, thank you." I picked up a toothpick and worked the mushroom off with my teeth while glaring at Jennifer with one eyebrow raised.

"That's pretty good." I chewed slowly while calculating how many hours I would need to stay up later to finish my paperwork if I couldn't escape until after the cooking demonstration.

Kyra gestured and said, "Follow me," as she glided to another low wooden table in the corner. She swept her arms over it a la Vanna White. "I thought I'd bring you here first, Tina, because, while I honestly love your suit and am well-aware that the dress-like-a-man, wear-a-tux-to-the-Oscars thing is very hot this year, women can always, *always*, add a special something to their outfit. Something that says, *I may be all business, but I'm well-acquainted with my feminine side.* And Tessa has some scarves here that, no matter what the season, can help you make a signature statement and create that Wow moment. Wait, where's Tessa?"

I looked down at my brown work suit. It was a more unfortunate, medium shade of brown than what I'd envisioned when I'd bought it five or so years earlier, more manure-of-horse-on-way-to-glue-factory than exotic, dark cacao. Had this suit always been this color and I'd only just now realized it? I never made time to shop, but maybe the situation was approaching dire. I sighed as I noticed a crumb stuck in the buttonhole of my lapel. A large crumb, the size of a small chunk of gravel, probably from the stale-ish crust of the hospital kiosk turkey sandwich I'd eaten for lunch. I flicked it away quickly and then looked up.

"I'm sure Tessa will fill you in on the possibilities, especially since, get this, she was a stylist to the stars!" Kyra's face filled with delight and then immediately switched to thoughtful mode. She tapped on her smooth forehead with a long black sparkly nail the same color as her backsplash. "Let me think, what else might you need? We have a mind-blowing eye cream that is scientifically proven to reduce crow's feet *and* puffiness, a spot remover which is fantastic for both wood-burning fireplace facades *and* grout, flavored olive oils, hand-crafted soaps . . ."

I nodded and thought about the fight I'd started with Daniel right before Jennifer rang my doorbell to pick me up for this party. How I'd been furious with him because my day had started at 4 a.m. and he had left the milk on the counter since breakfast. The babysitter hustled the kids into the backyard as I seethed, convinced that the warm milk on the counter was an irrefutable sign that Daniel was a careless, selfish man-child who was allergic to effort and would never amount to anything but the type of person who leaves milk on the counter. "I am coordinating and overseeing the surgical implantations of eleven products in three states! I've been on four flights in four days! And, and . . ." my hands quivered as I held them in the direction of the milk. My body was a neon sign blinking DISGUST as I turned away from him and the damning evidence and stormed up the stairs.

Ding dong.

"Oh shit, Jennifer," I'd said as I opened the door, still wild-eyed. Our bedroom door slammed above us.

Jennifer didn't seem to notice. "Oh yes, it's ladies' night, and the feeling's right," she sang as she hugged me in her wrinkled blue scrubs. "I got held up at work, but now it's time to move out!"

"I completely forgot about tonight's event-thing. I just walked in the door, and it's a monumentally bad time for me to leave. I've barely seen the kids."

"Yeah, my kids haven't laid eyes on me since yesterday morning, and guess what? They'll be just fine. *But I won't be fine* if I don't show up at this thing *with you at my side.*"

"But you don't understand."

"I understand that it looks like you could use a cold glass of chard and a night with low expectations and your favorite friend. Come on, there'll be plenty of wine there, but maybe bring a bottle, just in case. Something not by Charles Shaw. We gotta go! I sense Kyra is tapping her watch, even as we speak!"

I thought about running upstairs to say goodbye to Daniel or hustling out back to kiss the kids but decided it wouldn't fix anything and would more than likely make things worse. Instead, I grabbed a sticky note from the top drawer of the foyer table and wrote, "I'll be back later." "Don't miss me too much," I didn't write. I stuck it to the mirror facing the front door.

"Is there anything in particular you're shopping for?" I heard Kyra ask, possibly sensing that I had vacated the conversation.

"I'm, uh, I don't know. I guess I should walk around and take a look."

A woman in a black halter dress tapped Kyra on her chiseled bicep. "Excuse me, Kyra, but Pam's free now."

Kyra did a quick golf-clap. "Thank you, Jules! Tina, you will *love* Pam. Come this way, she's in my office."

I looked at Jennifer, who shrugged. "You first," I said to her as we turned to follow Kyra.

We stopped in front of pocket doors across from a hall bathroom. Kyra turned around and leaned against the door. The oversized glass sconces on either side projected stripes onto her face. "I have a psychic in here, and she's *incredible*."

My eyes and mouth widened as I started to protest.

Kyra smiled, raising her palm to silence me. "I know, I know, you probably think it sounds crazy, but I'm telling you, it's not. Just meet her! She's wonderful, and she's only charging five bucks for fifteen minutes! It's her SIS Special." She giggled and shrugged. "I predict you'll thank me later." She winked.

I glanced at Jennifer who suddenly looked nervous, like I might spontaneously combust, and she wouldn't know where to find the fire extinguisher. I didn't want her to worry. I also didn't want to burst into flames. *Screw it*, I thought. *It's not as though this day can get worse.* I closed my eyes and bowed my head in surrender.

Kyra turned and slid open the door. "Pam?" she called softly and tiptoed in. Jennifer and I followed. A woman looked up and smiled from the far end of the black leather sofa. She had bright blue eyes and long, straight, silver hair. Her simple gray t-shirt was soft and loose. Her flowing skirt was lavender with tiny silver and purple flowers. Her sandals were delicate, pretty, and also silver. She looked like she had just stepped out of an AARP ad, like she was simultaneously twenty-five and seventy-five. "Hi," she said, somehow making us feel unique and special.

"Hi," Jennifer and I responded in unison.

"Pam! I'm so so happy you are free," Kyra gushed. "This is my new friend, Tina, and my sister-in-law, Jennifer."

"It's nice to meet you," Pam said, oozing inner peace.

"Jennifer, let's let Tina go first, so she has time to circulate after. You can help me peel mandarin oranges in the kitchen. For the garnish."

"Okay," Jennifer said, searching my face for clues to my mental state. I smiled at her as I shuffled forward, tossing my purse onto the houndstooth ottoman and dropping onto the other end of the couch. *Not much longer now*, I thought as Jennifer slid the door closed behind her.

Pam turned toward me and pulled her legs into lotus position. She used her hands to scoot closer to me, reminiscent of a monkey. She stopped when she reached the middle of the couch, closed her eyes, rested her hands on her knees, and inhaled deeply. When she exhaled, she made the sound of an inner tube springing a leak.

After three loud breaths, she opened her eyes. "I'm going to shuffle some cards on this cushion between us." She patted the leather and carefully placed a stack of beat-up cards on it. "But first, let's hold hands and take some deep breaths together."

"Alrighty," I said, pushing my fingertips into my eyelids, willing myself to be polite. I deposited my clammy hands into her cool ones. Her fingers felt dusty, powdered almost, like a donut. I felt the hairs on the back of my neck stand at attention.

"Do you have any questions today, Tina?" she asked me softly.

I surprised myself yet again, this time by bursting into a spastic fit of laughter. I threw my head back and hooted. I let go of her hands and smacked the arm rest and zebra-striped ornamental pillow as tears of hysteria sprung from my eyes. "Do, I, have any questions?" I crowed. "Surely, you, already know the answer, because, you, *know things*," I put up finger quotes, "but, you're, you're breaking the ice! I, didn't, think psychics, needed to break the ice!"

She smiled at me, waiting.

"I'm, really, sorry," I said, trying to contain my guffaw. "I think, I've been, struggling a lot lately. I'm sorry, I should probably go."

"What do you mean by struggling?" she asked calmly.

I breathed again and wiped my eyes. "Well, you might, uh, already know this, but I guess I'm, uh, miserable, pretty much all the time. And, I'm not sure if I've, uh, created this unhappiness inside my mind, in some sort of act of self-sabotage. I guess I'm wondering if, um, I'm my own worst enemy. And I'm also wondering if I, uh, if I'm going to get divorced." I cringed as the words left my mouth. I hadn't said the D word in reference to my marriage out loud before. I suddenly felt small, like a kid sitting on a couch next to a wise elder.

"Let's start there," she said. I blinked and squirmed as she grabbed her stack of cards and mixed them up. I noticed she shuffled like an amateur. She flipped a few cards over and flicked them onto the couch. Flip, flick, flip, flick. Suddenly, she stopped. She looked at me, surprised, and gasped, "Divorce? Oh no, no, no, honey, far from it. Your journey with him has only just begun. Can you see this?" She pointed at a strange figure on one of the cards. "This right here is your creativity. Look how big it is! It's everywhere!" She flipped more cards. "And look here," she tapped a different card, "your creativity is about to make a move—a giant leap, more like it." She paused, then looked at me, eyes wide through silver lashes. "You will have a choice, a very big choice, between the path you are on now—the path you know—and the creative path, which you've barely caught a glimpse of. If you choose this creative path," her bangle bracelets chimed as she tapped the card, "you will have many adventures and wonderful experiences, including self-discovery and travel! See?" She laughed softly and hugged herself. "But this new path, it's unknown and will therefore be hard to choose." She inhaled and smoothed her skirt, folding her hands back together.

If skepticism were a building, mine was a skyscraper. If cynicism were a horizon, mine was a skyline packed with doubt-riddled skyscrapers popping out of the ground like blades of grass after a spring rain, too many to count. Yet, inexplicably, my eyes filled, and my throat constricted. I blinked and swallowed, blinked and swallowed. *Keep it together*, I reminded myself. *This is no time to lose it. Especially when you know this is all a bunch of hogwash.* But I couldn't help being transfixed.

"Do you have any more questions?" she asked.

I cleared my throat. "Uh, yes. When?"

"When what?"

"When do I get to choose the new path?" I unbuttoned my blazer and immediately re-buttoned it.

"I don't know when. Not too long, I suspect."

I scratched my legs through my brown skirt. "Okay then, how will I know?"

"Oh, you'll know." She made the *Oh, you'll know* face.

"But what if I choose the wrong path?" I blurted. "What if I see something that looks like a reasonably creative path and I choose it, but it's wrong? Will I be screwed because I've fumbled the trajectory of my whole life in error?"

She smoothed the already-smooth hair next to her face. "You know how you'll know you're on the right path?"

I shook my head.

"Because it's the path you'll be on." She stood and reached her hand out to help me up. "Come on, it's time for you to mingle."

I thanked her as I gathered my purse and she collected her cards. I was halfway out the door when Pam called from the couch, "Calista!"

I stopped and turned around. "Uh, no, I'm Tina."

"Yes, I know your name." She smiled. "Calista is the person who will bring you the journey. Keep your eyes peeled for Calista."

"Oh, but I don't know anyone named Calista."

"*Yet.* You don't know her *yet.*"

7.

The next morning, I found my skirt in a perfect oval at the top of the stairs where I'd stepped out of it. My blazer was strewn, inside-out, next to the front door; my new fuchsia scarf folded and placed on top of it. One tread-worn black flat lay behind a houseplant in the foyer. The other dangled off the third step from the bottom of the staircase. My cream-colored, pit-stained, only-wear-if-you-aren't-taking-off-your-blazer blouse was under a wet washcloth at the bathroom sink. I had apparently attempted my newly learned face washing technique with my newly purchased rose petal–n–apricot facial scrub. I found my purse, empty, on my desk chair in the office, the contents in a pile next to the file cabinet. I'd apparently checked email half-naked while searching for something at the bottom of my purse. Thankfully, I found nothing in my sent box from the time in question.

While I don't remember getting from Jennifer's car to my bed, I do recall the conversation and corresponding events once I got there. I woke Daniel by shaking both his shoulders while giggling. I remember feeling relieved when he looked more confused than angry. I silently scolded myself for my relentless case of hiccups because they made me seem drunk, as if none of my other actions would have led him to that assumption.

"You up?" I asked. Hiccup. Giggle.

"Huh?" he replied, not opening his eyes.

"You awake?" I said a little louder, tapping his arm.

"Mm," he said.

I leaped up and straddled him, grabbing his shoulders, first shaking them side to side, then, with more power, up and down.

"What is it?" He blinked several times. "What'd I do now?"

"You're not in trouble! (Hic!) On the contrary, I have excellent news, and it can't wait 'til morning. (Hic!)"

"Seriously?" He squinted at me.

"I'm dead serious." Giggle.

"What is it then?"

"We aren't getting divorced!" I bounced up and down on his stomach. "Isn't that fantastic?"

He paused. "You forgot to tell me the part where we were getting divorced before breaking the news that we're now not getting divorced."

"Well, we weren't so much getting divorced as on an unpleasant pathway that might have led us there. I mean, don't you agree?"

He looked at me, exasperated. "Is this why you woke me up?"

"No, um, I mean, I spoke to a psychic tonight."

He turned his head. "Oh for the——"

"I know, I know, it's nuts, but listen. She looked at these cards, and they told her stuff! She said we're going on an amazing journey. Together! And we'll also do some self-exploration, and she looked so sure! And I feel so relieved and happy! I mean, don't you think it sounds exciting?"

"I'm sure a person who buys into that stuff would think it sounds very exciting," he said, closing his eyes.

I grabbed his face gently and brought it back to center. "Most of me doesn't buy into it either. But what if it's true? What if she's right?"

"Tina," he said in a clear, flat tone. "I don't believe in psychics, or fairies, or Santa. I know you want me to, but I can't get there, okay? And I'm very, very surprised you can. Maybe this is what you needed to hear to stay married to me, I don't know."

"It's not that! I just . . . she looked so sure."

"Maybe she knew you needed to hear it. These people are experts at body language."

I let go of his hands and pressed my fingers into my temples. "But she was specific! She spoke about someone named Calista."

"I don't know anyone named Calista."

"Yet!" I whined. (Hiccup.)

He was silent, expressionless as he inspected me for a while.

"Look," I said softly. "Can you do me a tiny favor?"

"Maybe," he said.

"Can you believe it with me for one night? Then, tomorrow, we'll lock it away and never think about it again? I just . . . Please?"

He surprised me when he nodded with soft eyes and a small smile, as though appeasing a desperate child. "Yes. I'll believe it tonight."

I smiled and grabbed his hands, weaving mine into them, then suspending our hand knots between us. "What if we could go somewhere exotic, just our family, and do exactly what we want to do? I could write, and you could, oh I don't know, build robots or something, and we could watch our kids grow up and not worry so much that we were doing this all wrong. We could have the freedom to ponder and be instinctive and full of love instead of irritation, and, and be happy with exactly where we were at that very moment. We wouldn't need so much stuff and so much help and so many conference calls, and, and facial scrubs. And I could be nice." I leaned over and kissed him on the forehead.

He raised his eyebrows. "That would be amazing."

"And I'd donate my work clothes and wear cutoffs as a uniform and have a permanent flip flop tan." I kissed him on the nose. "Because writers wear flip flops, Daniel. It's in their by-laws."

He stroked my hair and leaned up to kiss me back on my nose.

FISH HEADS AND DUCK SKIN

I kept going. "And our kids would thrive and be multilingual Ambassadors for Good." This time I dropped my nose lightly onto his clavicle.

He chuckled.

"Why is that funny?" I pushed his shoulder softly.

"Because it tickles. But also, it rings funny to me: 'Meet our very small children, Piper and Lila, future Ambassadors for Good.'" He let go of my hands and raised my head. He pulled my shoulders slowly to the side and rolled on top of me, then located my collar bone and rested his nose on it.

"That tickles!" I squealed.

"I know," he said, giving me tiny kisses.

I resumed talking. "I'm saying our children would be doing something with their lives that feeds their hearts."

He looked up, mid-kiss. "Feeds their hearts? How sweet."

"Everyone needs a full heart," I smiled, kneading the back of his head.

"My heart's full right now, is yours? Let me check." He unclasped my bra.

"It is, it's full," I said, and sighed.

8.

Three weeks later, when my alarm beeped at 5 a.m., I smacked the off button but didn't get up. It had been a rough night—I hadn't fallen asleep until two hours earlier because the modern-day plague had descended upon our home and, for two nights in a row, the vomit fairy busily bestowed her gifts upon everyone but me.

At 6:45 a.m., I woke up again, this time to my phone ringing. I immediately flew into a level ten panic. I was late, extra, super late, on a Do Not-Be-Late! kind of day. My heart started thumping as dark sweat clouds accumulated in my arm pits. I could only think in four letter words.

"SHIT!" I screamed. Lila started crying. "HELL!" I hollered and shook Daniel's arm. He moaned like the ill man he was. I answered my phone.

"Hey, where are you? James is here," Mary whispered. Mary was my friend and also a nurse in the Cath Lab at Scripps. James was a mega-shyster and also a rep for my biggest competitor.

"JAMES? Are you kidding me? Who called him?"

"Dr. Burns must have called him when you weren't here by six."

"That asshole! I'm coming. CRAP!" I scrambled out of bed, tripping as I tried to unweave myself from the sweaty tangle of sheets.

"Uh, Tina, I don't, uh, think—" Mary stammered.

"I'm on the damn schedule, Mary! I'm coming!"

She paused. "You *were* on the schedule . . ."

"Mary, *please*, this is my livelihood."

"Yeah," she sighed. "Okay."

Forty minutes later I tipped my unbrushed, pony-tailed head into the doctor's lounge. James—tall, blond, and conniving, sat on the mauve, circa 1988 sofa, a double-layered box of donuts on the beat-up coffee table in front of him, every product in his catalog displayed around the box like it was the set of an infomercial. He talked at two doctors while they watched the news on the small TV and chewed on old-fashioneds.

"Hey James, may I speak with you for a moment out here?" I said in my sweetest voice while smiling with mouth only. I wiped the sweat from my upper lip.

He looked up with the only expression I'd ever seen him make—a cocky, detestable sneer. "Sure, Tina, be there in ten."

Ten minutes! I thought as I pulled my head back into the hall. *In ten minutes, he could sink my battleship.* I stewed. I paced. I went to the bathroom, twice. I told myself to stay calm. I said, *Tina, be rational. Be mature. Have an adult conversation.* But it wasn't lining up to be that kind of day. It was more of a hit-a-patch-of-black-ice-while-steering-with-your-greasy-thigh kind of day, and I had already careened off the road. I was now hanging upside down by my seat belt in a wet ditch, car wheels spinning.

When James finally sauntered out of the lounge, I met him with one hand on my hip, one finger pointed at his smirk and demanded, "Do you think you can just waltz in here and steal this account from me?" Before he could answer I blurted, "Because that is so not happening."

"Tina," he said, both palms out. "This place is huge. There's plenty of business here for both of us."

My eyes burned in fury and fatigue. "No, James. There's only enough business here for me. And I have the contract, I have the relationships . . ."

"But today, I have the donuts." He chuckled.

I threw my arms up. "I've had a bajillion donuts with these people! They are like family to me!"

James snorted. "It's true they choose you most of the time, but this morning they called me, ready to try something new."

"Are you listening to yourself? James, you're a one-night stand! You'll get slighted and then hurt and then boil the bunny! You're Glenn Close!"

"I don't think I'm the crazy one here."

"I'M NOT CRAZY!" I shrieked in what could only be described as a poor impression of Minnie Mouse. I glanced around to see if anyone else had heard it. "Look," I said in a low growl, "you need to leave."

James Santa-laughed, "Oh, ho, ho, ho," then said, "I'm not leaving, I'm on the schedule. Dr. Burns is using my product in OR 7 as we speak."

I felt my face turn purple as my eyes bugged. "That, is, a fluke. I was late, and you were staring at your phone, waiting for it to ring."

He laughed. "Was it a fluke? Or was it fate?" He shrugged. "Either way, I'm here all day," he said before turning and strutting away, like a rooster.

I was so furious, at James, at myself, and at the state of my household, I wanted to scream. But I couldn't give James the satisfaction of watching me be hauled away. So, I just sat there, hands fisted, watching him retreat.

Then my phone rang; it was Daniel. In my frenzied state, I wasn't going to answer, but he was sick and so were the kids, so I reconsidered right before it went to voicemail.

"Hi, how's everyone doing?" I asked, my voice suddenly scratchy.

"Better, I think. Kids are asleep, thank God. I feel like I'm on the mend. But that's not why I'm calling."

"What is it?" I said, wiping my forehead on my forearm and shuffling toward the exit closest to the coffee cart.

"Remember how I posted my resume on the grad school alumni board last week?"

"Uh, no," I said, smacking the square steel button that opened the double doors leading to the hallway. Caution tape extended down the length of the hall, keeping people from touching the milky, depressing, still-wet blue paint. *No wonder people stay sick in hospitals*, I thought. *They need to brighten their blue.* I took off my hair cover and spun it around on my pointy finger.

"That's right, you were out of town. Last Friday I posted my resume there but never checked it because of this whole flu thing."

"So what happened?" I asked while motioning to the guy at the coffee cart. I held my fingers in an L for large and then scribbled in the air to say, "Put it on my tab." He nodded. He knew what I wanted, and he knew I was good for it.

"Someone saw it and wants to talk to me. They have a unique position, and they think I'd be a good fit for it. I have a phone interview tomorrow at 10 a.m."

"What's the name of the company?" I asked, taking a lap around the coffee cart, grabbing a napkin and an insulated ring.

"There's no name yet, it's a start up—"

"Wait a second." I stopped mid-lap. "This sounds fishy. Is it even real? Or is it one of those shams where you have to 'invest in your career' before you can earn any money?" I started circling again. At lap three, my mocha appeared. I took a sip. On a scale of one to ten, for hospital mochas, this coffee cart usually produced about a 4. This one was no exception. I sighed and turned toward the lobby.

"It's real. The company's funded by Michael Hicks, a big-time alum from my grad school. His company went public last year, and he donated a mega-load of cash for a massive new library on campus."

"Oh right, I remember you telling me about that." I stopped to peer in the window of the hospital gift shop. It wasn't open yet, so I made a mental note to compliment Ethel, the volunteer buyer, later on her scarf selection. I was a recent convert to scarves, and these weren't half bad.

"Last year Michael sponsored a contest where students could submit their business plans, and he'd choose one plan and provide the funding to get it off the ground."

"Okay?"

"He picked a plan by a woman who graduated two years after me. She wants to import robotic toy sets geared toward little girls to spark their interest in robotics and programming since most robotic products on the market currently cater to boys."

"Sounds like a no-brainer to me, but why no name?" I turned toward the giant help desk in the lobby. It already had a line, even though visiting hours hadn't started yet, probably full of people looking for an update on their loved one. I looked at my pink clogs. I moved my toes to see if I could tell they were moving. Nope.

"The company originally had a name, I think it was Four Mighty Queens, but the initial response was better than anticipated. Now they want to launch globally with a name that appeals in every market. Apparently, names are very important in China, and the number four is unlucky there. So next week they'll vote on a new name."

"Why is four unlucky?" I looked back at the line of loved ones; it hadn't moved.

"It sounds like their word for death."

"Eek." I turned away from the line. "Alright, so they need something more China-friendly. Where do you fit in?" I walked to the window overlooking the ostentatious fountain blowing like Old Faithful at the front of the parking lot.

"If the interview goes well, I'll prepare a proposal and meet with Michael, then fly to China for a site visit. And, if I'm a good fit, I'll get an offer."

"Hold on, China?"

"Yes, Shanghai. That's where the factory is located and where they've opened the global offices."

"The office is in Shanghai, but you'd work here?"

"No, Tina. I'd work in Shanghai. I'd have a two-year contract with the option to renew."

I dropped into a seat against the window and leaned forward, putting my head in my hand. "Wait, what?"

"All the components will be sourced and assembled in China. I'd manage the whole process on site, from sourcing to manufacturing to quality control."

"But, China? Do you want to live there?"

"I don't really care where it is, I just know I really want this job—it's perfect for me. But I wanted to talk to you before I go further in the process. Do we want to live in China? Because I'm not going without you and the girls, I mean, unless you—"

"No, of course we'd go with you, but it seems early to assume this is a sure thing." I stood up again, turning back to the entrance.

"Callie suggested you join me for the site visit, if I—"

"Wait, who?" I stepped quickly toward the automatic doors. They whooshed open and I walked out, stepping off the sidewalk and into the grass.

"Callie—she's the president of the company; she holds the patent on the idea. It turns out she was in the Robotics Club that I started during Grad School. We didn't know each other, but she says she remembers my picture."

"Her name is Callie?"

"Yes. Why?"

"Short for what?" I turned to look up at the hospital, noticing how big it was. So many bricks, I could never count them all.

"I don't know, why?"

"Just, can you please look it up?" I squeezed the bridge of my nose.

"Yeah, wait a sec." Silence. "Okay, here she is—Calista Chen, recipient of the Michael Hicks Prize for Global Innovation. Why, do you know her?"

"Holy shit." I fell to my knees on the grass, then dropped onto all fours, and finally, slowly, rolled onto my back. I looked up at the sky, cloudless already—a clearer, more optimistic blue than the hallway paint job. I started laughing, at least I think I was laughing, except it included sounds I'd never made before.

"What is it, Tina? Are you alright?"

"I'm fine, I just can't believe it's true." I brought my legs into the air, perpendicular to the ground and then, as hard as I could, thumped them back down to earth again. "We're moving to China!"

9.

"Welcome to China Eastern Airlines," said the petite Chinese stewardess in heavily accented English. She wore a child-sized black polyester vest over a fitted white button down, a black pencil skirt, red stilettos, and a red scarf tied at the side of her neck in a bow the size of her head. "Please have happy travels."

I smiled at her and thought, *happy travels, that's cute.* It had been three months of whirlwind preparation and anticipation since Daniel received the job offer; we were finally on our way. I looked down the aisle where she directed us and stopped smiling. "Uh, Daniel? Is it just me, or does the aisle look really skinny? As in, only small children and ballerinas can fit down it?"

He shrugged. "The aisles are smaller, the seats are smaller, the leg room area's smaller . . ." He turned sideways and hiked Piper higher onto his hip, then crab-walked down the aisle toward our seats.

"But I'm not smaller, and you're not smaller," I insisted as I turned sideways to follow him. I lifted my right arm straight over my head so my giant carry-on wouldn't knock against every seat and hoisted Lila higher until her legs were straddling my ribcage. She whimpered. I bounced.

"You and I aren't their target market."

It was true. Almost every seat was occupied by a Chinese businessman.

"Wait, is the heat on?" I asked. "Please tell me Chinese business-men don't enjoy this temperature."

"No clue."

"Surely no one wearing a tie wants to sit in a flying sauna for fourteen hours," I muttered to myself as I scooted by a man who launched into a coughing fit that morphed into a throat clearing session lasting a full minute. I held my breath and scooted faster. When I finally caught up to Daniel, I whispered, "Reason #473 why this plane shouldn't be so warm. We're in a flying petri dish, that guy just coughed up the tuberculosis-riddled lining of his esophagus, and this is the ideal temperature for bacterial cell division!"

"Tina, I know you're anxious, but we have a long flight ahead of us; can we not start the hypochondriac thing right now? Try and relax."

My nostrils flared, as did the circumference of my eyes. "Never tell a person to relax, Daniel! Not unless they're getting a massage! You should know that by now."

"Why not?"

"Because you're basically instructing me to do something I'm incapable of. Be skinnier! Be taller! Be a concert level pianist! Relax! I can't do any of these things. And you verbalizing it only reminds me of my inadequacies and ends up having the opposite effect."

"Telling you to relax makes you less relaxed?"

"Obviously."

He rolled his eyes and pointed to the last row of four seats on our left where a female passenger was already fast asleep against the window. "You and the girls are there, and this is my seat." He dropped his laptop bag on the aisle seat two rows in front of us.

There hadn't been four available seats together, or two sets of two seats together, when we booked the flight—only a row with three seats adjacent to the lavatory and several empty single seats. After a heated discussion, we had decided that I'd start with the kids in the row of three and he would fly solo. We'd swap places halfway through the trip. I'd agreed to the first half with kids figuring I'd feel relatively fresh and energetic for the beginning of the flight. This was not the case however; my eyes stung with exhaustion from consecutive sleepless nights pondering our enormous life change.

The woman snoozing in the window seat in our row didn't appear to be struggling with the same anxious feelings. The upper half of her body was mummified in a dark blue airline blanket. She'd tucked another blanket around her legs and folded a third blanket neatly on her lap over her hands. Her eyes were shielded by a pink silk mask, and her sleek, black hair was banded by white, noise-canceling headphones. The only visible skin on her body was her forehead and her mouth. I recognized that it wasn't her fault she wasn't in a similar state of despair, so I only begrudged her clean, slumbering presence a little bit.

Lila started howling as soon as the wheels were sucked into the plane's underbelly. She continued for forty endless minutes. Poor thing, her ears must have hurt. Once the seat belt light went off, I walked her up and down, up and down the aisle, rocking and humming, bending and leaning to dodge the knees and elbows of the already sleeping, suited men. At long last, she fell asleep in my arms. Once she'd been asleep for about five minutes, I crept back to our row. Piper was sitting next to the sleek snoozer, watching a Chinese cartoon on her seat screen, arms crossed, frowning. I slowly leaned over my aisle seat to lay Lila down in a makeshift bed consisting of four blankets I'd pre-arranged into a nest on the middle seat with both arm rests folded up. When I finally got her situated, her little foot flopped out, tapping Piper softly on her thigh.

"OWWWW, LILA!" Piper screamed. She reached over, grabbed Lila's foot, and pinched it.

Lila startled awake and began screaming.

"Piper! Why would you do that?" I was mortified.

"She kicked me!" She pointed at Lila, her eyes fierce and accusing.

"But she was asleep, and she barely touched you!"

"Well it hurt." She attempted to fake cry.

"No, it didn't," I said, shaking my head. I picked up Lila and started walking again, up and back, up and back, until Lila's screams turned to sobs turned to whimpers turned to moans and her blinks got longer and then, silence. I tiptoed to Daniel's seat. His eyes were closed, his mouth open.

I tapped his arm and whispered, "Hey, wake up! Piper just pinched Lila."

He blinked several times. "Do you want me to talk to her?"

"No." I continued rocking Lila. "She's in a foul mood—I think from all the moving stress. Talking to her might make it worse—she could have a giant meltdown, and I don't want to wake up the entire plane."

"Why'd you wake me up then?" he said, rubbing his face with his hand and turning his head away from me.

"Because you're their dad! And I need to talk about it with somebody!"

"Talk to me later; it's my turn to sleep," he said, closing his eyes again.

I turned to continue rock-pacing, feeling miffed.

Back at my row, I leaned over and set Lila back in her nest. I looked at Piper. Her eyes were tightly sealed, and her head rested at an awkward angle on the arm rest she shared with Sleeping Beauty. Once again, I wasn't fooled. "Piper, please look at me," I whispered. No response. "I know you're used to having more space, but you have to share this row with your sister while we're on this plane. You need to let her sleep."

There was no response until two minutes later when Lila readjusted her sleep position. She rolled over and kicked her foot out again, grazing Piper's leg.

"LILA! STOP THAT!" Piper screamed as her eyes popped open. She grabbed Lila's foot and pushed it hard away from her.

Lila hollered.

"Piper!" I shrieked. "You have to stop this!"

"No. Lila has to stop this," she whimpered.

I stood up with Lila, and walked, bounced, rocked, and shushed, straight to Daniel's seat while Lila wailed.

His eyes opened in alarm. "What is it? What happened?"

"Piper can't share a row with her! It's not working!"

He paused. "There isn't another option unless you think she can sit alone."

"I know, and there's no way she can sit by herself! But this is hard, and I'm frustrated!" I stormed away to burn a deeper path in the aisle carpet while I problem solved. Daniel's eyes were still open when I returned after a few minutes.

"Will you please hold her for a few minutes while I try to reason with Piper?"

"Sure," he said.

When I got back to our row, Piper was face-down on the floor, her front half wedged under the seat in front of her, her tiny butt in the air, and her legs folded underneath her. She was going for invisible, ostrich-style.

I was reaching down to pull her out when I stopped myself. *Hold on*, I thought, *this could be the fix! I'll leave her there, and I bet she'll fall asleep.* I sat down and let my head drop back and my eyes close. *This might be the solution.*

Suddenly, the man sitting in front of Piper sprung up, turned around, and glared at me, red-faced. "Hey!" he pointed his finger at my nose. I looked at him in a panic. "Tell your kid to stop tickling my feet!" he spat.

"Oh no! I'm so sorry!" I reached down and picked up Piper. She was evil-chuckling. I heaved her onto my hip and stepped into the aisle. I sidled sideways to the first open space and spun her down in front of the lavatory. I squatted so we were nose to nose.

"Why would you tickle that man? Why?"

"Because his feet were in the way!" she cried.

I paused. "They weren't in the way; they were where feet are supposed to be. You were in his space." I looked away from her, then blinked and looked back. "There must be a consequence for this, like Miss Amy said." I glanced around—every seat was packed. I noticed the green lavatory light. "You can sit in this potty for a one-minute time-out and think about your actions." I stood, reached over her head, and slid open the accordion door.

"No, Mommy! I don't want a time-out!" She wailed.

I looked around. A few people were craning into the aisle to see the commotion. This didn't deter my plan. "Then I hope you'll show me different behavior when you get out," I said, leading her in and closing the door from the outside by the white plastic handle.

"Mommy, it's dark in here!" The door started shaking as she knocked and pushed on it.

"Just slide the knob that locks the door and the light will turn on," I called through the door.

"But I can't see it, Mommy!"

I opened the door. "Look, it's right there." I pointed to the lock. "Just slide it over."

Piper made a break for it under my arm. I grabbed her by the waist mid-run, and she howled.

"Piper! Stop fighting me!" I yelled. She screamed louder, kicking wildly in mid-air.

The flight attendant with the gargantuan neck bow walked up.

"Excuse me, Madam," she said. "I see you have trouble? I have special activity bag to help you? For your daughter. I put on her seat now, okay?"

Piper had stopped screaming to listen to the stewardess. "I don't want to go to the bathroom!" she blubbered. The stewardess smiled in pity and walked away.

None of this had gone as planned. And there was no plan for the rest of the flight. Or for once we landed. Or for the rest of our lives. For a second, I couldn't breathe. I put Piper down and pressed both hands against the wall between the bathroom and the food prep area. I took three shallow breaths. I closed my eyes and opened them again, then squatted. "I really need you to be good, Piper," I said in a soft voice. "Can you please try?"

She sniffed and nodded. "Yes, Mommy."

I squeezed her hand. "Then let's go see what's in the bag."

It was the size of a standard brown grocery bag except it was made of shiny bright blue plastic with a glittery, puffy purple airplane on the front. And it was filled, almost to the top, with candy.

I was horrified, but Piper's face lit up at the gold strike. "Mommy look at all this chocolate! Can I eat some, please? I promise I'll be so good!" she begged.

I would love to say I made the right parenting decision at that moment, but that would be untrue. Instead, I did the opposite. Less than halfway through my half of the trip, I surrendered to that bag of tooth-rotting distraction, pushing it toward her with no words. Not a, "Only have one," or a, "Take two and hand me the bag," or a, "Let's save this for after dinner." Nothing.

She didn't hesitate, tearing at the bag like a ravenous buzzard who'd just witnessed a giant elephant take his last breath.

I guess I assumed she'd stop eating at some point. That it wouldn't taste good after a while, and then she'd push it away and fall asleep. Or maybe I thought that, at age four, she was old enough to make reasonable choices, sort of like the kind I was modeling for her.

I turned my head away and closed my eyes.

I nodded off, which is strange because I don't normally sleep on planes. It seems I only make exceptions to this rule when it's a terrible idea to do so.

I woke with a start and a feeling that something was dreadfully wrong. I turned toward Piper. She was pale, staring straight ahead at the map on her screen. The little red dots and tiny red airplane indicated our position was over the North Pacific, near Canada.

Piper held an unwrapped piece of toffee in her hand. She wasn't putting it in her mouth.

A clear sign of fatigue! My plan is working! I thought, like a fool. Our row-mate was still asleep when Piper suddenly sat up straight, blinking. She looked at me and then grabbed her arm rests. In what looked like slow-motion, she turned toward her sleeping neighbor and vomited all over her lap. Without a cry or any other peep of warning, I could only assume that Piper had been caught off guard, too. She dropped her head onto the arm rest and moaned.

I flew out of my seat and ran to Daniel. He and Lila were both sleeping. I grabbed his head and shook it frantically, "Ohmygodohmygodohmygod. DanielDanielDanDanDanDanDan!"

He looked up at me, startled. "What? What happened?"

"Piper just barfed all over the woman in our row!"

He stood quickly and handed me Lila. I shuffled out of his way. He took two steps back and surveyed the nasty scene. I tiptoed in to review the damage, to confirm it was real.

"Holy shit!" he said, staring at the mess while running a hand through his hair.

"I know! What are we going to do?" I stood there, holding sleeping Lila with one arm, the other hand covering my mouth, cringing, waiting for this woman to open her eyes and start hurling abuses at me while I nodded, "Yes, YES!" because I deserved anything she had to say.

"Wait," he whispered, pointing at the large puddle of regurgitated candy bars. "Piper only barfed on the blanket covering her hands. Her skin's completely clean, and she's miraculously still sleeping. Hurry—pick up Piper and clean her off in the bathroom. Then put her in my seat with a barf bag. I'll hold Lila. Quickly."

I did as I was told. Piper, zombie-like, did not resist. Once in Daniel's seat, she dropped her head on the aisle-side armrest and closed her eyes.

Daniel tapped me on the back. "Go get a stack of clean blankets. They're usually in the carry-on compartments above the seats in the front."

I ran back with the blankets. "Should we wake her now?"

"Who?"

"The woman! So we can change out her blanket!"

"No, I have a plan." He glanced around to see if anyone was looking. He then squatted and slowly, very slowly, pulled the soiled blanket still folded over her hands down a half an inch. No movement. He pulled again; she still didn't move. Puke started streaming down the blanket, dripping onto the carpet by her feet, so he pulled from the sides in a containment effort. He continued until the blanket was off her lap and on top of the puddle.

"Blanket!" he shot his hand toward me and I pressed a clean one into it. He turned and dropped it onto her lap, patting it gently into place. Then he pointed his right foot and dragged the dirty blanket backward into the aisle.

"Put another blanket on the ground here," he pointed next to her feet, "so she doesn't slip when she wakes up. I'll take the evidence to the hamper in the back."

"Okay," I said.

When he came back, I asked, "Now what? Do we sit down again? And pretend that didn't happen?"

"I'm sure no one would want to switch seats with us, so yes, you sit with Lila. I'll check on Piper."

I lay Lila down on the seat where Piper had been sitting and sat next to her. She snuggled her head into my lap. After a few minutes, Daniel sat next to me.

I put my head on his shoulder, my nose gravitating toward his collarbone. "Is she okay?"

"Yeah, she's sleeping now."

I sighed. "You amaze me," I whispered.

"Oh, come on."

"No, I mean it. You stayed so calm, cool, and collected, I could never—"

"It wasn't that big of a deal, I mean it worked out, right?"

I lifted my head and looked at him. "Yeah, but it was almost atrocious, and the entire thing was my fault."

"What? No, it wasn't."

"Yes, yes it was." I paused, then blurted, "I'm suddenly feeling like this whole thing might be a horrible mistake."

"What do you mean? The flight's been rough, but we're going to—"

"Not just the flight, I mean this whole quit-our-life-and-move-to-China thing. We have absolutely no idea what we're in for, and I've just ended my career and signed up for full-time parenting! Me!" I laughed and shook my head. "I suck at parenting!"

"How would you know if you suck at parenting? You've never been with the kids by yourself for extended periods." He squeezed my hand. "You'll be fine! I'm sure of it."

"No, I won't. I'm a mediocre mother—I don't have innate talent there. Maybe it's genetic, I don't know, but I lack a strong maternal compass."

"You're wrong."

"I'm too selfish to be a good mom! To improve anyone besides myself."

"You don't have to improve them, Tina, they're children! You just have to love them."

"Of course I have to improve them—I can't just stand by and watch them destroy each other! I mean, let's be honest—Piper's life was ruined the second her sibling was born. She knows it, I know it, this entire airplane knows it. She signed up to be an only child, and now she has to share. She'll spend her entire life thinking of ways to make her baby sister, a.k.a. her competition, vanish." I laughed and cried simultaneously. "And to think—we wanted three kids!"

"Tina, please. You're freaking yourself out."

"I won't know what to do with myself in China, Daniel! It's illegal for me to work."

"Which is fine because you need a break, you said so yourself."

"But what else does a workaholic control-freak do? Who will I be? I don't cook, and I don't play dolls. I don't speak Chinese, and I won't know a soul."

"You'll meet other people in the same situation. There are 100,000 expats in Shanghai, Tina."

I shook my head and squeaked, "I'm scared."

"And that's fine," he said. "You're facing a lot of big changes; we both are. It's normal to be scared."

I looked at him and cocked my head. "Are you scared?"

He shook his head. "Not really. I'm excited."

"Ugh," I said.

"What?"

"That's either insane or brilliant."

He smiled. "Can we get back to me being amazing and how we narrowly escaped needing to placate a barf-covered woman?"

"Yes," I said. I smiled, kissed him, and put my head back on his chest. But inside, I was still petrified of all the unknowns that lie ahead and unsure if I could handle them.

10.

ourteen hours and 6,500 miles later, I found myself in an
alternate universe, one where I was floating in a Jello-like
substance, unable to complete a thought or move without Hercu-
lean effort. I could hear everything—the incessant horn-honking,
the taxi driver screaming incomprehensible words into my face,
the harsh, repeated whistles of the dozens of surrounding traffic
attendants. I definitely could see everything—the spit bubbles
accumulating in the corners of the mouth of the ruffled driver. His
ill-fitting, faded black blazer and short white gloves. The rust surrounding the wheel well of his white Volkswagen Jetta taxi idling in
front of us. Daniel attempting to cram our tower of luggage into its
trunk. My eyeballs burned like they'd been plucked out and rolled
in margarita salt. I couldn't identify the smell, but it registered as
revolting. I had so much to say, but I couldn't move the messages
from my brain to my mouth.

The girls were crashed out in the double stroller, observing
none of these things. It was 6 p.m. at the Shanghai Pudong airport,
3 a.m. at home.

"There are no seat belts," I croaked.

"What?" Daniel lifted his head from the trunk and wiped his
wet, red face on his forearm.

"I can't attach the car seats. No seat belts."

"Oh. Well, it's probably a short drive. I'm sure they'll be fine."
I blinked painfully in assent.

"I'll have to put the pack-n-play and stroller in the front seat," he said.

"He won't like that," I said, jabbing my thumb in the direction of Mr. Grumpy Gloves, who waited for his meter to commence ticking, fists on hips, muttering, foot tapping.

Daniel shrugged. "Something tells me that's not much of a departure for him."

We plunked ourselves in the back seat of the Jetta—Daniel and I pressed against the doors; kids arranged in a slumbering pile between us. Our driver slammed his door and glared at us.

"What does he want?" I asked, the words coming several beats after the thought, like thunder after distant lightning.

"This," he said, pushing a full-sized sheet of paper through the slit in the plastic shield between us and the driver. He looked at me, pleased with himself. "Directions to the hotel. In Mandarin. I also got enough currency at the mall to pay the fare."

"Oh. Why are the directions printed so large?"

"My guidebook said to print them as large as possible since the taxi drivers can't see."

I looked out the window at the mirrored glass walls of the massive terminal and the congo line of luggage trolleys that stretched from one end to the other. The whistle-happy traffic attendants wore heavy, hot-looking gray rompers and matching uniform hats. I noticed they wore white gloves, too.

"Can't see or can't read?" I said, finally identifying what had bothered me about his last statement.

He looked at me and shrugged. "Hopefully read."

The driver gunned it. Our heads snapped back, hitting the white slip-covered seats.

"Holy crap," I said.

"Holy shit," Daniel said at the same time.

I thought, *we might die today*, but didn't feel the fear that would normally accompany such a thought. Daniel put his arm across the girls and grabbed my hand, squeezing it. Several seconds later I squeezed back.

A few more things stood out from that first taxi ride: I remember wondering what was in the jar of clear liquid that the driver slurped loudly from besides floating leaves, grass, and twigs. I remember trying to breathe shallowly when he lit his first of several cigarettes. I remember wondering how to ask him to roll down the window and then almost laughing as I realized I wasn't even sure how to say hello correctly—I'd been too busy exiting our old life to properly prepare for the new one. I remember thinking I'd never seen a brown sky before, and that it almost looked like a poorly painted backdrop.

I don't remember falling asleep, but I do remember waking up about an hour later with the awareness that we were still driving and the Sahara Desert had somehow relocated to my tongue. I longed for a sip of his liquified garden-clippings.

Our hotel was a twenty-five-story Pepto Bismol–pink cuboid, one of many identical structures on the same block. Light blue twinkle lights framed every filthy window. Bright-orange neon lights were fashioned in a rainbow shape over the rusty, revolving door marking the entrance.

Daniel stood next to me. "This was the best hotel in my budget that was sort of close to my new office."

I nodded and shrugged, looking up at it again, pushing the stroller up and back a few times, too overwhelmed and exhausted to cast judgment.

"Pancakes!" Piper hollered while yanking on my thumb. It was 1:30 a.m. She jumped on the mattress between Daniel and me.

"Mattress" is a generous term for what felt like a sheet of plywood covered in burlap. Lila's pack-n-play was wedged in between the corner of the room and the corner of the bed. She lay in it, making happy noises.

"Mm. Daniel? Do they do pancakes here?" I pushed on his shoulder gingerly with my pinky. Every piece of me hurt.

"Where's the remote?" he asked, his head still under the pillow. He patted his hand around the tiny bedside table blindly until he located it. "Here, Piper. Go."

Chinese language channels flicked onto the small screen. News. A variety show. A rom-com. No cartoons.

I sat up. "If they don't have pancakes, we can probably find eggs. Chickens are everywhere, right? Hey, is there a Bible in here?" I blabbered. I was suddenly fully alert and starving even though my vision was blurred at the edges. My mouth had an unfortunate metallic taste, and the one water bottle that came in the room was long empty. I clicked on the light.

"Since when do you read the Bible?" Daniel asked the mattress.

"I don't read it, Daniel, but this is an anthropological moment. We're in China." I sprung out of bed and started ripping open the drawers. "And what do you know—no Bible. First time in a non-Christian country, kids. Take note."

"First time the girls have left the US," Daniel reminded me.

"Right," I said. "I'm famished. Do they do coffee here? I don't see a pot."

I pulled open the drapes. They resembled aluminum foil but felt like plastic. Like a marathon blanket. Or a cheap, reflective shower curtain. We were on the tenth floor. Beyond the outline of blue Christmas lights stretched a blackish-brown night—the color of the warm drink I was craving. I could see nothing else.

"It's too early to walk around. Let's try to sleep a little longer, or we'll feel awful by 3 p.m.," Daniel said.

Lila squealed in response and then giggled.

Ten minutes later, we waited as Piper pushed the down button on the elevator.

"There has to be a twenty-four-hour convenience store, don't you think?" I asked when the door clanked open on the ground floor.

"I don't know, and we can't ask." A man stared at us from behind his computer station at the front desk. "That's the same guy who checked us in; he doesn't speak a lick of English."

We filed silently past the collection of brown velour couches and through the emergency door since the revolving door was blockaded by oversized cones that matched the neon lights buzzing loudly above them.

"Did the guidebook say it's safe here?" I blinked and yawned, pushing the double stroller in Daniel's wake down the dark street.

"Yep. No weapons, no violent crime. Some petty theft but punishments are harsh."

"Harsh? As in what?"

"I'm not sure, the details were vague." He continued, stepping over a large hole. "No predatory behavior, unless you're a Chinese woman, because, you know, they're in short supply."

The stroller wheels jammed on a sidewalk crack as I maneuvered the hole. "Dammit, I can already tell I brought the wrong stroller."

"Did you ship the jogger?"

"No, I sold it."

"Oh, too bad."

"Do you know where we're going?" I asked, looking up. The shop windows were closed, blocked with metal grates. Streetlights cast a dull glow on the sidewalk. From what I could tell, everything was gray . . . the worn-down, two-story buildings lining the sidewalk, the lamp poles, even the occasional tree poking out of holes between the gray cement sidewalk squares had a gray trunk and grayish leaves. Many of the squares were missing or broken. A few older men walked by in the gutter, staring at us. When I looked back at them, they didn't look away.

"We're walking around the block, taking a tour of the neighborhood while looking for a convenience store."

"Oh. Good idea," I said, suddenly feeling itchy everywhere. I stopped to scratch my elbows. I considered pushing the stroller to the gutter, where the men were walking—the path looked smoother there. Then a military vehicle banged loudly by us, trailing a black cloud of exhaust. Never mind.

"Lots of cars out. Plus trucks. Big trucks."

"Big twucks," Piper said.

"Gah!" Lila hollered, throwing a cracker, one of the last of our travel stash, onto the ground.

Daniel said nothing as we started our march again. "They sure like their horns here," I said.

"Beep beep!" yelled Piper.

"Nothing on this block, let's try the next one," Daniel said thirty minutes later as we dragged our feet up to the corner nearest our hotel.

"Yeah, okay." We turned to cross the street. Waves of fatigue crested on my brain, followed by waves of alert, jittery energy, puffs of nausea, and tremendous thirst. The smell of raw sewage wafted in and out. I stepped over several piles of what looked and smelled like feces, but I saw no dogs. I didn't ask.

"Let's try this direction," Daniel said as he pressed the crosswalk button on a street called Huai Hai Lu. It was only 4 a.m. but it already felt like we'd traversed the entire city. The street in front of us was six lanes wide and busy with both car and bike traffic. The road rules weren't clear. As men and women of all ages rolled into the intersection on ancient-looking bikes, they sped up, seemingly unafraid of the cars that barreled toward them with no sign of braking, regardless of whether the light was green or red. At the last second, the cars screeched to a halt and blasted their horns as the bikes continued. No one seemed fazed by this.

"I'm not sure I want to cross here," I said. "The cars don't seem to care that this is a red light."

"If they don't care here, they won't care somewhere else."

I looked at him. "That might be true, but I don't want to die."

"The bikers don't want to die either, Tina, and the system works for them. Come on, you're going to have to cross the street at some point while we're living here." He grabbed the stroller from me and pushed it into the road, standing next to it. He held up his hand in what I hoped was the international signal for STOP.

"I can't walk into that road, Daniel; I'm really scared," I said to the back of his head.

"Yes, you can, follow me," he said, plowing ahead. A car stopped abruptly next to him. "See? It works."

"Okay, I'm coming," I called, suddenly more scared to be by myself on the corner than in front of oncoming traffic. I hustled up next to him, grabbed his arm with both of my hands, and closed my eyes. "Tell me when to step up," I said.

"I see one!" Daniel said an hour later, pointing to a street corner in the distance. A red and blue neon sign glowed in front of it.

"I can't read the sign," I said, squinting at the characters.

"It doesn't matter, it's clearly a convenience store," he said. "Finally!" He pulled the doorknob. Locked. "Damnit!" We peered through the window. Magazines. Kleenex. Bike tires.

We turned around, feeling sunk. On the street in front of us, we saw a rickshaw, pedaled by a man who looked twelve, packed with a twenty foot tall mountain of Styrofoam, held together by ropes and random pieces of string. The rickshaw inched slowly forward, but it looked like the smallest gust of wind would convert the collection of Styrofoam into a sail that could pull the rickshaw rapidly backward, or even sideways.

"There's another one," Daniel said, sounding less enthused. This was our fourth convenience store spotting in several hours. The first two were closed, the third was open, but the cashier had hollered and waved us away when we walked in.

"It's open!" I screeched, pulling the door open and lunging inside. "And it has AC!" I said, shivering in delight as I felt the dampness of my shirt sticking under my arms and down the center of my back.

"Do they have coffee?" Daniel asked.

"I don't know what they have," I said looking at the counter by the cashier as he walked toward the cold case. "I see a large pot of brown water, but it doesn't look like a vessel for coffee, and I think there are eggs floating in it."

"I see Coke!" he said.

"And muffins!" Piper called.

"And water!" Daniel said. "Um, the Coke is warm, do you care?"

"No, I don't even drink Coke, but it's caffeinated so bring it here." This moment felt like our first victory, bringing us a step closer to finding our way and moving forward in our new life.

We carried two Cokes, four waters and eight muffins to the counter. The cashier grumbled something and shook his head. He started to scan and place our early morning breakfast into a thin white plastic bag. As he picked up the second Coke, a cockroach, half the size of my palm, ran across the counter. It scurried from behind the cash register toward the vat of brown water.

I screamed.

"What is it?" Daniel asked.

I pointed while backing away.

The cashier noticed it too. *Thwack!* He smacked the roach with the bottle of Coke and swept its remains onto the floor with his other hand. Without stopping, he waved the same Coke in front of the scanner. *Beep!* He dropped it into the bag, on top of the muffins, and began scanning the waters.

"Wait a, whoa, whoa, whoa there, guy." I stepped in front of the stroller, both hands raised. "Stop!" I said.

The cashier did not slow down.

"NO," I said, "I won't buy this." I put my hands over the top of the plastic bag. "Stop. I said no." I made eye contact with him and shook my head.

He threw his hands up in the air and started yelling, gesturing first at the bag, then at the cash register, then at me, then at Daniel. Then he started the cycle again, this time louder than before.

My ears rang, and my knees felt wobbly. I thought my brain might explode. I wondered if the man would brush the contents of my skull onto the ground the same way he'd brushed off the dead cockroach. Would he wash his hands after? Would he take a moment to contemplate the incident, or would he get right back to cashiering? I felt woozy; my vision started to blacken at the sides. "I can't do this right now. I need to go outside." I walked to the door and pulled it. It screeched against the dingy white tile floor in protest.

"What do you mean you can't do this?" Daniel followed me, irritated. "Come back here, Tina. You have to do this. My job starts in two days; I'll be traveling to visit factories every week. You need to be able to operate here, by yourself, with our children. This was our decision, and I know you can—"

"I need to sit down," I heard myself say in slow motion.

He paused to look at me, his face full of annoyance, and then, concern. "Are you okay? You don't look well."

I took a deep breath, and another, and another. I squeezed my eyes shut and opened them again, twice. I attempted to swallow the dryness, the stinging, the tears, and the vomit, all of which were poised and ready to make an appearance.

"I'm not sure," I started to say, and then I saw black.

11.

When I woke, supine on a large, perfectly manicured patch of grass under a tree, I thought for a moment it had all been a dream. A crazy, first-world nightmare, actually, where I'd given up:

my identity
my home
my car
my cat
my best friend
my hair stylist/colorist
my dry cleaner
my life goals, and
my robust and rewarding albeit challenging career

for a noisy chunk of the planet that smelled like a gargantuan toilet and operated under a whole new set of rules that I couldn't, for the life of me, comprehend. Until a man in a camel-colored romper, matching hat, and white gloves leaned over me and blew his whistle.

I startled, and Daniel leaned over me from the other side.

"Apparently we're not allowed on the grass," Daniel said. "I saw a sign, but I couldn't read it. Here, let me help you get to this bench."

My neck felt glued to the grass, but I said, "I can get there by myself, I'm fine."

He looked at me, eyebrows raised. I lifted my arms, and he pulled me up like a rag doll, propping me on a cement rectangle on the sidewalk.

My feet felt like they'd been wedged into Barbie shoes and my skin was so itchy, I yearned to molt. I looked around. The foot of the sky was beginning to lighten. A few people were starting to mill around, all of them on the sidewalks and large concrete areas, no one on the illicit grass.

"What time is it?" I asked.

"Almost 5 a.m."

"Oh." I suddenly stood up, frantic. "Where're the kids?"

"Don't worry, they're fine. When you fainted, the cashier called his grandma, or possibly his great-grandma, who speaks a speck of English. She hustled over and led me to this park. She even pushed the stroller so I could support you because you were like a drunk sailor. By the way, she asked me if you'd been drinking *bai jiu* and I just shrugged because I didn't feel like explaining the convergence of jet lag, panic, dehydration, and cockroach guts that had sidelined you. So, if she treats you like a booze-head, just go with it."

I moaned and put my head in my hands.

"At least I think that's what got to you, is that what you think it was?"

"That sounds about right," I said, squinting at the playground on the other side of the grassy area. "Is that her?"

"Yep."

Grandma was galloping like a horse and bouncing Lila on her hip as Piper slid down the world's most treacherous-looking slide. "Oh jeez."

"I'm not sure she's ever seen blonde hair; she can't stop touching their heads."

"You're kidding me!" I started to laugh and winced.

"No, and I think she's taken about a hundred pictures of each of them. Piper finally growled at her, so she put the camera away."

I shook my head. "Why am I not surprised?"

"Here, drink this," he said, handing me a plastic bottle with neon yellow liquid inside.

"What is it?"

"Some type of Chinese Gatorade. Pretty good actually. I already had two."

I opened it and guzzled half immediately. "Did the kids get anything to eat?"

"Grandma picked out some snacks at the shop. I have no clue what they were, but they gobbled them down. Piper said they were 'the best snacks she'd ever had'."

"I bet." I laughed. It felt better this time.

I stretched my arms overhead and looked around. "What's going on over there?" I pointed to a group of older men and women assembling under a large, dead-looking tree. There were about thirty of them. A woman with dyed black cotton-candy hair held a boom box and a microphone. She set the boom box down and stood next to it. She called out instructions into her mic, waving her arms like a conductor as the group arranged themselves into some semblance of order. When she pushed play, they began ballroom dancing on cue around the tree, circling and swaying, up and back, round and round.

"How great is that?" Daniel laughed.

"Seriously."

From our vantage point, a slight incline by the playground, we could see a few other groups of seniors assembling. Behind us, next to a low wall of rocks, a group of seven men stood, each holding a bird cage. They hung their cages on the lowest branches of a nearby tree and then commenced a variety of calisthenics.

"They walk their birds to their exercise session?" I asked.

"Apparently," Daniel said.

FISH HEADS AND DUCK SKIN

Another group stood on the large central square near the danc-ers; they were the oldest group by far. They were small in stature and moved slowly, many of them hunched over. The men wore sensible pants and button-down shirts tucked in, the women wore equally sensible pants and colorful sweaters, the kind you might see at an ugly sweater contest. Most of them had let their hair go gray.

"What do you think they're up to?" I asked. They set down their bags and pulled small metal pails out of them, followed by large paint brushes. They situated themselves in a row at the farthest cor-ner of the concrete, almost to the main sidewalk, then squatted and went to work. "It almost looks like they're painting the sidewalk with water, but that doesn't make sense."

"I need to get a closer look," Daniel said. "You feeling okay enough to come with me?"

"I think so," I said and stood up slowly.

Keeping the kids in our sights, we walked closer. Close enough to see each person in the group dip their brushes into their pail of water and then draw on the concrete patch in front of them, slowly painting from bottom to top, right to left. Their brush strokes were smooth, measured, and precise. They focused on their work, not taking breaks to look up or around. They seemed like the only peo-ple at the park who didn't notice we were there.

"It looks like they're painting Chinese characters," Daniel said.

"How can you tell?"

"I took a Chinese Civ class sophomore year. It was supposed to be an easy A but after the first week we got a new teacher and it became a tough C. Anyway, I remember what the characters look like. The stroke order is apparently crucial."

I smiled and rested my head on Daniel's shoulder. "I wonder what it says."

Just then Grandma walked up holding Lila. Piper ran in front of her. "Mommy, Lila needs a new diaper."

Lila looked at me and wailed.

"Wet!" Grandma hollered, pointing at Lila's bottom.

"I see that, thank you," I said. I reached my arms out to take Lila but Grandma stepped back.

"No. I help you. I *ayi*," she said.

"Excuse me?"

"I work for family, help you, I ayi." She pointed at herself. "Baby cold. Wet. I help. For whistle training."

"Whistle training?" I shook my head. "That's very nice but I don't need help."

"What's your phone number?" Daniel asked her, holding up his phone. He looked at me and shrugged. "Just in case."

"Ah," she said, taking a scrap of paper from her own sensible pants as Daniel handed her a pen. She scribbled down her number and handed it to me, frowning. "Baby cold. Wet."

I looked at Lila. Her cheeks were bright red and the fuzz on her head was plastered down with sweat. "She's not—"

Right then, a man wheeled between us on his bike and stopped. A large antennae-like structure swung from the back of his seat. Dangling from the antennae were hundreds of tiny, round, hand-woven baskets. A loud screeching sound emanated from his rolling basket collection. He stepped off his bike and held the handlebars with one hand. He stretched his other palm toward Daniel and me.

"*Wŭ kuài!*" he said.

"What?" I looked at Daniel. He shrugged.

"Wŭ kuài!" he repeated.

"What's he saying?" I said, this time looking at Grandma, who had walked around and stood frowning with her hands on her hips next to me.

She hollered and then stepped right up to the man's face and initiated a heated exchange, which is a nice way to say screaming match. They ranted at each other for a while, gesturing, finger-pointing, snorting, stomping.

Finally, the man waved his arms in dismissal and muttered

something. He untied one of the baskets and handed it to Grandma. She opened the basket and pulled out a large cricket, holding it up to Daniel in her fist so he could see its face.

"This one have nice song," she said. "I tell him four kuai, local price. He say okay."

"They're seriously trying to sell us a fifty-cent cricket?" I looked at Daniel.

"Oh Daddy, please! Please can you buy me the cricket? I'll take good care of it, Daddy. I'll even name it Mr. Tinsey!" Piper said.

Daniel laughed. "Mr. Tinsey, who is Mr. Tinsey?"

"My new cricket is Mr. Tinsey!" she said, jumping up and down.

"Piper," I said. "Please be reasonable. We don't have a home yet, and we haven't even had breakfast. Let's look at the crickets later, when things are more settled, okay?"

"I'm not asking you, I'm asking DADDY!" she bellowed.

I looked at Daniel. "Can you please tell her what I just told her?"

"I say we get the cricket." He shrugged. "We're in China, might as well."

"Mommy, please, it will be so fun!" Piper said.

I looked at her and back at Daniel. Their expressions communicated a shared sentiment—I was the biggest wet blanket on planet Earth. The spoiler. The one who turned fun into work, who lacked spontaneity, who could never seize the moment, even when it shook me by the shoulders. I felt sick and tired of being that person—Mrs. No, the snuffer of fun. I thought, *here we are, in a new setting, I can start now and be the new Tina—Fun Tina.* So I stuck a smile on and said, "Sure, let's get the cricket," because new, Fun Tina thought, *what could possibly be the downside of insect ownership?*

12.

"I'm sorry about the cricket. I don't know where else to put him; I don't want him to get smushed," I explained to Richard, the local "realtor for expats" who sat across his desk from us, blinking behind black Buddy Holly glasses, blinking so much that I thought he might have sand in his eyes. Daniel and I were wedged together on a miniature wooden bench facing Richard's cubicle. Daniel's knees scraped the underside of Richard's desk, and when he sat straight, his head grazed the wall behind us.

I held Lila, passed out in my arms, while Piper snoozed in the stroller by the door. The cricket chirped loudly in his tiny basket in the center of Richard's desk.

Richard was maybe 5'5" with a twenty-four-inch waist on a fat day. He had spiky black hair and wore a red long-sleeved button up, jeans, and loafers. He could have been eighteen, but then again, he might have been fifty. Neither age would have surprised me.

Richard patted the top of Mr. Tinsey's basket with several blinks and a small smile. "It's okay, he has a nice song."

"I don't know how he can chirp nonstop at the top of his lungs like that." I wrung my hands and shook my head. "I mean, don't crickets need to breathe?" I looked at Daniel. He shrugged while casually sucking on his fourth Chinese Gatorade.

"His song comes from his legs, not his lungs." Richard looked at me, confused.

"Oh, that's right. I can't even think with all this chirping. Don't his legs get tired then?"

"Perhaps not," Richard said and then turned and fluttered his eyelashes at Daniel. "What's your housing budget?"

"I read that we could find a decent place in Puxi for about $2,000USD per month, so I've created my budget off that number," Daniel said.

"I don't recommend Puxi. It's no good for Americans. Too difficult. Too old. Only Chinese people live there, people like me."

"But——" Daniel started.

"You won't like it." Richard shook his head. "I suggest a foreigner enclave in Pudong. It's more like America there. Much better for Americans to live in those communities."

"I like the sound of the enclave." I looked at Daniel with hope in my eyes.

"We need to live in Puxi; it's closer to my office," Daniel said, ignoring me.

"You can commute. Get car, driver, ayi for kids—all Americans do it like this."

Daniel paused. He looked at me and then back at Richard. "How much is the enclave?"

"Starting price, $5,000 per month."

Daniel laughed and shook his head. "That's a non-starter. What do you have in Puxi?"

Richard sighed and started typing furiously on his keyboard.

"This might be a long shot, but is there an apartment complex with, you know, some sort of play area?" I called to Richard who sat shotgun in the cab. The sun had begun to set, and I was sweaty and exhausted after three petrifying taxi rides to view three dirty, dark, and depressing apartments. Lila whimpered as she watched Piper roll Mr. Tinsey's basket up and down the length of her arm while he continued rubbing his godforsaken legs together.

"Yes, the next place has a playground and a pool," Richard said over his shoulder.

"Oh thank God," I said, dropping my face onto Daniel's shoulder.

He pulled away. "And this place with the pool is in our budget?"

"Little bit higher, not much," said Richard, turning to look ahead.

"We need to stay in the budget, Richard." Daniel looked at me. "You know what happens when you test drive a nicer car than you can afford."

"Oh, let's just look at it!" I begged. "I mean, we haven't seen anything remotely habitable yet. And there's a playground." My voice cracked. "Please?"

Daniel paused. "It's a slippery slope, Tina; that's all I'm saying."

"And in a Chinese taxi, so is life," I said, closing my eyes and hugging Lila to me as we blew through yet another red light.

The driver pulled into a circular, polished travertine driveway lined with tightly clipped azalea hedges. Over-sized, wrought-iron lanterns sat on travertine pillars surrounding a fountain that sparkled and splashed, beckoning all tired apartment-hunters. Straight ahead, we saw it—a mirage-like playground, shiny and pulsating with primary colors. Beyond it lay a gated, resort-like pool, complete with a huge water slide and cascading rock fountain, surrounded by lounge chairs in neutral tones and wide red umbrellas. Three gleaming high rises fringed the complex. I spotted two people sitting on the perfect grass area between the buildings. "There is a spa downstairs and a bar on the third floor," Richard said.

I nearly wept with joy. "Now we're talking!" I whooped.

Richard smiled. "There is an apartment available on the sixth floor. Won't last long."

Daniel looked ahead in silence.

The inside didn't match the outside. For starters, the entire apartment could have fit in our kitchen in the US, or possibly our pantry. There were two doll-sized bedrooms. Only one person could fit in the kitchen at a time. No dishwasher. The mini-cube of a washing machine sat in an itty-bitty closet by the front door. No clothes dryer. A square dining room table was wedged into a space that almost blocked the entrance to the kitchen. On the other side of the table was the living room which contained a love seat, two stools, and a low coffee table the size of a Monopoly board. A newish flat screen TV was attached to the dingy gray wall above a skinny credenza. The furniture was baroque-style and had apparently just been polished—the whole place smelled like varnish. A bare, dusty patio sat beyond a glass sliding door on the far wall.

"This is perfect!" I said, spinning around like Maria in *The Sound of Music*.

"Are we looking at the same place?" Daniel snorted.

"Yes, and I love it. The playground is fantastic."

"We can't move into the playground."

"No, but we'll go there a lot, Daniel. And since I'll be with the kids all day, their entertainment is my priority. This place is a thousand times better than anything else we've seen," I said.

"But there are more places on his list!"

"I don't need to see anyplace else, and I can't bring myself to get back in a cab. We've already skirted death a dozen times today. At some point, our luck is bound to run out."

Daniel exhaled loudly. "Tina, you're going to feel cramped here, I guarantee you."

"So what if I'm a little cramped? We've never needed all the space we've had, I know that now. I can live with less, Daniel. That's part of why I wanted to come here—to learn to live with less. Less is more, I say!" I picked up Lila and flew her in a circle. She squealed.

"My turn, Mommy!" Piper said.

Daniel sighed and turned to Richard. "Looks like we'll take it."

"This will be mine and Mr. Tinsey's room!" Piper yelled, scampering down the mini-hall.

"And Lila's room, too!" I called after her.

13.

"**D**on't look now, but at nine o'clock, there's a little boy pooping on the sidewalk," I said to Daniel out of the side of my mouth. We'd been in China for ten days and were walking near our hotel. Two men in pajamas had stopped whatever they were doing to stare at us as we walked by. Being the object of stares from men cruising town in pajamas already felt semi-normal. The sidewalk pooping did not.

"What? Where?"

"I just told you, nine o'clock. Don't look. His grandma's next to the fence and she's holding him in a squat on her thighs. His pants are split open at the seam in the back, and, oh man, I just got the chills."

"Look away, Tina. We don't need you fainting right now." He glanced at the boy and then back at me. "Welp, I guess that eliminates using the five second rule."

"It suddenly makes sense!" I smacked my forehead. "No wonder the convenience stores don't have diapers—this isn't a diaper culture. Daniel, we only have six diapers left. What do we do?"

"I don't know, teach Lila to squat, I guess."

"That's not remotely funny!"

"Tina, they must have diapers here. There's no way—"

"But I've looked everywhere!"

87

"They'll have them in the grocery stores."

"But we haven't found a grocery store! I don't think that concept exists here either!" I stopped in my tracks and allowed the panic to seep in. "We need to go to the consulate."

"What? Why?"

"To find out where to buy diapers. They'll know if there are grocery stores here, right? They're the consulate!"

"The consulate's where you go in an emergency—when your passport is stolen, or you need to extend your travel visa. They aren't a concierge."

"That's it!" I clapped my hands to my face. "You're a genius!"

"I am?"

"Yes! Didn't Richard say there's a Ritz-Carlton near here? Let's ask their concierge! They must speak English, right? Maybe their gift shop even sells diapers!"

I could see Daniel was weighing whether this was a good idea, and then, unable to suggest a better solution, he shrugged. "I'll find the Ritz in the guidebook."

"There it is—that tan building straight ahead," Daniel said forty-five hot minutes later. I had refused to take another death-defying taxi ride, so we had walked the two miles in the hottest part of the day. Sweat stung and blurred my vision so I squinted to see where he was pointing.

"Wow, it's so out of place." My breath caught in excitement. "Do you think they'll have ice?"

"If they don't, the place right next door will."

I grabbed his arm. "Is it a mirage?"

"Nope." On the front of the two-story cinder block building adjacent to the Ritz, the green mermaid of Starbucks shone in her benevolent circle of love, beckoning us with her tail.

I gave Daniel a side-hug. "I can't remember ever feeling this happy."

◎◎◎

Twenty people were waiting to order when we walked into Starbucks. We arranged ourselves in a huddle behind the last person in line. "What should we get, one of everything?" I hugged myself in glee. "Ouch!" I yelped as something dug into my kidney. I turned to see a woman with sharp elbows glaring at me. She then blazed past me, shouting her order at the barista. He nodded his head without looking at her. Daniel and I looked at each other as another man approached the counter from the other side and did the same thing.

"Wait, this isn't a line?" I said.

"There's no such thing as a line in China." I heard this and turned around. There she stood, a smile in her eyes even as the corners of her mouth turned down in pity. "You must be new," said my first friend in China.

Kristy was tall and thin with light-brown hair cut in an adorable pixie around a pretty, postage-stamp face. She was half Japanese and had grown up in Alaska but moved to Shanghai six years earlier for a job teaching English. She'd subsequently met her husband, Andrew, who was British and taught "maths" at the British International School. Kristy and Andrew had a son named Jeremy who was the same age as Piper.

"Where's Jeremy now?" I asked, scanning the room for Piper's potential playmate.

"School," she said. "But even if he wasn't, I'd never bring him here. He'd rip this place to shreds and then drop a match on it."

"Oh," I said, looking at Piper who was busy emptying the second napkin container.

"He doesn't love school, but his Mandarin is great."

"Do you speak Mandarin too?" I asked.

"Out there I speak just enough to get by." She pointed at the door. "In here, I'm fluent. What do you want? I'll order for you." She looked at her watch. "I have a few minutes, school's almost out."

"Do you know where we can find a grocery store?" Daniel asked Kristy once we were outside.

Kristy looked confused. "You mean, like the one directly below us?"

"Seriously? There's a grocery store below us?" Daniel said.

"Do you know if they have diapers?" I blurted.

"Yes, but they're imported, so they might as well be dipped in gold. Your best bet is to have your next visitor bring a suitcase of them from home."

"We won't have a lot of visitors," I said.

"Then you should ask your ayi to whistle train her."

"What is this whistle training?"

"It's Pavlovian potty training. You whistle in their ear every time they pee; pretty soon they pee whenever you whistle in their ear. Works like a charm, even on tiny babies. The Chinese have been whistle training since the beginning of time. Just ask your ayi—"

"I don't have an ayi." I shook my head.

Kristy regarded me with open-faced horror. "Oh sister, you live in Shanghai now—you must have an ayi if you want to survive. If you walk away with one kernel of wisdom, make it this."

I looked at Daniel. "But we're on a budget."

"Who am I, Kristy Warbucks? Trust me, an ayi will save you more money than she'll cost you. They bargain, pay the local price for everything, erase bribes, call in favors. This is their scene; they get how it operates. Where do you live?"

"In a hotel right now but we're moving into Century Club next week."

"The place with the ornamental playground?"

"What do you mean?"

"That playground is always closed."

"What? No way! It wasn't closed when we were there."

"Oh really? Were kids playing on it?"

"Uh, no."

"That's because it was closed."

I looked at Daniel. He shrugged. "We'll talk to them," he said.

Kristy stopped and pointed at the escalator descending underground in front of the Ritz that I'd assumed was going to a parking garage. "That's how you get to the grocery store. Remember, anytime you need groceries, look down. All grocery stores are underground."

14.

Tina!

I demand an update. It's been three weeks and I haven't heard boo from you. Are you alive? Are you well? Are your hands so greasy from stuffing wontons in your face that you can't drag yourself across the carpet, drop yourself onto a stool, and bang out a brief message to me? I know you suck at communicating (!!!), but a reply will require thirty seconds of your time and allow me to rest peacefully knowing that you're thriving in your new life on the opposite side of the planet.

-Jennifer

P.S. Your cat is an a-hole. I can't believe you talked me into taking him. HE SUCKS. But I'll probably forgive you once I know you're alive. The reply button is typically in the upper left corner of your screen. Click it now or the beast pays . . .

■ ■ ■

Jennifer,

Wow—your timing. The internet serviceman just left our new apartment. Actually, servicemen. It took five hours and seven men to get it up and running. You would have thought they were launching the internet satellite from our gross little patio. I'm not convinced any of them had set up an internet connection before. No one seemed to be in charge. It was a real headscratcher, but hey, I can't complain—I'm connected! At the speed of slugs crossing ice, but I'm working on being less irritated by that, or anything related to speed and efficiency. I came to China with several goals, one of which is to be less aggravated by events out of my control. I can already see that this intention will be tested many times a day. And that I may need to add sanity preservation to my list of aspirations.

Before I begin my journey toward serenity, allow me to quickly list a few of the irritations I've uncovered:

1) Our new apartment has no oven. Somehow, we forgot to check for one on the walk-through, which, according to Daniel, was my fault, since I'll be the one using it, and he was busy haggling. In my defense, I was more concerned about finding A/C, which thankfully does exist—it's near the ceiling in a slim rectangular box in the corner of the living room and both bedrooms, and you need to situate yourself directly underneath it to feel cool. But not too close, because it drips. Back to the oven. Apparently, no one bakes here; all food is stir-fried. I can come around to this, but between you and me, I'm not sure how strongly I'll identify with a culture that doesn't appreciate chocolate chip cookies. Or banana bread. Or lasagna! Gulp. No wonder they're so grumpy! Which brings me to,

2) These people, their grouchiness, good grief. My anger issues? They don't hold a candle, not the wick of a tea light, to the fury I witness here at almost every exchange. I've been here two weeks and have already seen three fist fights. Grown men rolling on the ground, scratching at each other! It stresses me out. Most of the time the people here are barely civil to me. Although, I'll admit,

when I'm with the kids, which is pretty much always, I get a much softer reception. This is because,

3) My kids are celebrities here. I don't jest. Any time we go to a public space, CROWDS of people emerge and surround them. They laugh, they point, they snap pictures, they tug at my clothes and ask me to take pictures, of them, hugging my kids. The first five times, this felt fun, even flattering—like someone else noticed that my kids were special. But let me tell you, the bloom isn't just off the rose, it's been chewed up and spit with gusto into the sewer. Piper now twists up her face and screams when locals so much as turn in her direction. And they don't care! They touch her anyway! Forget subtleties, these people miss direct signals, every time. Speaking of direct signals, I'm not getting a lot of them on the TV because,

4) All of our TV stations are in Mandarin. All eight channels. Wait—I exaggerated. There's one channel that broadcasts news in English—it repeats the same six-minute segment for the entire day. Oh, how I yearn for news from home. I'd watch fifty-five minutes of commercials to get five minutes of English-speaking commentary about anything. I want to hear someone, anyone, outside of my own family, speaking English. My head hurts from all the foreign sounds flying around it. I'd probably be too tired to watch TV, except that,

5) The playground at our complex is not meant for actual use as intended. The pool is always open, which is great, but,

6) No one swims in it! The pool's a virtual ghostland, all day long. Not one kid frolicking! Not until 4 p.m. anyway, and then holy smokes, it's a mob scene. But 4 p.m. is the middle of nap time so we have yet to show up for the party. Maybe someday. It's good to have goals.

Here's my list of good things about this place (It's short, but I'm determined to make it longer):

1)   We're alive and in one piece
2)   The girls and Daniel seem happy
3)   I made a friend. Yay! We're having coffee tomorrow. Oh yeah:
4)   I found coffee!

So there you have it. Your turn. What's new on your side of the world?

-Tina

15.

"**I** don't know how a despicable creature like you, who might cause a grown woman to bleed from the ears, could be considered a pet to anyone, anywhere, at any time," I snarled as I crept slowly toward the corner of the room. It was 3 a.m. We had been in our apartment for four nights, and Mr. Tinsey had escaped from his basket, again. This time he chirped while hanging like some kind of deranged circus cricket from a ceiling tile in the corner of the kids' room, a location which dramatically amplified his already excruciating sound. When it jarred me awake, I honestly thought it was a smoke alarm. But our apartment didn't have a smoke alarm, due to different or possibly non-existent building codes. It was just Tinsey's damn song piercing the night again.

Piper sat up in bed, rubbing her eyes. Lila continued to lie on her back in her crib, wailing.

"I'm coming for you," I said and picked up the desk chair. My words came out in a fierce yet desperate whisper, as if I were impersonating a B-actor in a horror movie. And like any good (or more likely, bad) horror movie, the time had come to slay the beast and roll the damn credits.

"Tina, let me do it, I'm taller than you," Daniel said, mid-yawn. He stood in the doorway in his boxers.

I turned to look at him. "If you promise you'll M-U-R-D-E-R-H-I-M, then I'll let you do it. Otherwise, you can turn around and head right on back to bed."

"I will," he said without hesitation.

"You will what?" I cocked my head.

"I'll do what you just spelled." He scratched his stomach.

"You promise?"

"Yes. I promise." He held his arm out.

"Fine," I handed him the skinny chair.

He propped it against the dingy gray curtains, then stepped on it and wobbled.

"Oh for the love," I said. "Let me do it."

"No, I've got it," he said, grabbing the wall to steady himself.

"Just, please be careful, Daniel. The last thing we need is for you to break your arm again while catching the damn cricket."

And that, right there, is what some people call famous last words.

16.

4 a.m., Renai Hospital

"**E**ven the hospital smells like pee," I said in awe, my head on a swivel as I pushed the stroller into a poorly lit entry hall the size of a hotel ballroom but much filthier than any hotel ballroom I'd ever encountered. "Are you sure you don't want to look for the expat hospital?"

"I'm positive—it's forty-five minutes away, and I have no idea how to tell a taxi driver to find it. We just need to take care of this as fast as possible," Daniel said while wincing and shuffling next to me. The linoleum floor was maroon with brown flecks, although it's possible the brown flecks were ancient clumps of mud. Or something else.

"At least you killed the cricket," I whispered in case the girls could hear me from their slumber. "I mean, not that I'm glad this happened, at all, but you know what I'm saying. Thank you."

He didn't respond. About twenty rusty folding chairs sat near the center of the room where people had congregated to watch cartoons on a flat-screen TV balanced on a hodge-podge of side tables. There weren't nearly enough chairs for the other hundred or so people who waited, perched against the walls, shifting their weight from one leg to the other, many of them wearing large visible bandages on their head or torso. A dozen people sat in wheelchairs also facing the TV; another dozen squatted against the wall in the far corner, smoking.

From what I could tell, there were three reception areas. We headed toward the least crowded one.

"Do you speak English?" I asked several people who all looked away uncomfortably. The last guy finally picked up a phone and yelled into it. A short, plump woman in blue scrubs hustled over. "Hello, how may I help you?" she said.

"Hello! I'm so happy you can understand me. My husband broke his arm. He's in a lot of pain, and we don't know where to go."

"How you know it broken?" she asked.

"Well, he's broken it before, in the same spot, and he says it felt just like this, so—"

"Go for x-ray." She pointed to the farthest reception area. "You must first wait there."

"Uh," I stammered.

"Come, follow me." She scurried in front of us, hollering as she pushed through the sea of people loitering around the desk. I attempted a futile manipulation of the double stroller behind her, through the masses of humanity, but ended up reversing out and circumnavigating the crowd.

"First you get number!" our hostess cried once we found her, pointing to a stainless-steel pole with a mechanism at the top that dispersed pink paper numbers from a roll.

I paused, confused at first. "Oh! Like a deli!" I said, proud to have grasped the concept. I looked at Daniel for his approval. His eyes were closed, his face, pale. I pulled number 74 and looked at the screen above the desk—it said 47. "Wait—I think the numbers are reversed," I said. Then the number changed to 48.

The wait was eye-opening, although to be fair, nothing in Shanghai to that point hadn't been eye-opening. For starters, the hospital setting didn't preclude my kids from being celebrities. Neither did the fact that they were asleep. People crowded around us, reaching into the stroller to shake their feet.

"Uh, please don't touch. Sleeping." I put my palms together and put them to my ear, tilting my head to rest on them. They ignored me, which made we wonder if either, 1) this wasn't the universal sign for sleeping, or 2) they didn't give a hoot that this was the universal sign for sleeping. They just wanted to touch my kids.

For my job at home, I'd attended many a five-day conference where the sole focus was the minimization of hospital-related infections. The lengths we would go in the US to keep germs far from any orifice were astounding, but also, necessary. At this hospital, I marveled at the sheer number of patients waiting in the lobby who were either actively oozing blood, attached to an IV pole by a mountain of dirty, peeling steri-strips, or sneezing and/or coughing without covering their mouth or nose. Several people were engaged in all of the above. I'd noticed a remarkable amount of people walking around Shanghai wearing surgical face masks and had assumed it had been for protection against the air pollution, which was significant. However, I then realized they may have also been protecting themselves against disease and infection. I wondered where I could procure four of these face masks, and how I could coerce my children into wearing them.

At 6:57 a.m., number 74 flashed onto the screen. My eyes burned as I ran toward the desk and yelled back at Daniel, "Hurry up!" Our English-speaking comrade must have been following our progress because she hustled up, too. She explained to the man at the desk, in what sounded like tremendous detail, Daniel's situation. The man nodded with no words. He slowly pulled open the drawer in front of him and extracted an 8" x 6" book of triplicate forms. He inserted an ancient piece of cardboard between the first triplicate and the rest of the book. Then he filled every last millimeter of the top sheet with characters. He removed the blue copy, slowing at each point of perforation, and finally handed it to me.

"Wait one moment," said my comrade and then spoke to the man in a stern voice while he filled out a second triplicate, this one half the size of the first. When he was finished, he tugged out the pink copy, also with great care, and slid it toward me.

"Take pink paper to that desk to pay," she said, pointing to the only desk in the lobby we hadn't visited yet which apparently housed the cashier. "Then take blue paper to third floor."

My shoulders sunk as I saw the line for the cashier curve around the desk and turn at the wall. "Please, is there any way to speed up this process?" I pleaded. "My husband is in a lot of pain."

"Not much longer now, okay?" she said brightly, as though we were waiting in line for Space Mountain. Then she leaned down and squeezed my sleeping kids' feet.

I walked over to the cashier's desk with notably less bounce and enthusiasm and pulled another number. I looked at the monitor; twenty-three spots until our turn.

"What's that?" I whispered two hours later, eyes bulging from my head as I clutched our third paper number du jour. Daniel moaned softly in the chair next to me. Piper was taking laps around the waiting area with her eyes closed. Lila blinked her big blue eyes and played with her toes, entertaining throngs of idle sneezers.

We'd finally made it to the third-floor x-ray department, which felt both like significant progress and no progress at all. I felt despair enter my throat and begin to seep toward my chest when I noticed, out of the corner of my eye, a small movement in an empty gurney parked against the far wall in the x-ray waiting room. Then I rejected the ludicrous notion—movement in an empty gurney! Until I saw it again, one tiny motion.

"Oh my God, Daniel. I think there's a cat in that gurney."

"What?" he mumbled from his pain-induced haze.

"There's an animal in that gurney. I think it's a black cat; I'm going to look. Holler if you see your number come up, okay?"

He didn't answer. I stood, feeling the vinyl chair peel away from the backs of my thighs like a sweaty band-aid. I tiptoed forward and poked my head over the corner of the gurney. I stood abruptly and quickly walked back.

"Holy CRAP," I said.

"What? What is it?" Daniel asked, opening his eyes.

"It's a baby," I said. "There's a baby in that gurney."

"A human baby?"

"Yes, a newborn human baby. Where's her mother?" I stood and looked around. "Daniel, I don't think anyone's in charge of that baby. I just noticed her, and we've been here for a while. No one else has gone close to that gurney."

"Don't jump to conclusions. Her mom is probably in the bathroom. Or getting an x-ray. I bet she's on her way back to her as we speak."

I looked at him, feeling the furrow between my eyebrows deepen. "Let's hope you're right."

"That does it," I said, three minutes later. I stood and put my hands on my hips. "I've waited long enough. No one's on their way back to that baby. I'm going to find someone to tell me what's going on."

Daniel closed his eyes and shook his head.

Needless to say, there was not a lot of English being spoken in the X-ray department. Or anywhere. But I'm nothing if not persistent, and so finally, an old guy who'd played peekaboo with Lila earlier said he could translate for me. He was confined to a wheelchair and his head was wrapped in gauze. I pushed him toward the reception window where he struck up an argument.

"What did he say?" I asked him once the yelling tapered off.

"He say baby have no mama. No baba. This morning baby left at back door of hospital."

"What? But why? Just look at her! She's gorgeous!" I swallowed and pointed emphatically at the gurney where she lay, blinking, not making a peep, her cheeks pink, her head covered in an explosion of black fuzz.

He shrugged. "Girl baby," he said, as if that was some sort of explanation.

"But girl babies are good! I have two girl babies!"

"Yes." He looked disappointed for me.

"Can you ask the man where this baby will go? Who will take care of her?" My mind jumped to the women I knew at home, so many of them battling infertility. I was all too familiar with that struggle myself. And here lay this perfect baby, unwanted, a casualty of her sex. I could have named five women off the top of my head who would give their right arm to love this baby. I leaned over and grabbed the vinyl pads of the wheelchair armrests, bringing my face close to that of my translator's. "You tell the man I want this baby. I can take her, today." I glanced at Daniel after I said this. His eyes were closed again. He had no idea what I was doing, but that didn't bother me in the slightest. In my naive little fantasy world, my commitment to finding a family for this child was all I needed. Women all over the globe yearned for this unwanted child lying in front of me, swaddled in a rumple of sheets, so quiet and all alone. She could have a good life, this gurney baby; I could bring that to her. I felt energized as I waited for my translator's permission.

"Baby stay here," he said after speaking to the man at the window.

"What? No! For how long will she stay here? And then where will she go?"

He shrugged.

"Can you please ask the man?"

He shook his head. "Before, I ask him; he say he don't know. Later someone pick up baby."

"But that's ridiculous!" Spit flew from my mouth as I yelled. "No one's even paying attention to her, and I can help her now! I can find her a good family!" I wiped my chin and burst into furious tears.

Daniel shuffled up. "My number." He pointed with his good arm at the monitor, either not noticing or ignoring my distress. I turned to look at the monitor, but my attention was drawn to the red sign above the door behind it—Emergency Exit. My tears evaporated as my brain worked a plan.

"Yeah, okay. See you in a bit," I said. I didn't tell him that once he was finished, I would enlist his help to steal this baby.

17.

I didn't steal the baby. As the plan was hatching in my mind, the girls suddenly, urgently needed to go to the bathroom. When we returned, the baby and gurney were gone. I burst into tears as Daniel told me a woman in a white outfit had just come and pushed the baby down the hall and around the corner. I sobbed and tore at my hair for a while as Daniel looked on, glassy-eyed. Apparently, while prepping him for his x-ray, they had given him something for the pain. He told me in a jumble of thick-tongued words to get over myself; he needed to wait in one line to get a cast, and I needed to get downstairs with the kids to wait in another line to pay for it.

"You'll need this," he said as he dug a crumpled pink slip out of his shorts pocket with his good hand.

"I don't want to go back down there by myself," I said, sniffing, wiping my eyes with my t-shirt.

"You won't be alone; you'll have the kids. Besides, if we don't divide and conquer, we'll be in this dump all night," he said. "And, today's—"

Right then Lila started crying.

The sweat inside my fist dampened the fourth deli number of the day as I closed my eyes and tried to picture my happy place. I drew a blank. I eventually paid twenty dollars for a cast I would have paid 100 times more for had it been available ten hours earlier, when we'd first arrived at this abysmal place.

I felt a draining sensation in my heart as we pulled away from the hospital. I looked at Daniel and my eyes filled. There we sat, he, broken-armed and I, broken-hearted. Our legs were touching, but I felt miles away from him. That was when I realized what he'd been trying to tell me earlier—it was his birthday.

I took a deep breath and attempted to sound upbeat. "How should we celebrate?" I smiled at him and then looked out the window. It was 4 p.m., and our taxi idled on a raised, six-lane road in a mass of black-cloud spewing, horn-blaring, immobile mayhem.

Daniel scratched at his cast and turned toward me. "You know what I really want? A good Chinese meal," he said. "I know we've been avoiding it because the smells make you gag and the mysterious meats—"

"Because I don't want to eat somebody's dog, Daniel."

"Just to clarify, no culture eats their pets."

"What's that supposed to mean?"

"It means you wouldn't be eating somebody's dog; you'd just be eating a dog."

I sighed and closed my eyes. "That's not comforting."

He nudged me with his good elbow. "I can't eat microwaved pizza from the Century Bar again. Please? I promise not to order from the dog section of the menu, okay?"

"Sure." I nodded at him. "Whatever you want." It was his birthday after all and so far, all he'd gotten was an arm wrapped in twenty pounds of plaster, an old school cast from the seventies. The back of his neck was already pink and chapping from the weight of his cast in the pleather sling.

"Do you know what restaurant you want to go to?" I asked.

"No," he said. "I could call Richard—"

"Wait, I have a better idea." I grabbed my phone and dialed Kristy.

"Yo! New kid!" she sang into the phone.

"Quick question, Kristy. I want to take Daniel to dinner for his birthday tonight. Can you recommend a decent Chinese place walking distance from our apartment?"

"If I tell you, can we come?" Kristy asked. "It's Saturday, which means we're all just sitting around, pushing each other's buttons."

"Of course! That'll be fun."

18.

"This restaurant has the best duck in all of Shanghai," Kristy's husband, Andrew announced in a British accent so thick that, initially, I wasn't sure he was speaking English.

I cleared my throat and looked at the fish tank next to me. It hadn't been cleaned in perhaps a decade. It didn't smell, or at least I couldn't smell it over the cigarette smoke. When a hostess approached Andrew, he beckoned for us to follow him.

We walked by row after row of tables, each covered in a maroon tablecloth and under their own dusty brass chandelier. When we got to our table, Andrew directed everyone to their seats.

"You should sit here." Andrew looked at me and smiled, patting the chair on the other side of him. "I can help you order."

"Doesn't Kristy know how to order?" I looked at Kristy, trying to sound casual, to keep the begging tone from my voice. He seemed friendly enough, but I had a pounding headache and didn't want to strain to understand someone. I did that all day long.

Kristy shook her head. "He's way better. Plus, you and I should be on either side of the kids. You know, in the interest of containment."

"True," I said. I felt uncelebratory.

Daniel sat on the other side of Andrew, his giant cast resting between them. The girls and I had decorated his cast when we got back to the apartment from the hospital. It boasted a large purple castle adorned with many red flags, a moat, a drawbridge, several upside-down Ws (a.k.a. flying birds), and two pink princesses. Plaster had its upsides, or at least, an upside.

Piper had already unleashed herself from the stroller and plopped into a chair next to Jeremy. They stared at each other for a while, sniffing. Then Piper poked Jeremy's arm and smiled, perhaps because it wasn't broken. He looked confused at first but then poked her arm and smiled back.

Jeremy turned to look, first at Andrew, then at Kristy. "Mama, I can please go look fish with him?"

Andrew responded first. "Look *at* the fish, Jeremy. And Piper is a her, not a him."

"*With* her, *with* her! *At* the fish! Please, Baba!" Jeremy bounced in his chair.

Piper crossed her arms and shook her head. "I don't want to look at the fish," she grumbled, a straight-up lie, one I recognized from my own DNA. She just wanted the fish-viewing to be her idea.

"I go with me then, okay Mama?" Jeremy said.

"I'll go by myself," corrected Andrew.

"*Duì de*," said Jeremy, nodding.

"Don't go out the door," said Kristy.

"*Shénme?*" Jeremy said.

"*Bùyào cóng nàgè mén chūqù!*" Kristy barked.

"*Hǎo de*, Mama," Jeremy said and ran between the tables toward the front of the restaurant. I pulled Lila onto my lap.

"What'd you tell him?" I asked.

"Not to leave," Kristy said.

Andrew exhaled. "That's the downside of local schooling—if you want them to follow instructions, you need to say them in Chinese in the loud, stern voice a Chinese teacher would use."

"Wow, that's something else," Daniel said.

"The language acquisition is eventually supposed to even out, at which point they'll speak both languages fluently," Kristy said.

"When does that happen?" I asked.

"It depends on the child," Kristy said. "Most kids Jeremy's age are already there. Some of them switch between three or four languages depending on who they're talking to. But Jeremy just seems more confused by all of it."

"He'll get there," Andrew said, skimming the menu pages. "I'll order duck for all of us plus a few other plates since I can see we're getting quite hungry."

Daniel said, "Oh man, thank you, I could eat a horse."

"Really? Because I think they have horse here." He skipped ahead a few pages.

Daniel looked at me nervously. "It was just a figure of speech."

"I'm familiar with the figure of speech; I just wasn't sure how adventurous you might be feeling."

I cleared my throat. "On the adventurous scale? We're a one. Maybe closer to a zero than a one. Mainly because this," I waved my hands in the air, "this whole thing is an adventure. So I'd rather keep the menu unexciting if at all possible." I opened my menu. "I can't read this." I closed the menu, dropped it back on the table, and dropped my chin into my hand, moping.

"What are you looking for?" Andrew asked, leaning over.

"You read characters?" I asked him.

"Yes, well, menu characters and street signs," he said.

I paused and looked down. "This will probably sound strange . . ."

"Oh?" Andrew said, his smile fading slightly.

"I know this is a Chinese food place—"

"Not just *a* Chinese food place, *the* Chinese food place!" Andrew laughed and drummed the table with his index fingers.

"It's just that, I'm not crazy about Asian food, and I'd give anything for a salad. Nothing elaborate, just your basic side salad."

"But this—"

"Don't get me wrong," I raised my hand and smiled. "I'll try the food you order, but it's been a rough day and it's really warm and smoky in here. I just feel like crunching down on a fresh piece of cold lettuce."

Andrew frowned. "In China, they don't eat raw vegetables."

"I know, I know, and I don't mean to be high maintenance, but since this restaurant is more upscale than any place we've been so far, I was hoping they could accommodate my craving."

"It's really not a good idea," he said as the waitress walked up and stood between us.

I craned my neck around her waist and smiled. "Thanks, Andrew, I so appreciate it."

When Andrew went to the bathroom and Kristy took a phone call, Daniel came over and squatted between the girls. "You okay?" he asked softly as he attempted to position his cast between the chargers.

"What? Yeah, I'm great. I just asked Andrew to order me a salad."

"A salad? Do they even make those here?"

"I'm pretty sure they do."

"Tina . . ."

"Hey, what are these little things?" I tilted a large white plastic bowl that had been plunked on the table toward myself. It was filled with what looked like a mixture of peanuts and small, unidentifiable silver objects the same size as the peanuts but flatter. I picked out a few of the nuts to sample. "I'm not sure—"

Piper hollered, "Mommy don't hog it!" She pulled on the lip of the bowl, nearly toppling it.

"I won't hog if you won't grab," I said and held the bowl for her. She reached in with both hands and smashed the contents into her mouth.

"What are these silver things?" I passed the bowl to Daniel. "Bleh, they're really salty. They almost taste like—"

"Fish heads," Daniel said, holding one up to the light.

"Holy crap!" I wiped my tongue with my napkin.

"Look, Piper!" Daniel took a fish head and air-swam it onto her plate. "I'm delicious!" he said in a Donald Duck voice.

"They're so cute, Daddy! And yummy!" She grabbed the nut bowl and deposited it in her lap, wrapping one arm around it for protection as Lila screamed.

"You can have the bowl later," I said to Lila, patting her chubby fist as she pounded it on the table.

"No, she can't," Piper mumbled as she hunched over the bowl, picking out the fish heads and creating a stack of them on her plate. "There are millions and millions of fish heads in here, Daddy! And look, this one has a body!" She picked it up and held it an inch from her nose. She made her voice squeaky and said, "Hello there, Mr. Fish, how are you today?" She switched to her deep voice. "Well, I'd be better if I was just a fish head. This body's too heavy." Back to squeaky, "Well here, let me fix that for you." She ripped the head from the body, tossing the body onto her plate and the head into her mouth. "Look! It's raining fish heads!" she proclaimed, picking up a pile and sprinkling half of it around her plate. "And even in my mouth!" she dropped the other half onto her tongue, looked up, chewed, and smiled.

Andrew came back and didn't notice the fish head puppet show. He sat down, crossed his wet hands on the table and turned to me. "Daniel tells me you'll be spending a lot of time alone with the kids."

"Yes, he'll be traveling a lot, and that's, uh, always been my job until now."

"So you've swapped both family positions and global positions." I smiled. "Exactly."

"I bet you wake up wondering both who and where you are some days," he said.

I thought about admitting that even though our circumstances had radically changed, I'd often wondered the same things at home.

Instead I said something that was also true, "I think I've been too overwhelmed to wonder much of anything about myself."

"Well, I know Kristy wants to help you when she's not working, but most of the time, you'll need to lean on your ayi to pull you through."

"I, uh—" Two waitresses balancing massive serving trays approached. They began to unload enough food for a mid-sized wedding on the lazy Susan.

Daniel rubbed his hands together in delight. "What are we looking at?"

Andrew pointed at the plates as they were set down. "This one is fried chicken with chilis which will make your tongue go numb but are also strangely addicting. Here we have broccoli with delicately sliced beef. This one is stewed eggplant braised with pork. Here are eggs delicately scrambled with fresh tomatoes. This is my personal favorite—sliced potatoes with peppers. And here's the fried rice with mixed meat and vegetables."

"What exactly do they mean by 'mixed meat'?" I asked.

"The usual I guess," he said.

"But what's usual?"

He ignored me and continued. "Here are noodles mixed with onions in a sauce that *mmm*, smells like heaven. Three varieties of dumplings. Fresh cucumbers, peeled, sliced and drizzled with peanut sauce. Sweet and sour fish—"

"Complete with head and tail," I interrupted.

"Because that's how fish is served in China and many other places in the world." He paused. "And finally," Andrew said as the largest platter was placed on the lazy Susan in front of his seat. "The duck— an 800-year-old Imperial Palace tradition." He spread his arms and looked up. "Happy birthday, Daniel. It's a pleasure to meet you. Please enjoy—" the waitress came up and whispered in his ear, handing him a small plate. He turned to me. "Your salad." He set it down in front of me—a rectangular side plate with four leaves of soggy white iceberg, sheer at the ends, three slimy-on-the-inside, pruney-on-the-outside tomato wedges, and a small bowl of lukewarm white sauce.

I looked at my pathetic attempt at comfort food as the aromas from the rest of the table wafted into my nose. I closed my eyes and inhaled, stretching my nostrils up and over my plate toward the delicious scents. "Cheers!" Andrew called and the three of them drank beer as I continued to enjoy breathing through my nose.

"Uh, Tina? Cheers," Daniel said and held his glass toward me.

"Oh, sorry!" I opened my eyes and lifted my glass. "Cheers, honey. Happy birthday." I air-kissed him.

"This is family-style eating so please, help yourself," Andrew said and then leaned toward me. "You may want to pretend that salad never came."

"Oh no, I don't want to waste it." I said, looking around my plate. "But, uh, do they have forks?"

"I'll ask," Andrew said and waved at the waitress.

"Behold, the skin of the duck," Andrew held up a stiff translucent sheet, the color of baked honey, with his chopsticks.

"Wow," Piper said.

"Nice," Daniel said.

I leaned toward Kristy. "Does Chinese food in Alaska taste like this?" I slurped the last bite of my third serving of eggplant off my fork. "I won't even touch eggplant at home!"

"I won't touch Chinese food at home," she said, flicking the fried rice with her chopsticks directly from her bowl into her mouth.

I admired her dexterity.

"Please place your plates on the lazy Susan, and I'll do the honors," Andrew said.

"No skin for me, please," I said as I plunked down my plate on the rotating circle. "Does duck have white meat?" I asked Kristy.

She shrugged.

"Just the tiniest slice of the best part for you, Tina," Andrew said as he spun my plate toward him. He then grabbed a small circle of rice paper, a tiny spoonful of plum sauce, a slice of two different colors of meat, and a sprig of the stalk of a green onion—the part I'd always thrown away. He arranged them carefully on the rice paper. Next, he took his chopstick and broke off a piece of the skin the length of a toothpick and not much wider. He dropped it cautiously in the center of the pile and sent the plate back to me.

It was delicious.

"Can we go back there tomorrow?" Piper asked when I tucked her in that night. Lila was already passed out on her belly in her crib. She'd slept through half of dinner, too. That child could sleep in a train station.

"To where, that restaurant?" I asked.

"Yes, Mommy, that place has all my new favorite foods," she said with a serious expression.

"Really?" I sighed and smiled, remembering the flavors. "Which ones did you love best?"

"The fish heads and duck skin, Mommy. They were so-ho-ho-ho-ho good. I'll dream about them tonight," she said and turned onto her side.

I brushed her hair back from her forehead. "I'm glad you liked it. We'll go back there soon, okay?"

"Okay, Mommy."

"Kids are amazing," I said to Daniel as I lay next to him in bed.

"Hmmm . . . How so?"

"I mean, Piper and Lila haven't missed a beat here. They're exactly the same people they were before we left, but somehow, they get here, where everything about their life is different, and crazy, and befuddling, and confounding, and jarring, and they love it. I don't know how, but they've already accepted this place."

"Except the people touching their hair."

"Right, but outside of that, did you know Piper already calls this her home? Shanghai is *home* to them, Daniel. She doesn't ask about anything back in the US, not the kids, not the preschool, not the cat. How is that even possible?"

"Because they have us," Daniel said. "Everything feels like home to them as long as we're in it."

I sighed. "I'd like to take credit for it, but I think it's bigger than us. They're adaptable, Daniel. They've adapted."

"You're right. They have."

"I'm too rigid to adapt," I said.

"Well, you're an adult."

"I'm a rigid adult. I'm stuck in my ways."

He said nothing.

"And I'm highly judgmental. I'm like a mean-spirited robot."

He laughed. "Robots don't have spirits."

"That depends on what movie you're watching."

He paused. "Why does your kids being good have to mean that you're being bad? Why are you comparing yourself to them?"

"It's an observation," I said. "They're not like me, and that's good." I paused. "Have you adapted?"

"Hmmm. I think I will adapt, but as of this moment, not really. You wouldn't believe what I've already seen in the factories—it's beyond comprehension. The bathrooms . . ."

"Everything here is beyond my comprehension, and I'm not getting used to it," I said. "Not any of it."

"I know, I can tell. But you will, Tina. You can do anything; you can certainly do this."

I sighed. "I hope so." I grabbed his good hand.

"Just wait; you'll be queen of this place before you know it."

"I'd be a great queen," I said and smiled as I closed my eyes.

I was Queen of the Latrine a couple hours later when the first wave of food poisoning hit me.

"Tina, what happened? Are you okay?" Daniel asked, flipping on the lights in the bathroom. I was curled around the base of the not-so-clean toilet, whimpering.

"No, I'm not okay," I said. "Turn off the lights."

"Do you have the flu?"

"No, I think it was the salad." I felt another wave of nausea rise. I scrambled to sit up in time and drooped my head over the bowl.

Daniel turned off the lights and sat on the tile next to me. "Andrew told me this might happen."

"He's a fucking Know-It-All," I said and sagged my head onto the tile again, heaving my right arm up and locating a cool spot on it to rest on my temple.

"You said he was nice!"

"He is, I'm just mad at myself."

"He said we need to start eating like the locals. We haven't accumulated enough of the local gut bacteria to combat whatever might show up on uncooked vegetables here. He also said we should never eat anything that depends on refrigeration to not spoil. That white sauce . . ."

I scrambled up and vomited again. "Can we not talk about it? Seriously. I'm sick enough." I rested my head on the toilet seat and closed my eyes. "Can you please go now?" I said. "I want to wallow in misery by myself."

Daniel stood and walked out of the bathroom, closing the door behind him.

"Wait!" I cried with my last reserve of energy. I looked up with my head balanced on the rim of the bowl. He opened the door again and looked down at me with an expression I couldn't read, but it wasn't adoration. I wanted to tell him that I changed my mind. That

I didn't want him to leave me alone, not at all. Because I needed him more than I ever had. But then my hair felt suddenly heavier. The reason hit me as I considered the unfortunate proximity of my head to the basin.

"Can you get me a hair tie?" I squeaked and vomited again.

19.

The next morning found Daniel on a train to a distant factory and me at the playground in the park with the girls, alternating between sweating, shivering, and yearning for a friend. I felt anxious and terrified because we were alone in this corner of the park and the playground equipment resembled the kind that had been banned in the US since the '80s. Teeter totters that arced high, allowing ample room for finger squishing. Spinning platforms with greasy bars for kids to cling to as they kicked off, spinning faster and faster. Tall, steep metal slides with barely a lip on the sides. If I encouraged them to play on something more safe, they dissolved into tantrums on the ground—the foul, phlegm-riddled ground. I had choices to make and none of them ended well. It was the setting of a parenting horror movie.

When I wasn't gripped by fear and isolation, I reflected on how much my life had changed in the last month. Suddenly I realized it had been exactly one month since we'd arrived. It felt like we had been in Shanghai both longer and shorter than that. Longer because so much had already happened and every day brought new adventures and experiences we didn't understand. Shorter because I still had so much to learn, and the more I learned, the more I realized I didn't know. I wondered, would I ever be able to do this well?

I suddenly wanted to talk to my boss. To drop myself briefly into a space where I was considered excellent. It couldn't wait. I looked at the girls, who were taking a break from near-death fun to stare at a group of seniors who were slowly ambling toward the crumbling badminton courts on the backside of the playground.

"Hello?" Chuck answered in a scratchy voice. Oops. It was 1:00 a.m. his time.

"Hey. It's Tina."

"Tina? Hi! Where are you?"

"I'm in China," I said. "Remember?"

"Of course," he said. "I thought for a sec it was all a dream and you were still here insomniating."

I laughed. "I don't think that's a word." I heard him struggle and turn on his light.

"So, Tina, how may I help you at this fine hour?"

"I just wanted to know how everything is going there, you know, without me."

His voice perked up. "Well I can't believe I'm saying this, but I really like your replacement. I'm so glad you found him for me; he's going to do a great job."

"A great job?" I snorted. "I mean he's nice, and I'm sure he'll work hard but—" I turned to pace toward an arrangement of rocks behind the rusty swing set.

"No, he's a real go-getter! Remember that deal you were trying to close at Loma Linda? He landed the contract last week. It's going to be huge—a hospital-wide conversion! Even bigger than you and I were expecting."

"I created that opportunity, Chuck. It was in my pipeline. I was just keeping your expectations low so you wouldn't ride me about it." I clenched my jaw as I reached the closest rock and spun back around. As I planted my first return step, I glanced up at the kids. Lila had chased Piper to the sky-high monkey bars. Piper had climbed to the top and swung herself up to sit on the bars, dangle

her legs and tease Lila, who was on the ladder reaching, reaching
. . . I started to run, but I was too late.

BAM. A full faceplant.

"Wahhhhh!"

"Well I think—" Chuck started.

"Chuck, I gotta go. I, I gotta go." I hung up just as I got to Lila
lying on the ground wailing.

"You okay, Lila? You okay??!!" Piper screamed. She was rocking
back and forth above us, leaning over the side of the monkey bars to
get closer to her sister.

I picked up Lila and looked up at Piper. I couldn't reach her if I
put my arm up and jumped. "Piper, she's okay. Just be still and stay
where you are. I'll come get you in a minute, okay?"

Piper whimpered and continued rocking. "Please just wait, Piper.
Please please please be still."

I knelt down to rest Lila on my knees and examined her face.
Her eyes were wide in hysterics, but her pupils looked even. I wiped
the dirt gently from her lips, eyelashes, and hair line as she heaved
and sobbed. A small trickle of blood ran down her chin and a savage
road rash bloomed on her forehead.

"Oh baby, I'm so sorry. I'm so, so sorry." I held her to me and
closed my eyes, stinging with escaping tears, and rocked both of us.

Then I felt a cool shadow envelope us and looked up. It was one
of the men from the group of seniors. He stood next to me under
Piper, leaning on his cane, assessing the situation, nodding.

He raised his cane to the bars. "Please turn and put your hand
here," he said, tapping one bar closer to the ladder. He had such a
sense of peace about him, I could only watch and listen.

Piper quieted down and did what he said. He tapped on the side
of her hand.

"Other hand here."

She followed his instructions. He tapped her all the way back to
the ladder then stood under her as she wiggled her legs down to the

top rung where his cane rested, then tapped her all the way down to the ground. She waited for his taps to move. I sat speechless, watching, rocking. As Lila's screeches turned to whimpers, she pushed back so she could see what I was watching.

Once Piper was down, he turned to smile at Lila with scarce teeth.

"You speak English?" I asked him.

He nodded. "*Yi dian dian*," he said and held his fingers close together.

I smiled and wiped my eyes. "Thank you very much."

He knelt down and scanned Lila's face.

"I have band aids," I said. "Is there a water fountain?"

"Follow me," he leaned hard on his cane as he walked to a bench near the badminton court where he had a small leather satchel.

"Water no good here. Clean with this. Boiled." He handed me a glass canister with tea leaves floating in it.

"Are you sure?"

"Sure. Clean."

I took a Kleenex from my pocket and poured tea on it. I dabbed the dirt from Lila's forehead and then pressed the tissue to her chin. I held out the canister and he took it from me.

"You like tea?" he asked Piper. "Make you strong and healthy."

Piper nodded, and he poured her some in a small steel cup he detached from the top of his canister.

She sipped it and looked at me. "Yummy," she said and handed the cup back to him as Lila nuzzled her head into my shoulder.

A woman from his group hollered at him over the sound blaring from a cassette player. She stood in front of the group slowly swinging her arms forward and backward to the beat of a man's voice counting from one to five in Mandarin over and over again. Everyone in the group gently, barely dipped their knees as they swung their arms on number five.

"I go to my exercise class now," he said and turned to walk slowly away.

I wanted to thank him for his kindness, for shifting our morning from disastrous to peaceful. But I had a feeling he didn't care to be thanked again, so instead we watched him walk back to his friends who were waiting for him, and I realized it was time for me to make greater efforts to find some friends of my own.

20.

"The toy stores here are all crap," Kristy said a week later at Starbucks. She mouthed the straw protruding from her iced coffee like a horse procuring a carrot, and then slurped the remnants of her cup loudly without breaking eye contact. "You can buy imported toys at the mall, but they'll cost you a small fortune. Your other option is to buy local toys at one of the street markets, but they'll break within five minutes." She bit into her giant muffin and started slowly chewing, then stopped to say, "Are you sure you don't want anything?"

"Yeah." I dabbed at my face with a napkin from the stack Piper had pilfered. I was sweating profusely and generally felt unwell. "It is seriously humid here," I said. I looked at the girls, both passed out in the stroller.

"That's August for you," she said.

"So, you're telling me not to buy toys?" I asked.

Kristy paused. "Look, can I give you a word of advice?"

"That's why I'm sitting here. My kids are driving me bananas and Daniel's been gone for a week. I need some toys!" My voice had grown progressively louder until the word "toys" ricocheted off the skyscrapers surrounding us, filling the hot wet air with its echo. People at the other tables glanced over as toys . . . toys . . .

toys . . . bounced off the blacktop, the windows, and the concrete. I wrapped a napkin around a piece of ice from my coffee and held it to my forehead.

"Listen, you don't need toys, you need school. All kids in China go to school as soon as they can walk. Do you ever see kids playing here during the day?"

"No, never," I said.

"That's because they're all in school."

I looked at her like she was pulling my leg. "Really? I thought we were just going to the wrong places to play."

"Nope. And another thing—do you want Piper to learn Mandarin?"

"Yes, definitely. Someone in our home needs to be able to communicate."

"Then stick her in a local preschool, like the one Jeremy goes to! It's by far your cheapest option."

"'Cheap' has never been a big selling point for me."

"Does Daniel's company cover schooling?"

"No."

"Then trust me, it's a selling point. Listen, if she's not in school, you'll be staring at each other all day long, and that's not good for anyone."

"But I just quit my job!" I whined. "I haven't had much time with her or Lila until now."

She took my hands. "Tina, deep down, you and I both know that you and Piper will be happier with a little school time. Look at you—no offense—but you're a mess! A few hours of separation during the week isn't a *bad* thing, it's a *life* thing, okay?" She squeezed my hands and let them go. "Come with me to tour Jeremy's school; I'll set up a meeting with the principal. I'm working tomorrow, but I can take you next Thursday."

I cocked my head. "What's your job again?"

"Cross-cultural communication. I consult expats sent to Shanghai by large companies on how to adapt. This advice I'm giving? I usually charge for it."

As we stood up, I said, "I have my doubts about a local school. I mean, I haven't been inside one, but I've walked by plenty. The uniforms freak me out. Does Jeremy wear a red neckerchief?"

"Yeah, and trust me, they're great. It looks like you could use a neckerchief right now. You've blown through an entire tree's worth of napkins wiping the sweat off your face. Neckerchiefs are useful in this climate."

I pushed my wrought-iron chair under its matching table and then leaned heavily on it. "What about the morning calisthenics on the playground? I can't picture Piper following the instructions of one man with a megaphone doing head, shoulders, knees, and toes while counting to eight over, and over, and over."

"You'd be surprised."

"Ha! You may have noticed—my child is not much of a rule follower. She needs a school that lets her believe she is in charge and that everything that happens is her idea. She sees herself as the supreme leader, and I don't see that going over so well in these parts." I paused. "What about the international school where Andrew works? They learn Mandarin there too, right?" I asked.

"That's a good one!" She slapped her leg.

"What?"

"No one puts their kids in an international school unless they're a client of mine and have been sent here by a huge corporation. Those schools are outrageously expensive! The families who send their kids there have allowances to pay for it. They also have housing allowances of ten thousand dollars a month, minimum. And cars with drivers who wear white gloves."

"But everyone wears white gloves."

"My point is that those schools aren't for normal people. I couldn't afford one day of tuition there."

FISH HEADS AND DUCK SKIN

"Oh." I looked down. "Not for normal people."

"You know what I mean. How about we meet in front of your place at 8:00 a.m. on Thursday? We can walk to Jeremy's school together."

"Sure, that works," I said, feeling the unintended sting of being average and unexceptional.

21.

"I can't do it," I told Daniel the following Thursday night. I dropped my head onto the plastic throw pillow adorning our love seat which, much like the playground and the grassy areas in the parks, was not intended for use. The love seat, covered in an unfortunate lavender floral print, felt like it had been pushed through a laminating machine. At that moment I didn't care though; I felt exhausted and needed to be horizontal without actually going to bed. It was only 7:30 p.m., and the kids had just fallen asleep. I couldn't admit defeat that easily. My legs hung off the end of the mini couch from the knees down, and my butt was wedged into the crease between the foam cushion and the arm. Daniel walked in with a beer, saw that I had assumed ownership of the love seat, and lowered himself onto a glossy wooden stool. I usually preferred the stool—it was better for all my wiggles—and he preferred the love seat. But on this night, I simply couldn't hold my head up for another minute.

Daniel rested his cast across his thighs, took a swig of his beer, and sighed. "Thank God China makes good beer."

"Beer can't erase what I saw today, Daniel. Or smelled. The stench of that school! I'm pretty sure the acrid aroma of urine has permanently lodged itself into the lining of my nostrils, never to depart."

"Did you ask Kristy if it always smells like that?"

"I asked that exact question, and do you know what she said? 'Does it always smell like what?' She doesn't smell it anymore, Daniel! She's adapted to a world that reeks of piss."

"Okay, so besides the pee smell, what was it like?" he asked, stretching out his legs and then re-crossing them.

"Well, I'd tell you, except I have no idea! They wouldn't let me in! There's this weird little hut right inside the gate where the administrators work; they took us there to discuss the school. I asked if I could see a classroom and they said, 'No, that would be disruptive, and we don't allow disruptions.' Not even for prospective parents! And, get this, parents must drop their kids outside the gate at 8 a.m., and pick them up outside the gate at 4 p.m. Parents aren't allowed inside the gate between 8 and 4, unless they have an appointment, and then they're only allowed in the hut."

"That's different," Daniel said, shifting from one butt cheek to the other on the stool.

"Especially when you're trying to decide if your child would be a good fit there! I, for one, would like to know how they punish the kids who are naughty. What if Piper bites someone and they pull out a paddle? Or one of those medieval stretching machines? We don't know what they'd do to a child who's not afraid to use her teeth!"

Daniel shifted again. "I'd like to put that couch through a stretching machine."

"Get this—Kristy says they give the kids candy all the time, especially the foreign kids. She said Jeremy's teeth have rotted from all the candy he eats at school."

Daniel looked at me. "Is there anything you like about it? Because it sounds like you hate it."

"I made a list of pros and cons. And you're right, the con list is significantly longer. But the school is really cheap; that's a pro. And the kids become fluent in Mandarin, fast, which, as we both know, would be hugely helpful."

"I thought you decided that Piper learning Mandarin was our primary objective."

"But not like this! We can't squelch her spirit! I think she'd be a terrible fit there."

Daniel stood and shook out his legs, then sat again. "We don't have to decide this right now, do we? Can't we think on it?"

"No, we need to decide right away. We have to sign up three days before the end of the month because kids can only start at the beginning of every month. Today's the twenty-third. If I miss this window, I'll have to find alternative ways to entertain Piper for another month. She needs stimulation outside of the apartment. And friends! You know how social Piper is. She dominated the playground back home."

"She dominated everything back home."

"True."

"So, what are you thinking?" he asked, taking a slow swig.

"Well," I paused and looked at him. "I made an appointment to check out an international school, the one where Kristy's husband works."

He suddenly looked alert. "Wait, isn't that school outrageously expensive?"

"Yes."

"Tina, you know I don't make a lot of money, right? We can't spend the way we used to. This is a start-up operation I'm working for—"

"I know, I know, I just need to see all of our options."

"But that school's not an option."

"I know! I just want to see it, okay!" My head was pounding, and I sealed my eyes shut.

Daniel polished off the rest of his beer in one giant glug and stood. "That doesn't make a whole lot of sense."

"It doesn't have to make sense; I just need to know what's out there."

"It's a waste of your time."

"You forgot—I've got nothing but time—all kids all the time," I said.

He paused and crossed his arms. "When's the tour?" he asked.

"Monday, at 10."

"I'm coming with you."

22.

"This is amazing!" I said as we pulled up to the glossy new campus of the British International School. The exterior façade of the three-story main building was sleek and modern with dark wood outlining large windows overlooking a courtyard. The trees lining the driveway were tall and healthy; the lawn was perfectly manicured with no rope around it. A group of children were playing Duck Duck Goose on the grass. A full-sized soccer field lay to the right. A separate but equally modern kindergarten complex lay to the left, in front of which bloomed a sizable veggie garden lined with roses and lavender. I strapped the girls into the stroller as Daniel perfected his frown. I nearly skipped in the front door.

"May I help you?" the beautiful Chinese receptionist asked in perfect English.

"Yes, we have an appointment at 10?"

"Oh yes, you must be Miss Tina. I'm Amber," she said. "Would you like some tea while you wait for Heather to lead you on a tour of the campus?"

"Tea? I love tea!" I almost clapped. "Daniel, would you like some tea?" I looked at him, eyebrows up, silently begging him, willing him to accept the tea.

"No, thank you, I don't drink tea." He looked at me and rolled his eyes. He dropped into one of the soft leather chairs arranged for a civilized conversation about elegant topics and grabbed a magazine from the sparkling glass coffee table. He flipped it open.

"You're looking at the monthly publication that goes home to our families, the BIS Chatter. That is last month's Chatter. Every month we highlight students for their academic achievements, musical pursuits, and of course, their social consciousness. Last month our eighth graders rebuilt an orphanage." She beamed.

"An orphanage! Daniel, isn't that incredible?" I said.

"It is," he said, looking bored. He dropped the magazine back on the table. "Do you have sports teams?"

"Oh yes, once our students are in middle school, they can choose from a wide variety of sports. Our teams compete against the seven other international schools in Shanghai. Our best teams travel to Beijing to compete at higher levels. But for our primary school students, like Piper, we offer a comprehensive physical education program every day followed by daily violin lessons. Do you like the violin, Piper?" she leaned over and stroked Piper's head, tucking a stray strand of hair behind her ear.

"Ribbit," Piper said.

"Piper, please use your words, honey." I smiled at Amber. "Piper loves music, don't you, Piper?"

"Ribbit," she repeated.

"Hello, my name is Heather," said a throaty voice from the doorway.

We all turned to look at her. Heather made Amber look like she'd just napped in a foxhole. She was approximately eight feet tall and stunning, nay, flawless. Her sleek black hair was rolled into a perfect bun on the top of her head. She wore cat eye glasses and tiny diamond stud earrings. A silky white blouse glimmered under her fitted black suit. Pinned to her lapel was a brooch with BIS written in cursive diamonds.

I suddenly felt under-dressed. I looked down at my favorite shirt and realized it had seen better days. The week before I'd worn it to coffee with Kristy and felt pretty put together. Smart even. Now I felt like I'd dressed myself in the dark in something I'd plucked from the bottom of the hamper.

"I see you have two children," she said with disdain, looking at Lila on my lap. "Amber, please prepare a packet on our toddler program for the Martin family."

Amber rushed from the room.

"Oh no," I said. "It's okay, we're really only looking for a program for Piper right now."

"We'll see about that," she said and smiled at Daniel. "How are you today, Mr. Martin?"

Daniel smiled back. "Doing great, thanks. You can call me Daniel."

I noticed he hadn't shaved, probably since Friday. I pulled Lila's finger out of her nose and looked out the window, away from all of them, silently listing off the areas I would address the minute we got home.

"Follow me, please. I'd like to show you the classroom for our K3 program. This is the class Piper would join. Right now, they're preparing for a play they'll perform at the end of the month."

"A play! How wonderful! Which play is it?" I gushed.

"A Midsummer Night's Dream; have you heard of it?" She smiled at me and then winked at Daniel. "The junior version. One class prepares a play each month to perform for the entire school. This gets the students comfortable speaking on stage and teaches them to be a good audience. At the end of every term, the primary students perform in a violin concert. Three hundred children gather on stage to play the songs they've practiced in their daily lessons. It's truly a sight to behold."

"I'll bet it is," Daniel said and looked at me with eyebrows raised.

We headed toward the Kindergarten complex. I walked behind Heather and Daniel, pushing the stroller.

"Mommy, I want out!" Piper shouted.

"Okay, honey, we're almost there," I said.

Heather opened her arms as she whooshed through the automatic doors of the kindergarten building. She swung her head out as she spun to face us. "This complex was built last year. It houses all four levels of preschool students. The toddlers receive instruction in a separate area with the ratio of one instructor to every three toddlers. They study early language development, science, puzzles, violin, and maths."

"Math?" Daniel said.

"Yes, mathematics is an essential part of our curriculum. We believe an early introduction is critical to every child's development. By the end of the year all of our K3 students can multiply and divide."

"Wow, that's wonderful," I said. Piper was red-faced, thrashing and bucking in the front of the stroller, working to extricate herself. She'd spied a group of kids her size on the lawn and was desperate to move herself there.

"Piper, please just wait—"

Heather interrupted me. "It's alright, she can play with her schoolmates." She looked at her slim watch on her minute wrist. "They have five more minutes of physical education before play practice. Why don't we let her join the class for a bit and then continue our tour? I can tell you about our language acquisition program while she makes friends."

Piper ran over to join the game. They had moved on from Duck Duck Goose to Red Rover. Piper sprinted up to a red-headed boy on the far end of the chain and grabbed his hand. He looked at her and ripped his hand out of hers. She grabbed it again.

Heather started talking. "Each of our classrooms is run by two teachers, one native English speaker and one native Chinese speaker, ensuring they have a full immersion experience in both—"

The boy ripped his hand out of Piper's again. I heard him yell, "Don't!" Piper grabbed his hand again anyway.

"On Wednesdays, the children get an hour and a half of Latin—"

"Hold on just one sec, Heather, I really want to hear this," I said and hustled over to Piper.

"Piper!" I beg-whispered. "Don't force it! You should ask before you grab someone's hand." I kneeled to get eye-level and smiled at the boy. "Hi sweetie!" I said in my happy voice. "This is Piper, she'd like to join your game. Is it okay if she stands here and holds your hand?"

"NO!" he yelled loudly.

I raised my eyebrows. "Okay then, uh, Piper, let's find another place to stand," I said, looking for an empty-handed kid who was less fierce.

"NO!" Piper hollered back, louder than the boy. "I want to stand *here*."

"But why?" I pleaded while glancing back at Heather and Daniel. "We're only playing here for a few minutes. There are plenty of other, nicer kids you can hold hands with." I looked around. "Look at that little cutie over there!" I pointed to a girl holding her crotch in front of a lavender bush. "Oh wait, I think she needs to go potty."

Piper turned to face the boy squarely. She got a few inches from his face and yelled loudly, "My mommy says I don't have to play with a meanie like you!" Then she kicked him, hard, in the shins and walked toward the sideline.

"AAH!" the boy screamed and fell onto his back, writhing and grabbing his leg. "She kicked me!"

"Oh no! Piper! Apologize right this instant!" I sputtered.

"No, I won't say sorry! He's a meanie, you even said so!" she screamed.

"I, I did not say so! You apologize right now or you're in huge trouble, Missy, more trouble than you've ever been in EVER!"

"NO! I won't say sorry because I hate him!" she yelled and sprinted toward the center ring of the soccer field.

◎◎◎

Silence enveloped the taxi as we idled in traffic heading toward our apartment. With this particular taxi driver, it was either all brakes or all gas. Our heads pressed against the seats during bursts of acceleration, flying forward when he stopped. Start, stop, start, stop, we pitched forward and back like passengers on a boat in a storm. I looked to the right, out my window at the concrete barrier of the raised road. Piper sat on the far left with her face buried in her dad's shirt. Lila whimpered in between us.

"I hated that place, Tina," Daniel said.

"You hated it before we got there, solely because of the price tag," I said, addressing the concrete barrier.

"Wrong. I hate it because it's stuffy and ridiculous and they teach 'maths' to babies," he said.

I turned to him, glowering. "Well, I think that if you put 'perfect school' into Google and hit images, there'd be a picture of that school staring back at you." I turned away again. "But whatever, it doesn't matter if it's perfect since it's no longer an option. We can cross that school off the list with a big fat red pen."

"It never was an option," he said.

We sat in silence for a while as the list of things I wanted to change grew longer and longer.

Daniel paused. "Why don't you go for a run when we get home. I'm leaving tomorrow for three days, and it looks like you need to blow off some steam. I'll stay with the girls for a while," he finally said.

"I'll probably get lost. I only know how to get to Starbucks and back," I grumbled.

"Run to Starbucks then," he said.

"Fine."

23.

Running to Starbucks did not improve my spirits. There were too many roads to cross, bikes to dodge, staring people to maneuver around, and nasty puddles to jump to maintain any speed or glean any sort of mind-numbing groove. The large white city buses, and there were loads of them on every block, farted steady black clouds of exhaust. *This will be the day I catch cancer,* I grumbled to myself before sealing my lips, puffing out my cheeks, and crossing a single lane street behind a line of buses shoe-horned with people.

When I finally arrived at Starbucks, I stood facing the door and crossed my arms—I didn't reach for the handle. I sensed that neither a warm nor cold drink would provide the antidote to my grumpitude. I sighed and looked up, silently addressing the green mermaid oracle, *what does a person banished to this dreadful town do for distraction?*

Lady Serendipity was apparently friends with the Starbucks Siren because at that very moment, I caught sight of a chalkboard out of the corner of my eye. It was about waist high and perched against a pile of cinder blocks at the entrance to the alley adjacent to Starbucks. The answer I was seeking spoke to me from this chalkboard in large capital letters:

MASSAGE
65rmb

A small arrow scribbled in the corner of the chalkboard pointed to an unlit, unmarked door. It looked derelict. I thought about walking away but hesitated. Seeing the word "massage" reminded me of the tightness on both sides of my spine, reminiscent of a set of over-tuned guitar strings connecting the base of my head to the crest of my butt. Our mattress was barely more than a plank; my right arm fell asleep every night before I did. *I need this*, I thought and marched up to the door, pressing my forehead against the glass, blocking the light around my head with my hands. Pitch black. *Figures*, I thought, but pushed on the door just in case. A string of bells tied to the inside handle jingled as I nearly fell in.

"Hello? Um, *ni hao?*" I called into the darkness.

As my eyes adjusted, I could see that the room was empty except for two old red vinyl couches facing each other.

A small man dressed in black stepped out from behind a faded old curtain on the far wall. He pawed at the air in silence and disappeared behind the curtain again.

Is he motioning for me to follow him? I thought. *I'm not sure. This is sketchy. Why aren't the lights on? I should leave. Following a stranger into a dark room is something I would instruct my children to never, ever do.*

The man reappeared and pawed at the air again, this time smiling at me. I walked toward him with a shrug.

I mean, what's the real risk here? Look at him—he's five foot nothing and half my weight. He's wearing slippers for Pete's sake. What could he actually do? If he attempted to grab me, I could reach around and snap him over my knee like an anemic scrap of kindling.

Once behind the curtain, the man led me to a tiny closet lit by a bare lightbulb hanging from the center of a spider-webby ceiling tile. He looked me up and down quickly, then reached onto the top left shelf to grab faded but clean-smelling blue and white striped pajamas. He handed them to me with both hands and a small bow. Relief flooded through me because this stack of pajamas meant I didn't have to get naked, removing a variable I had just started to panic about.

Next to the closet, he shoved aside a dingy pink towel which hung by two nails from a board attached to the corner of the ceiling, revealing a small triangular changing area. A square plastic stool sat against the wall. He plucked the pajamas from my hands and set them on the stool. Then he stood and smiled. His teeth were sparse.

In a low voice, he said something I couldn't understand and bowed again, this time turning and walking away, toward yet another curtain on the wall near the opposite corner.

I paused, watching him leave and the curtain swing back to its resting position. *It's not too late to leave*, I thought. *And do what?* I snapped at myself. *Find something else to be miserable about?* My back chimed in. "Get your ass in the pajamas," it said. I stepped inside the towel, pulling it closed. There was a large gap between the towel and the walls on both sides. I changed in record speed.

When I stepped out, I clutched my running clothes in a ball in one hand and hung my shoes from the middle fingers of the other. A pair of fuzzy, not remotely new, black slippers had been placed in front of a folding chair that was backed against the wall closest to me. The man walked up and pointed to them.

I mounted my final protest. "Do I have to?" I whined, knowing he didn't understand. "I'm freaky about my feet and I'm guessing these crusty dogs are rife with someone else's fungus." I pointed at the slippers.

He smiled and wagged his finger at my feet.

I surrendered, sitting heavily in the folding chair. "Do my socks come off too?" I looked at him. "Like this?" I pulled off my socks and he nodded. "It's a good thing I packed my foot spray," I murmured as I slipped my feet into the slippers. I looked at him and nodded, indicating we were on the same page. He smiled and turned to lead me down the hall.

Behind the curtain lay a large dark room filled with about fifty back-to-back massage tables—a virtual massage factory. Four of the tables were occupied, all by men laying prone in pajamas matching mine. At least one of them was snoring. I followed the man to a vacant table near the other men. He stopped to fold a hand towel around the face ring, and then he walked away.

I kicked off the slippers and pushed myself backward onto the table. I saw the man washing his hands at a tiny sink in the corner of the room as I turned to lay on my belly. I flopped around like a fish on the vinyl to position my nose into the center of the face hole. *At least his hands are clean*, I thought and attempted to quiet the alarm bells ringing in my mind.

I looked up as the man padded back to me. "Not too strong, okay?" I whispered. Even though I knew he didn't understand, I felt better for having said it. I looked down and felt his presence at my head before he reached out to smooth my hair. Then he took a deep breath and lay his fingers lightly on my temples.

So began the best massage of my life.

In a near-trance, I paid the equivalent of eight dollars for my massage and stumbled out the door, the bells jingling, this time signifying gratitude, on my way out. I crossed the road with significantly less fear than usual and ambled in the direction of home. Halfway through the first block, I stumbled onto a pedestrian pathway.

Kristy had been telling me about this path, but I hadn't noticed it before, probably because I always fled to the other side of the road for this section of the route home to avoid the fermented tofu vendor who was usually stationed here.

Nothing compared to the funk of fermented tofu. One whiff would induce a gag reflex in me so powerful, my arm hairs would stand at attention for a solid fifteen minutes as I tried to regain composure and stop my eyes from watering. But on this day, stinky tofu man wasn't there and thus, I stayed on that side of the road and noticed the path, which at that moment was softly lit like an angel's passage and nearly empty, nothing like the sidewalks and gutters of my normal high-traffic route. *What the heck*, I thought and turned down the path.

A few old trees lined the pathway which was mostly dirt and small rocks with the occasional blob of busted-up asphalt. After walking for a few minutes, I noticed what looked like light green ceramic tiles peeking through a thin layer of dirt on the ground. I bent down to take a closer look when an unexpected voice nearly caused me to jump out of my skin.

"It's a fine day for a walk, isn't it?" a man's voice said. My first reaction was to look up, into the tree closest to me. Why would I search a tree for the source of a man's voice? I have no idea. Maybe I was expecting to see the Cheshire Cat peering down at me, all magenta stripes and giant grin. The voice chuckled (just like that cat would have) and that's when I spotted the source—an old man tucked into a shadow—in a corner where the path turned, between a chain link fence and an apartment building covered with the same light green tiles that were on the path.

I recognized him right away—he was the same man who had helped Piper down from the monkey bars at the park a few weeks prior. He sat on a flat rock, and on his lap rested an accordion. He crossed his hands on his instrument and blinked at me. He was so earnest and unexpected, plunked on this path in his black beret and baggy gray jumpsuit, I had to stifle a laugh. I turned toward him.

"I'd like to play a song for you," he said, and suddenly, "Happy Birthday" boomed from his accordion. For squeezebox neophytes, the accordion has two volume settings: LOUD and EXTREMELY LOUD. The song blared from his instrument as his hands maneuvered the bellows back and forth and his eyes literally twinkled. I couldn't make this up. I also could no longer stifle.

It wasn't a polite tee-hee type of laughter that bubbled up. It was a shriek, howl, snort type of laughter. I doubled over and crossed my legs for fear I'd wet myself. I must have been overdue for a good laugh because this moment wasn't particularly funny; he could really play that thing! Plus, I didn't want to insult him. I tried to stop and listen, but every time I slowed my laughter down, I would guffaw again, hooting, tears streaming. I had no control. The laughter was my master.

He stopped playing. "You don't like this song?"

"No, I do!" I crowed. "It's a wonderful song, an important song! Keep playing! Don't pay attention to me!" I wiped the tears from my eyes and tried again to get my act together.

He waited for me to quiet down. "This song is American, like you," he finally said, nodding.

"How do you know I'm American?"

"I can see," he said.

"Really?"

"Of course. It's easy to see—Americans are happy. They smile," he said, grinning at me with a straight line of gums. "Even their bodies are happy. Their knees bounce and their arms swing when they walk." He let go of his accordion to flap his arms. "And Americans look up, not down. Not so serious. Very happy. I can see."

"Well that may be how I'm walking today." I flapped my arms back at him and smiled, "But on most days you probably wouldn't guess that I'm American because I'm typically grouchy."

He looked confused. "Eh?"

"I mean I'm not always happy."

"Yes, yes you are," he disagreed. "You're happy in here." He thumped on his chest with his palm. "Happy in your heart, because you're lucky."

I smiled. "I didn't know we Americans did all that bouncing and moving."

"It's true. You could ask anyone in my building here, but they can't speak English like I can."

"How did you learn English?"

"I learned it a long time ago. And now that you're my friend, I can practice it with you," he said. "Soon you come back here, speak

English with me. I'll play *shǒufēngqín* for you again, make you laugh more. Trade favors we will."

I felt it coming again, from just below my lowest ribs. My eyes widened and I raised my hand. "Please don't talk like Yoda. I'll laugh again."

"I don't know this Yoda," he said, replicating Yoda.

I blinked and pressed my lips together. "I have to go. Thank you." I turned to walk away and stopped. "Wait, what's your name?"

"You can call me Mr. Han. What is your name?"

"I'm Tina."

"Very nice to meet you, Miss Ting-ah. When will you walk here again?"

"Hopefully in four days," I said, already dreaming of my next massage. "Goodbye, Mr. Han."

"Goodbye, my friend." He paused, then called after me, "I call you Ting Ting, okay? See you soon, Ting Ting!" Then he launched into a slower, sadder song, one I didn't recognize.

24.

Dear Jennifer,

I bought a bike today—a cruiser—because it's now November, which means rain—pounding, sleeting, dumping rain. San Diego hasn't experienced a whole day of rain like this since its inception, and we've been drenched by water cascading from the sky here for two straight weeks with no sign of let-up. The bottom floor of my apartment building is one giant murky, slippery cesspond. It's cold to wade through, even in rain boots, and it smells like dead things.

I bought a bike because guess what taxis do when it's raining? Drive other people. Anyone but me. I see how it is. The people who win taxis in rainstorms aggressively assert themselves in the center of the road with an all or nothing approach; you either take me, or you kill me. But I just can't do it. I mean I'm gutsy enough, but I've got a stroller, and it just feels wrong. Also, I tried it once, and we all nearly perished. Besides, it didn't work—the driver weaved and then picked up a person ten feet beyond me. Someone without two screaming kids and an extra-large, extra-wet apparatus for transporting them.

Enter: the bike. It has two child seats—one in the front, one in the back. The back seat is less a seat and more a basket. To be clear, it's an actual basket—woven probably from some form of bamboo. *Factoid Alert* There exists a species of bamboo that grows three feet in one day. If the amount of rain equals the amount of growth, I get it. Do I see bamboo growing here, in the concrete jungle? No. But it must grow (and rapidly!) nearby, because so many things are made from bamboo here, including, but not limited to: ladders, scaffolding for high-rise buildings, and child bike seats. It's strange to me that the strongest, most durable material around here is not a metal. But who am I kidding? It's all strange. Strange and wet.

I bought a large plastic poncho to complement my bike. It has a long train, kinda like Princess Di's wedding dress, except it's long in the front, too, and also see-through. I mount my bike and flip the back train over Piper in the back seat, the front train over Lila in the front seat, et voila! The kids remain dry. And they don't suffocate! Which is a plus. I stay mostly dry too, except for my face, which is wet, frozen, and feels like it belongs to someone else when I touch it.

I ride my bike cautiously in the gutters and on the sidewalks slammed with people, ringing my bell with abandon. People love me! Okay, not really, but I'm too cold and wet to care. Plus, bike rides entertain the kids for long stretches. And without school or friends or more than a small collection of toys which have all lost their luster, child entertainment is my raison d'être right now. My friend Kristy has sensed my desperation and kindly agreed to accompany me to a local market—one specializing in knock-off toys—for shopping and translation assistance. We've had to reschedule this much needed outing for two straight weeks because of the deluge. But things are looking up—the forecast says no rain for 1.5 days! Toy status improvement is imminent. Can you feel my joy over this crappy excuse for a modem?

-Tina

P.S. My clothing status improvement is not imminent, and I will tell you why once my PTSD has subsided. In case you're wondering what to send in my first care package, make it a cute shirt. And chocolate bars. And diapers. And cereal. And chocolate bars. What can I send you from Shanghai? How about toads and water snakes? They sell them on the street in front of my house. For dinner. I guess everything is delicious somewhere. xxx

25.

"There's a fly in my nose!" I blustered the next day, halting mid-stride in the teeming local market to shake my head wildly while exhaling in bursts through flared nostrils, blowing hard enough to dislodge an insect without releasing shrapnel. The ground in the market swarmed with people; the air abounded with flies.

Kristy stopped and turned around as locals bumped, shouted, and wriggled around us. "Keep walking," she barked. "We'll get it out when we get to the handbag shop."

"What? I'm not here for a purse, I need toys for the kids!"

Kristy faced me with her hands on her hips and her brows in a V. "I know, but the purses are on the way to the toys, and I need to buy a Frauda backpack for my mother-in-law today if I'm going to get it to the UK by Christmas."

A man stopped directly in front of me, well within my personal space. He bent over and reached for Lila's feet. "No!" I yelled at him. He looked at me with a blank expression and kept reaching. "I said no! No, no, no!" I pushed his shoulder away. He stepped out to get his balance, then stood, muttering, and shuffled away. I turned to Kristy. "This place is terrible. I've never in my life seen so many flies."

"Two things," Kristy said. "One, it's only fly-infested because we're by the meat, and two, you should say *bùyào*."

I looked at her for a moment. "Huh?"

She continued. "Bùyào is how you say 'no.' Well, one of the ways . . . but if you say bùyào when someone is doing something you don't like, they'll understand you, and you won't need to shove them."

"I'm still back on the meat."

"Right, well, this is the meat area of the market so you'll see lots of flies and probably a rat or two."

"You've got to be—"

"But today's larger lesson is bùyào. In this context, it's how you say 'no.'"

I cocked my head. "I get that they use a different word here, but isn't 'no' universal? Don't most people on this planet understand what 'no' means?"

Kristy's eyes widened. "This is China, not Europe. Or the Americas. So no, 'no' is not 'no'. Bùyào is 'no.'"

I closed my eyes, put my hands in front of my face, and then spoke through my fingers. "Why does everything have to be so complicated?"

"Come on, Tina! Don't get stuck—we're almost out of this quadrant! It's much more pleasant by the purses and toys. Plus, you can't live in Shanghai without experiencing this market. Many Americans come to Shanghai solely for shopping right here."

"I can't imagine that's true, but I'm still following you," I said, slowly pushing forward again and then stopping to raise my hand. "But if the kids wake up and start melting down, point me in the direction of the fake Barbies, or the My Little Phonies, or whatever knock-off they will sell me to provide amusement."

"Here we are," Kristy grinned seven minutes later, "at the best handbag shop in all of Shanghai, possibly all of China."

We stood in front of a low-ceilinged, dusty shack festooned with a gazillion heinous-looking handbags. Every color, size, and configuration of satchel hung from every available cranny. But I didn't see one I would hang off my arm.

"This is the best handbag shop in all of China?"

"No, dummy, this is the facade. Follow me," she said, pushing past a table piled high with every color of plastic coin-purse.

"But my stroller can't fit," I said. Right then a chunky woman wearing a yellow sweater dress, pink sunglasses, and maroon high heels hustled out clapping. She rushed to the stroller and crouched down.

"Don't wake her, please!" I said as she went straight for Lila's feet. I'd already forgotten the word for 'no.' Too late. Lila blinked and rubbed her eyes. She stretched and looked at me, then looked at the lady tickling her toes. The woman smiled and reached out to her. Lila looked at me again and then back at the lady and put her arms up. Piper continued sleeping.

Kristy spoke Mandarin to the lady holding Lila. The woman nodded emphatically and hollered something back at her.

"This gal will watch your kids. If there's an issue, she'll bring them inside to you," Kristy said.

"Excuse me?" I said.

"This is what she does, Tina—watches kids so expat women can shop. Trust me, the girls will be fine. She wants to increase her odds of making a sale, not destroy her livelihood."

"But I'm not buying anything!"

Kristy shrugged.

"How do I know she won't take off with my kids?"

Kristy chuckled at my folly. "Come on, Tina! There's not a chance in hell that one of the 1.2 billion citizens of the People's Republic of China would steal or harm a foreign child. It would never be worth the punishment! Any person who harms a foreigner, or even gets accused of harming a foreigner, would get shot before you could utter the words Amber Alert. Plus, they don't want girls here, not even to marry all their single boys. You're nothing but a photo opportunity to them, you know that, right? Trust me, no one wants your little white girls but you."

I looked at her for a long moment. "They shoot people?"

Kristy shook her head. "I keep forgetting you're new."

"Like, in the streets?"

"Of course not! They'd take her out back. Look, don't worry about it; I think they've slowed that whole program down. Maybe she'd end up in prison for life instead, moving rocks from one pile to another and back again. Either way, your kids aren't going anywhere."

I looked up, took a deep breath, then exhaled loudly for effect. "If you promise to never bring me here again, I'll run in for a quick look. Tell the woman not to take her eyes off my kids; remind her of the punishment." I slid my finger across my throat.

Kristy barked at the woman before pushing through the rainbow landfill of bags.

We stopped at the back wall of the booth. I leaned forward with my knees bent so the purses hanging from the sloped ceiling wouldn't nuzzle my head.

"*Xiàng sheng! Wǒmen yào jìnqù hǎo ma?*" Kristy bellowed.

A man hustled toward us clutching a key on a dirty string. He kicked a pink plastic footstool against the wall, stood on it, and reached up, grabbing an unattractive white pleather purse from the highest hook. Behind it was a tiny keyhole. He pushed the key into the hole, then pulled with both hands to the right. The entire wall slid open.

"Wow," I said and stepped in.

The interior of the illicit space consisted of three small whitewashed rooms connected by a cramped, dark corridor. The rooms were filled with metal racks separated by skinny aisles. On the racks sat neatly-arranged luxury brand bags, smallest in front, largest in back: Gucci, Prada, Louis Vuitton, Hermes, Chanel, Fendi, Balenciaga, plus a few I didn't recognize. The wall slammed shut behind us.

"These are all this year's styles and colors. I think the next room has the older models. And luggage. And shoes——"

"Wait, these are all fake?" I whispered.

"You don't have to whisper, we all know what's going on here, right?" she remarked to a middle-aged blonde woman walking by clutching a fake Gucci wallet. The woman glanced at her and then looked away.

"How much do they cost?"

"Oh, I don't know, twenty bucks for a wallet, more for a purse? It depends on the size and how well you bargain," Kristy said.

"Sheesh." I walked around as Kristy ducked over to the "Prada" area on the next rack. I picked up a fake Louis Vuitton Speedy bag and smelled it.

"It even smells like real leather," I called to Kristy in amazement.

"That's because it *is* real leather. The good fakes are almost exact replicas of the real thing, down to the paper they're stuffed with, the lock if they have one, even the care instructions. But check the zipper on anything you like, because if it's a bad fake, that'll be the first thing to bust apart."

"Oh, I'm still not going to buy anything, I need to get back to the kids. I didn't even bring my wallet in."

Kristy dropped the bag in her hand and strode straight up to stand in front of me. "You're kidding, right?"

"What?"

"You left your wallet out there?"

"You told me my kids were safe out there, Kristy, so why wouldn't my wallet be? Besides, it's under my kids—in the bottom of the diaper bag which is crammed in the basket under the stroller where Piper's sleeping."

She shook her head in confusion. "Tina. You can never leave your wallet anywhere."

"Then what was the whole song and dance about how safe it is here! 'People get shot,' you said!"

"Yes, *you* are safe, and your children are safe, but your wallet is not anywhere near safe. *Fu wu ren!*" she yelled, knocking on the exit door. "*Kuai yi dian!*"

A woman hustled over to unlock and slide the door open.

Piper was awake and out of the stroller, watching a Chinese cartoon on a TV wedged under a body length mirror in the back corner of the hut. Next to Piper, the lady in the yellow dress bounced Lila on her hip while Lila chewed on the arm of her sunglasses. The stroller was parked toward the front of the hut, the front half of it wedged under a folding table showcasing every configuration of fanny pack. The diaper bag was nowhere to be seen.

26.

"There's something wrong with this place!" I hollered into my cell phone as I steamrolled over toes and elbowed the butts of innocents on the sidewalk outside of the market. I held my phone to my ear by my cocked left shoulder. People scattered around me, expressing their dissent with high-pitched percussive commentary, clucking, and fluffing, then rejoining their traffic patterns behind me.

"What happened?" Daniel asked.

"My diaper bag is poof! Gone. Vanished. No trace. My wallet was in it. I have nothing." I jumped the stroller off the sidewalk and into the gutter to get around an army of men sweeping the street corner with brooms formed from a collection of tree branches banded together with string. The girls squealed in joy.

"Is that the girls I hear?"

"Uh, yes."

"Then you don't exactly have nothing," he said.

I thought about hanging up but couldn't figure out how to do it with my chin, so I stayed on the line and fumed silently.

"Was there a lot of money in it?"

"Not really. About fifty bucks."

"Your passport?"

"No."

"Apartment key?"

"No."

"Any credit cards?"

"Just a debit card with my picture on it. I already cancelled it."

"What else?"

"Other cards. Health insurance. Driver's license. Triple A——"

"Those cards are worthless here."

A horn honked behind me. I shook my fist at the driver of the Jetta taxi riding my tail with two of his wheels on the sidewalk. "Shut up!" I hollered.

"Uh, was that directed at me?" Daniel asked.

"No. I mean, sort of! I know the cards are worthless here, okay?"

"Then why were they in your wallet?"

"Are you serious right now? I'm telling you my personal property——"

"And I'm telling you it could be worse."

I looked at my watch. "This isn't helpful. I just got to our building, and I need to identify an English speaker who can help me replace my pool pass."

Ten minutes later, I hit redial. "Our apartment is flooded."

"What?"

"I started the washing machine before we left, and I don't know, maybe I crammed too much stuff in it, but it has literally split open at the bottom—not even at a seam. It looks like the metal ripped, or like someone took a dull cleaver to it—one of those cleavers I just saw people using to chop chickens into bits at the wet market," I whimpered.

"Where's the water?"

"Everywhere. The kids are standing on the couch."

"I'll call Richard."

◎◎◎

Five minutes later, I picked up before it rang.

"Richard called our building manager. He says it's our responsibility. We need to replace the washer," Daniel said.

"What? That's ridiculous. Give me his number." I sloshed down the hall.

"It was apparently part of the rental contract. We fix, maintain, and, if need be, replace appliances. That's what the contract says; I have it right in front of me. It's non-negotiable."

I smacked the bathroom door jamb with my hand, feeling the sting, and then blaming the entire city for it. "There's something wrong with this place!"

He let me vent and then spoke again. "He said to go to Carrefour. They have the best prices for appliances."

"What's Carrefour?"

"It's a French grocery store, the second largest chain store in the world after Walmart. There's one about 45 minutes outside of Puxi."

"They sell appliances at a grocery store?"

"Yes, and they're cheap! Richard says they'll pick up the broken one when they deliver the new one. I'll send you the address now. Grab money from the top drawer in my nightstand."

"Daniel, my consumer experiences in Shanghai have been pretty terrible up to this point, and that's being generous." I laughed with acidity. "I don't have the patience for shopping here. It's been a long day. I think it would be better if you go to Carrefour when you get back."

"Tina, I have a job. And I'm in back to back meetings next week about a new factory—"

"Wait—what new factory? I thought you were already working with a factory?"

"We were until our accountant paid them a surprise visit last week and discovered it was a shell factory. A phony."

"Last week? Why didn't you tell me?"

"I was going to, but it seems like there's always a fire to put out."

I stomped my foot, splashing water on the walls in the hallway. "They even knock off factories?"

"Yep," Daniel said. "I think it's safe to assume that everything here is fake."

I clenched my fists. "This is ridiculous. I'm going to Carrefour right now, and I'll leave there with a new washing machine, today!"

Several hours later I called Daniel again. "I did it! We have a new washing machine!" I sang into the phone. "It was painful, it took far too long, it might not even be a washing machine because I can't read anything on the dial or in the instruction book, but guess how much it cost?"

"I've got a conference call in two minutes, can I—" Daniel said.

"Ninety bucks, brand new. NINE ZERO!" I ended the word "Zero" with an off-tune vibrato.

"That's great, honey, uh—"

"Daniel, are you hearing me? Until today I haven't had the patience to buy a banana off a guy at a food stall, and I just bought an appliance. Can you smell that? It's called progress! Please acknowledge me! This is tremendous!"

He paused. "Uh—"

"Oh never mind, I'll call Kristy."

I hung up and dialed her. "I bought a new washing machine today, and I only paid ninety bucks, I ROCK!"

"Ninety bucks, geez, you didn't get one of those top-loading pieces of crap, did you?" she said.

I felt like a bird, experiencing the joys of its maiden voyage, waving to all my feathered friends, chirping, "Look at me, I can do this!" and then BAM. A window.

"Please don't pop my balloon, Kristy. Yes, it's a top loader, but it's the latest model with the newest technology. I think they said it's a great choice."

"Did I not tell you explicitly when you called me in a snit on the way to Carrefour that under no circumstances should you buy a top loader?" she demanded.

She might have told me that, and I might have ignored her.

"I feel good about it, and I think it's gonna work. It's being delivered today at 4 p.m."

She exhaled her disgust into the phone. "I can see that you're the type of person who insists on learning lessons on your own and resists any form of help or input, even when you ask for it. And that's fine. My brother's the same way and he's limping by, so it can work. It's just more difficult your way, which makes it often frustrating to watch. But, because you're my friend, I'll try not to say I told you so. Except I did."

I ran the new washer umpteen times that night. I coaxed it lovingly, then firmly, then with profanity. I even tried a load of only four socks and two pairs of underwear. But every time I lifted the lid, clumps of powdered soap were still there, undissolved. Hems were still muddy, pits still offensive. I tried every setting on the dial. Nothing got clean.

I couldn't call Kristy.

"What do I do?" I wailed to Daniel. "I can't return an appliance in a taxi!"

"Didn't you say it cost ninety bucks?" he asked. "It's not worth the aggravation. Just roll it to the curb, someone will take it."

"I will NOT roll it to the curb. They sold me a bum washer! I'm returning it first thing on Saturday and leaving the kids with you."

27.

A s soon as the doors to Carrefour were unlocked on Saturday, I hopped on the escalator up to the appliance floor. "Hello, can you direct me to an English-speaking manager?" I asked an employee in a blue jersey who idled at the front of a vast display of rice cookers on level three—the appliance level. She ambled off and whispered to a group of co-workers who had huddled close by to stare at me.

A man in a yellow jersey approached. "Hello," he said while feverishly scratching the inside of his left ear.

"Hello, are you a manager?" I asked.

"Yes," he worked his mouth like there was food stuck in his molars.

I squinted at him and his internal itch. "Okay, uh, good. I bought a washing machine the other day, and it does not work very well. I would like to exchange it for this one." I tapped the lid of the $350 front-loader, the most expensive option. "I'll pay the difference. Is that possible?"

"One moment."

He hollered into his walkie-talkie. An extra tall, acne-riddled youth, also in a yellow jersey, strode up. I re-explained my situation to him. He smiled and nodded.

"I bought this one yesterday," I told the third yellow jersey, tapping the lid of the $90 display model and making an exaggerated frown. "It does not work at all." I spoke slowly and shook my head. "It is at my home now. I want to exchange it for—" He walked away mid-explanation as a woman in green Carrefour coveralls strolled up. She looked me up and down and muttered something. About a dozen nearby employees burst into fits of laughter.

I was about to storm home and kick the washer out the window when the first yellow jerseyed man trotted up.

"Yes, okay, we will exchange," he said.

"Oh thank God," I said, feeling the tiniest bubble of hope.

I followed him to the nearest cash register, trailed closely by a gaggle of jerseys and coveralls. Once there, we all huddled around the cashier to watch her enter the information. The group alternated between watching her and watching me watch her as she slowly tapped on her keyboard. Tap, pause, tap, pause, tap, tap, extra-long pause. Why was she typing so slowly? Isn't typing a basic skill set for a cashier? I wondered these things as I tried not to think about how badly I had to go to the bathroom. I couldn't bear the thought of walking away to find a place which could only hit ten out of ten on the stink scale, and risk needing to start the transaction over from the beginning. I couldn't hack starting over; I could already feel myself crowning into Crazyland.

I took breaks from watching the cashier to close my eyes and count to ten over and over. It didn't help. As I counted, I noticed that Twinkle Twinkle Little Star was playing over the loud speaker, more agitator than lullaby.

Finally, a yard-long triplicate receipt burst forth from the bubble jet. The cashier ripped it at the perforation with a flourish, circled the total on the bottom with the pen she wore on a piece of brown yarn around her neck, and handed it to me.

I squinted at it and then at her. "I see this is the total for the new washer, but I'm also returning a washer that doesn't work." I repeated the frown and the head shake. "How do I get my money back for that one?"

She looked confused as a yellow jersey translated. My entourage erupted into a shouting match. Everyone seemed to have a strong opinion, but I had no clue what those opinions were. Who had my back? Who thought I was an imbecile? Was anyone shouting about the fact that I desperately needed a haircut? Maybe I wasn't even the topic of their debate. Maybe they were bashing the world's slowest cashier, who also needed a haircut.

After several minutes, the manager interrupted. A hush fell over the crowd. "You get money back for that washer when we collect it. We can't give you money for that washer until we get it back."

"Oh, okay, I can see how that makes sense, but then who will give me my money?" I asked.

The soundtrack piping overhead switched to Oh Susannah! as another community debate launched. Finally, the manager said, "Delivery man will give you the money."

"Delivery man?"

"Delivery man." He nodded. "When he brings you the new washer, he will pick up the old washer and give you the money."

I paused and scratched my head. I was done playing the fool. "Can you put that in writing?"

"What?"

"I need you to write down how much the delivery man will pay me, and, what is your name?"

He smiled nervously. "I am Mr. Li."

"Mr. Li, please also write your name and phone number on the pink paper so I can call you if I have a problem." I held out the receipt.

He took it and walked three steps to the cashier station where he turned it over, scribbled on it, and handed it back to me.

"Oh, darn it." I held it up toward him. "What does this say? I can't read characters."

"It says, 'Drop off new washer, pick up old washer, pay total of 700rmb.'"

"Great, Mr. Li. Now please write your name and phone number and also, please clarify that the delivery man needs to pay me at the time he picks up the old washer."

"Yes, okay." He took the receipt and scribbled on it again.

I had thought of everything. At least I thought I had.

The raised road was closed on the way home from Carrefour so the taxi wound toward our apartment through double lane, gray on gray back streets surrounded by every type of automobile—large, small, new, old—all of us barely moving in any direction. An inch felt like progress. I wondered if I would make it home by the following morning. I also wondered if any car in China could pass a California smog test. Both seemed unlikely.

The taxi driver declined my request, communicated via irate charades, to stop chain-smoking. The drizzle had turned to deluge so the windows were up. Even though my eyes stung and I could feel my lungs turning black, I couldn't disembark—I knew there was no way I'd be able to catch a different cab if I ran sputtering and coughing from this one. The surrounding car horns bleated in commiseration. The rain pelted my soul. I was sure it would have been both faster and less terrible to walk home wet. But I didn't know which direction home was. *I'm not going home*, I corrected myself, *I'm going to the place where I live with my family*. These felt like two vastly different concepts.

Back in the apartment, I felt exhausted, wrung out, and twitchy. Daniel had left a note on the dining room table saying he'd taken the girls to dinner. I thought briefly about going for a massage but decided a nap might be better.

Ding dong. A man stood on my doorstep with an appliance-sized box on a dolly—the delivery man. The nap would have to wait. I waved him inside. As he walked by me, dolly squeaking, he banged into the door and both walls, slowing down only to deposit his shoes near the wall, as was customary. I forced my shoulders to drop as I inhaled, closed my eyes, and rubbed the back of my neck. *This day is almost over, this day is almost over, this day is almost over . . .*

Except it wasn't.

Because once he'd deposited the box in the center of the living room, he stared at the note on the pink receipt I handed him, turning it this way and that as though he couldn't read characters either. Then he shoved it back toward me in a huff, shook the crumpled blue delivery receipt he'd brought, and yelled something while rattling a pen in my face. I grabbed my phone and speed-dialed Richard.

"Richard, hello! I need your help. You know how you suggested we buy a washing machine at Carrefour?"

"Yes—"

"Well the delivery man is here to deliver our second washer. He's picking up the first one I bought the other day, since it doesn't work, and is supposed to refund my money for it. Can you translate for us? We're having trouble communicating."

"Uh—"

"He's standing in my living room, Richard. Please?" I didn't wait for his response. I held my phone out to the delivery man.

He listened to Richard, hollered into the phone, and handed it back to me.

"He says no, he cannot give you any money," Richard said. "He's only authorized to pick up the old washer and deliver the new washer. You must go back to Carrefour for the money."

I threw up my hand and walked to the window. "But that's wrong! Mr. Li wrote it specifically on the receipt that the delivery man will give me the money. Tell him to read the note again. He can call Mr. Li and ask him; his name and number are on the bottom of the receipt."

"Okay, one moment," said Richard. I handed the phone back to the delivery guy with a pronounced frown and zero eye contact.

He listened, hollered, waved his arm around, and hung up the phone, dropping it on the table. He wrenched the handle of his dolly and swung it around until the wheels came to an abrupt halt in front of the seam of his thread-bare socks. He pushed the dolly toward the bad washer, muttering something. He shoved the flat base under the washer and tipped it back. I watched, frozen, as he rolled that ridiculous excuse for a washing machine toward my front door.

It's silly; I know this now. But at the time, it felt as though everything I valued in my life, including my self-worth and dignity, was balanced on that dolly as it rolled quickly toward the elevator. The fundamental truths of my being, in the form of a crappy washer, were escaping. Everything I'd worked so hard to be, to have, and to love was exiting in haste with my sanity at the helm yelling, "All clear!"

Fury entered my body, heating my head and then my chest and then my belly and then my fists, which curled, and my toes, which planted, and I shouted in an unfamiliar voice that could reasonably be described as a satanic baritone, "Like hell you're leaving with that washer!"

I ran around him and stood in front of the door, arms out and open, as though I were going to stop, wrestle, and pin the appliance on wheels barreling toward me, picking up speed. Am I ready to die for $90? I thought with my last ounce of reason. Not yet, I admitted, so I backed against the wall, leaving one foot out.

He slowed.

What else will prevent this man from leaving with this washer? I thought while frantically scanning his approaching person. I could snatch the truck keys sticking out of his pocket as he draws closer, or unclasp the fanny pack from his waist just after he passes . . . then I looked at his feet, padding toward me, his toes nearly pushing through the ends of his socks, and it struck me. I searched the ground and spotted them—a pair of beat up brown loafers on the opposite wall near the door. The perfect pair of hostages had been laid, quite literally, at my feet.

"Big mistake!" I screeched, emitting a witch-like cackle. I scooped up his shoes and sprinted toward the bathroom. With a loud *thump* I hurled the shoes into the bathtub, reached inside the door and turned the lock, then slammed the door shut. Then I planted myself in front of that door like it was the last hill left bearing my own personal tattered flag, because I knew without a shred of doubt that this man would not leave here without his shoes in a rainstorm. He would give me my money or one of us would suffer the consequences. I made animal noises through baring, clenched teeth. The moment I had never anticipated had come anyway— Tina's Last Stand.

He stopped and untilted his dolly, silent. He released the handle and walked back toward the table, toward my phone, which he picked up and hit redial.

He squeaked what must have been his interpretation of events to Richard, then listened, then walked over to hand me the phone.

My mouth felt as though it had been swabbed with cotton, but my purpose, my intention felt clear. I spoke to Richard without listening first. "Tell him I'll give him back his shoes when he gives me my money. If he, for some reason, did not bring my money, tell him to call Mr. Li, who can hop in a taxi to my house with my money. I'm not going back to Carrefour. We can wait for Mr. Li here, all night if we have to. If this has become a war of attrition, I'm afraid he's chosen the wrong adversary. Go ahead and tell him that now." I handed my phone back to the delivery man and licked my teeth to stop them from sticking to my lips.

He listened to my message as retold by Richard and then yelled back into the phone. He stopped to listen, then he shouted. I softly banged the back of my head against the bathroom door as he alternated between listening and hollering. The head-knocking felt soothing somehow, the rhythmic rocking of my brain as it smacked between the anterior and posterior of my skull. At some point, when I thought he was still listening, he must have hung up because my phone rang, interrupting my trance. I strode toward him with my hand out and my jaw set.

"Tina, are you okay? What's going on?" Daniel asked.

"I'm rectifying a nonsensical situation by taking my power back, that's what's going on." My breath came in puffs.

"Uh, Richard just told me you stole the delivery man's shoes."

I inhaled sharply. "And I did, because there was no other way to keep him here, and he's got my money. If I let him leave, I'll never be able to collect that money at Carrefour, I just know it. I have no documentation."

"Tina, honey, I get why you're frustrated, but you need to give the man his shoes."

"Oh, I'll give him his shoes alright, as soon as he hands over my money."

"How much is it, ninety bucks? I'll give you ninety bucks. You don't have to do this."

I looked at the delivery man; his eyes ticked around the room in every direction but mine. He shoved his hands in his pants pockets as he waited for his shoes to be emancipated. I turned away from him. My eyes narrowed as I growled, "You don't get it, do you? I don't have to do any of this. I don't even have to be in this god forsaken place dealing with these people! But, like an idiot, I chose to come to a place I don't belong to find and become someone I'm not, and now look at me!" A sob escaped, just one. *No you don't*, I chastened myself. I grimaced and took as deep a breath as my clenched body could accept. "This is not about the money anymore, Daniel. We could be talking about ninety cents, and I'd still be standing here, guarding this bathroom door. I'm here solely on principle. And on this principle, I refuse to back down."

Daniel paused. I could hear his fingers tapping on the table. "You do realize he's operating under a different set of principles, and he probably doesn't understand why you're doing this," Daniel said.

"He doesn't have to understand. I'm doing this for me."

"You're doing this for you," Daniel echoed.

"Yes."

His fingers stopped tapping. "The waitress is here to take our order. I guess I'll call you after dinner to see if you're still in a stand-off."

"Fine."

I hung up and re-commenced the soft head-banging. My phone rang again.

"I just spoke to Carrefour," Richard said. "Put the driver on the phone, please."

I held my hand out.

"*Wei?*" the driver said and then listened without hollering. He hung up the phone and placed it noiselessly on the table. He reached into his pocket and pulled out 700rmb, the equivalent of ninety bucks. He did not have to count it; it was folded in the exact amount owed to me with a yellow receipt wrapped around it. He handed it to me and stood there, staring at me with a blank expression.

I took a deep breath. And another. I said nothing.

I turned and reached above the door jamb for the pin to unlock the door. The unlocking process took a couple minutes because I couldn't convince my hands to stop shaking. I fished his shoes from the tub and walked past him to my front door. I pulled the door open and threw the shoes overhand as hard as I could. They bounced off the elevator door and dropped onto the worn-down carpet with a thud. He leaned the dolly back and pushed the bad washer out the apartment door. I closed and locked the door after him.

I turned around and leaned against the door. My butt slid slowly down, finally resting on the still-damp carpet. The sob that had tried to escape earlier came back again, this time with many friends. I rolled onto my side and let them have their way with me.

29.

"**P**ardon me," the chocolate-skinned woman called to me in an Australian accent, louder than necessary. She was sitting right next to me, wearing earmuffs over her dreadlocks; this must have prevented her from gauging her volume. It was two weeks after my washing machine meltdown. We were in the basement of an apartment building identical to mine except two blocks away, and it was cold, the type of cold that feels like a stingray just swiped its tail at your nose, ears, and chin. Not her ears though. I had ear-muff envy.

The two of us shared a plastic bench in a cement hallway, peering through a wall of scratched plexiglass into a cell-like room where our older kids were taking a ballet class. There were actually three of us on that bench. She was breast-feeding a child under her coat—a walking, talking, non-baby child. Lila sat on the ground with a cup of Cheerios.

From what I could ascertain, we were the only four English speakers in the hallway, and the two of us were the only parents. The Chinese nannies were clustered in a doorway down the hall gossiping. The Aussie and I had sat next to each other for the last twenty-five minutes without addressing each other. It felt too cold to kick start small talk with a stranger. Plus, the earmuffs. Plus, the lactation. I was just going to leave it.

"Do you have the time?" she bellowed.

"Yes," I said, looking at my wrist. "It's five 'til five."

"Perfect! She always ends class right on time. Daniela!" She tapped the head of the child on her boob through her parka. "Snack time is over, go put your shoes on."

I heard a muffled, "No!" through the coat.

"Yes!" her mom said. "Don't make me come in there and get you!" She looked at me and winked. "Name's Ellen," she said and stuck her hand out.

"I'm Tina." I smiled at her and then looked at Lila. "Where are your shoes, Lila?" She responded by grinning at me with a mouth brimming with mush.

The plastic door screeched open and Ellen's daughter, Rachel, ran out first. "I'm stah-ving," she proclaimed after leaping and landing on both feet in front of her mom, then sticking one hip out and jamming her fist onto it and glaring at her. She was about the same size as Piper, with two fuzzy, black pigtails posted on the top of her head like woolly antennae. Her crisp fuchsia tutu jutted out assertively from her tiny hips. Her pink turtleneck, however, looked like it had been dragged through a mud bog by a team of Clydesdales. Piper twirled up behind her. Her sweater looked like it had spent time in the same bog behind the same horses. As did her sweatpants. Besides the tutu, they were sisters of the bog.

"Do you mind if I ask you, do you live here? In this building I mean?" I asked Ellen.

"In this building, no, but in this complex, yes. This building is where we come for activities though, since our building has no basement." She shivered. "Been coming to this ballet class about four months now."

"Oh." I nodded. "I just found out about this class this morning—someone posted it on the notice board at the grocery store below the Ritz."

"Oh, you mean the outrageously-expensive-store-where-most-items-are-expired-but-we-shop-there-anyway-since-it's-the-only-place-that-sells-cheese?"

"Yes!" I laughed and nodded. "That's the place." I liked this woman, a fellow cheese eater and mother of two girls, the oldest of whom looked to be spirited, which is a nice way to say exhausting. "So, besides this class, are there any other fun activities for kids around here?"

"Well, there are a few things, but Rachel goes to school three days a week."

"School? A local school or an international school?"

"Neither, it's an adorable little Singaporean number down the way called Mother Goose. Haven't you seen it?"

I shook my head.

"I can show you some time. It's about as good as you can get around here, and perfect for this age. The children are very happy there," she said.

"Really? And are you very happy?" I blurted. "Here in Shanghai, I mean?"

Her eyes widened. "Uh, well—"

"I'm sorry to ask such a personal question, but I'm new, and I'm finding it really hard to adjust. As in, monumentally hard."

"Oh, right." She sighed and pushed her earmuffs back until they rested like a collar on her sweater. "I remember being new, all too well. How long have you been here then?" Her volume level, I noticed, remained above average.

"Seven months."

"I'm at two years, and it's only just started to get easier. Fun even."

I raised my eyebrows. "Fun seems like a stretch. I'm just going for bearable."

She chuckled and shook her head. "Well, it helps to meet some fellow outsiders, so you feel less alone."

"What's the best way to meet these outsiders?"

"I don't know, mate." She pushed on my upper arm. "Ballet class,

FISH HEADS AND DUCK SKIN

I reckon!" Just then her youngest dropped out from under her coat like one of Mother Ginger's children in the Nutcracker. She ran to the plastic wall, let out a giant, messy sneeze, and then smashed her lips and nose against the window and scuttled sideways to the right, leaving a trail of saliva and snot in her wake. Ellen ignored this window-as-Kleenex maneuver. "Also met a few mums at Mother Goose and then there's Mahjong Monday. I really try to put myself out there."

"What's Mahjong Monday?"

"Just a bunch of us outsiders who meet up at Malone's to shuffle bones and build walls."

"What?"

"Yeah, it's good fun. You should come! Why don't you meet me there next Monday at 4 p.m.?"

I paused.

"Or if this Monday isn't good, we're there every Monday. You can come anytime."

For the briefest moment, I thought about saying no—no to the energy it requires to meet a roomful of new people and then lose to them at an unfamiliar tile game. Then I realized that was ridiculous. This woman had just called Shanghai fun. I needed a sip of whatever she was drinking, even if it was both radioactive and hallucinogenic.

"I'll be there," I said, and right then, I resolved to get better at this.

30.

"Ting Ting!" Mr. Han called as I pushed the stroller down the pedestrian path toward the flat rock where he sat clutching a bamboo cane with both hands. It had been two weeks since I'd seen him. He leaned forward and peered into the stroller at the two faces staring back at him that had recently been stuffed, with significant resistance, into scratchy ski caps and puffy pastel parkas. "*Zhèxiē xiǎopéngyǒumen shì shéi?*"

I smiled. "I have no clue what you just said."

"What, you don't study *putonghua*?" He flashed his gums at me. "That's the Mandarin Chinese word for Mandarin Chinese. Or you can say *zhōngwén*."

"I need to learn the Mandarin Chinese word for everything, badly. Like today. Can you please teach me?"

He laughed. "Nothing worthwhile can be learned in one day."

"I know that, I—"

"Plus, you need a real teacher, a master. Then you will come sit on my rock for practice. We will alternate." He nodded as he described his vision. "Mandarin for you, English for me, you, me, you, me. We both will become *hěn lì hài*. Very strong, yes!"

I laughed. "Okay, but I think your English is already very strong."

"No, I forget many things." He coughed and then cleared his throat with such force that I stepped closer, holding my arm out to

174

him in case he fell off the rock while turning my face away from the spray of germs. When his fit subsided, he rasped while wiping his eyes with a Kleenex from his pocket that was at least as old as me. "Before, I asked you in Mandarin, who are your small friends?"

"Oh! These are my daughters, Piper and Lila." I touched their heads as I said their names.

"Don't!" Piper said, ducking her beanie-covered tangles to avoid my hand. It was apparently an off moment for affection.

"Pei Pei," he said, pointing at Lila. "And La La." He nodded at Piper. "Very beautiful."

"I'm Pei Pei!" Piper said as she raised her hand and graced him with her biggest gap-toothed smile. Maybe it was just an off moment for *my* affection.

"Ah, okay. Pei Pei, La La, do you already have Chinese names?" he asked.

"Uh," I said.

"Good! I will name you when I know you better. Beautiful names for beautiful girls!" Mr. Han leaned toward them. "Now I will watch my comrades; they dance here every Wednesday. Come, look!" He carefully touched his cane to the ground and then stood up slowly, keeping one hand on the cane and the other on the rock as he maneuvered himself near the fence. He wound his quivering hand into the chain link. "Come here for looking-looking, La La, Pei Pei—stand next to me."

I undid the stroller straps and the girls scrambled out. I picked up Lila and she hollered, "NO!" while squirming with straight arms pushing against my chest. I set her down and she ran for the side of Mr. Han that Piper wasn't occupying. I was 0 for 2.

On the other side of the fence, a woman stood in a football field-sized area enclosed mostly by tin siding and warped sheets of plywood. The field was filled with rubble. She bent down to lean her music player against a giant mound of dirt which had apparently been there a while because there were long and crazy weeds growing out the top of it, giving the hill a Muppet hairstyle. The only thing larger than the hairy hill of dirt was a neighboring mountain of trash, already picked through for anything recyclable or of any value, leaving mostly plastic wrappers and busted up cinder blocks.

"This is *jiě jiě*, my big sister, Xiǎo Qīng," Mr. Han said, extending his arm toward the woman. She growl-grunted in response without looking up.

A man rolled up on his bike, disembarked, and leaned his wheels against the opposite side of the dirt hill. He yelled loudly at the woman and then squatted to yank a sword from his bike basket.

"What's the——" I asked, alarmed.

"The sword is for the dance," Mr. Han interrupted with a smile.

"But are you sure? He sounds so angry."

"Not angry, just saying hello," Mr. Han said.

Xiǎo Qīng pulled her sword from where it was tied to the back of her hip by a faded black sash. Right then, two men and a woman walked up from the other side of Mt. Trashmore, also holding unsheathed swords. The next two men were the last two men. As soon as they arrived, the group stepped into a crooked line between the dirt and the trash and turned to face the fence with stern faces.

"The sword dance is, how you say, like magic." Mr. Han sighed as his sister pushed play with the tip of her sword. An unfortunate sound burst forth—a stringed instrument heavy on flats in duet with another stringed instrument being plucked. A Beethoven violin concerto this was not. To my ear it sounded like someone was rubbing a dull saw over a bike chain that was duct-taped over metal garbage cans—a symphony of sounds kids might make out of junk found in an abandoned shed and quickly discarded in the interest of ear health. I winced and looked at Mr. Han and the girls.

They were still. Captivated.

"Very beautiful." Mr. Han sighed, and I turned to see the dancers slowly stab their weapons at the air, then pull, twist, lean, step, and stab again, neither in time to the "music" nor in sync with the other dancers in the line. I blinked and looked at my watch.

"What do you think?" Mr. Han asked me with wet eyes once the extra-long first song had ended.

My most honest answer would not have furthered our new-found friendship.

"Well, it's nice, but, uh, I guess I'm not clear on the meaning," I said after an awkward pause. "I mean, I feel like I'm watching conflicting symbols. The dance itself is slow and deliberate, almost peaceful, but the sword looks heavy and unwieldy. Also, it seems dangerous to dance with a weapon, like they chose the wrong prop."

He cleared his throat again, this time with less force. "It's good you speak your thoughts. Americans are honest, even about things they don't understand." He nodded. "For me, the sword is not only a tool for war, but also a powerful symbol for the war inside." He thumped his chest. "Each of us has a quarrel in our heart, between who we are and who we want to be. It is difficult, but we must fight to uncover our own truth. We must harness our *qí* to succeed, which can be difficult, or as you say, 'unwieldy,' but the process is also very beautiful and empowering."

"What is qí?" I asked as the next song began.

He turned to watch the dancers. He didn't respond until the song ended. "Qí is this," he finally said. He pressed his hands toward one another but stopped them about a foot apart, as though he were a mime pressing on an invisible pillar in front of him. "Your life force." Then he dropped his hands and looked back toward the field as the music began again.

I didn't know what that meant, and I didn't ask for clarification.

"You should learn sword dancing," he said, this time speaking over the music.

"Me? No, I don't think—"

"Yes, yes. It is good for you. You can borrow my sword and dance with this team. My comrades."

"Oh no, I still feel lost here, so I want to learn Mandarin; I think that's enough."

"The dance will help you learn, teach you many things," he said.

"Yes, Mommy! And you can dance with these people in the magic field!" Piper chimed in.

I looked at her with a smile on my lips even as my eyes said STOP TALKING. "I'm sure it would be great, but I'm not very strong and I—"

"You'll start with tai chi only, no sword," Mr. Han announced as though it were settled.

"But I'm not—"

"Very good for your heart struggle. Bring you peace." He patted my mitten with his dry hand. "Don't you want peace, Ting Ting?" He smiled at me like he knew the answer.

Tears sprang to my eyes. "Of course I want peace," I said softly. "I always have. I'm just not sure I'm capable of it."

"Yes," he said, putting his hand on mine. "You are."

"But how do you know that?"

"I know," he said. "I know." He looked back at the dancers and then said, "Next Wednesday afternoon, 2:00 p.m., here, I will teach you tai chi. Soon you join this team, learn more. Gain control, gain power, gain peace."

You would have thought it was Mr. Han who had spent the last ten years of his life in sales, not me. Because somehow, he convinced me to try something I didn't understand and wasn't particularly interested in. I didn't know why I agreed to it. Maybe because he'd caught me fresh off deciding to say yes to more things and dive into China. Good timing on his part. Or was it?

31.

Dear Jennifer,

I almost rang your doorbell last week, no joke. Part of me still wishes I had, just to see your reaction. I can imagine your face opening up in shock and delight at the sight of your long-lost friend, then your brows dropping and chin pulling back in the transition to confusion, then your head tilting and eyes opening wide again, but softer this time, to say, uh oh, what happened? And should I hug you before or after you tell me?

I was this close (picture my fingers still touching) to traveling 7,000 miles for that hug. Which is ridiculous because I have access to unlimited hugs from Daniel, Piper, and Lila.

Unlimited is perhaps the wrong word. The following story problem will illustrate the actual situation:

Eighty percent of the time my family is more than happy to hug me, but twenty percent of the time I don't want them to touch me, and sometimes we don't want to be anywhere near each other at the exact same time. Therefore, sixty-eight percent of the time, I have access to unlimited hugs here.

I might have math-ed that wrong; you always had a stronger Venn diagram than me. But my point is, all I wanted was a hug on a different continent, which told me it wasn't about the hug. It was more about pulling the silver lever on the rectangular door with the rounded corners in the airplane exit row, and then inflating the giant yellow slide, and finally, hurtling myself face first onto it. It was about the escape.

Alas, the realist in me knows that escaping will only give me more problems than solutions (Was it my inner realist that said that or did you say it once in college and it stuck with me, but I forgot where it came from, and now I credit myself? That sounds more likely). So I will stay here, and today, I'm glad for it. Because even after eight months, this place keeps surprising me and revealing new sides of itself.

I won't mince words—at first glance, from my (limited, myopic) perspective, China is heinous. Almost irredeemable. But, like hidden facets in a concealed crevice on the underside of a raw gemstone caked in manure and buried during a natural disaster 10,000 years ago, this place looks (and smells) like a shitty old rock on the outside but there exist clandestine rainbows on the inside.

I'm going to make a concerted effort to tell you about the rainbows from now on. You, after all, are a natural rainbow seeker; you somehow find the good in all things. This habit of yours, which I have at times found annoying, I will now emulate. See? I do learn.

This must be my season for learning. I have a few exciting new things on the docket! I'll tell you about them soon, but not today. Today I'll keep you in suspense because that's fun for me and is also a great way to get you to open my next email. Hopefully it won't say something urgent, like, "Answer the door. Surprise!"

Thanks for being my transpacific rainbow-seeking dream hug.
-Tina

■ ■ ■

Wait, is it Christmas?
Dearest Jennifer,

How often does the above question get asked in the US? Hint: NEVER. Of course we know when Christmas is—we know the day after Halloween that an earthquake has struck off the coast of life and the green and red tsunami is rolling our way, featuring copious bouts of stress-eating and feelings of inadequacy. Plus, all the fun stuff! That gets kicked under the tree skirt of stress-eating and feelings of inadequacy.

Where was I? Oh right, I was about to inform you that PEOPLE IN CHINA DON'T KNOW WHAT CHRISTMAS IS. You're probably thinking, well duh, Tina, of course they don't know what Christmas is, but until you've lived through this Christmas-without-Christmas phenomenon, it begs description.

But first, a clarification: they sort of know what Christmas is. They know we westerners celebrate something they call "*Sheng Dan Jie*" and that it involves an obese man in a red suit. But that's about it.

If only it were so simple.

Anyhoo, today is Christmas Day, and here's what the lead up has looked like:

1. The shops were crowded in December, but not more crowded than any other time.
2. Only the tourist hotels are decorated. If you didn't walk by a tourist hotel (which is hypothetical because of course you would walk by a tourist hotel, how else would you get to Starbucks?), you would not know there was this holiday called Christmas causing melt-downs in every Costco parking lot across the Pacific right now.
3. No one in the megalopolis of Shanghai was in a state of panic yesterday, attempting to buy a last-minute gift for their spouse's cousin who just RSVPed "yes" to Christmas Eve dinner. The cousin who never says yes. Who definitely wants to borrow money.
4. Without the demand created by oddball cousins, no one was attempting to hawk over-priced, last-minute gifts.
5. All shops were open for business today, as though it were any other day.

6. The over-priced import grocery store was the only place that ran out of things—mostly (expired) baking supplies—which gave me the perfect excuse not to burn something in my toaster oven. SORRY KIDS, STORE'S OUT OF PIE CRUST.

And the kids didn't notice any of this! It's as though they never even knew that exactly one year ago, Christmas was a gigantic part of our life—financially, emotionally, perhaps spiritually if you caught me at the right moment. It impacted every aspect of our existence for at least one tenth of every year.

What did we do today instead of celebrate Christmas? Daniel took the day off, and we went on a bike ride with the girls. He rode Piper and I rode Lila. We cruised through town as though it were a day like any other, but with no agenda and no plan. We ate delicious noodles from a street vendor on the next block, and dumplings from the guy on the corner. I did break into Christmas songs during bath time, I couldn't help myself. Piper's memory was jogged—she joined me for Rudolph. Then each of us opened a very small something before we went to bed. Daniel gave me a knock-off Mont Blanc pen; he said it's so I can finally start writing again. He is really very sweet (You should remind me I said that next time I complain about him). I gave him a Starbucks mug that says "Shanghai," but only because I want it as a future keepsake. I am perhaps less sweet.

It was a very refreshing, very merry un-Christmas, which I will try to replicate next year, and maybe even once we move back home.

I hope you had an equally lovely day, my friend. Merry, merry to you and yours.

xxT

32

"**N**o kids allowed," the woman called in a Cockney accent that sounded like a sneer as I crested the final stair butt first, having finally arrived after hoisting the stroller up one step at a time backward for three flights. It was the first Monday of January, and I'd made it a resolution to finally attend Mahjong Monday.

We were at Malone's, the large, wood-paneled, American-themed bar near the Ritz-Carlton. I turned to locate the source of the bad news and spotted her, smoke seeping from her nostrils to hover above a red pashmina that had been tossed over her right shoulder and attached with a bejeweled brooch, casually on purpose.

Her hair was steel gray and bobbed. All angles on her face were pointy. She was giving me the slow once-over, capturing my purple ski jacket with the ripped side-pocket, faded jeans baggy in the knees from months of wear without a clothes dryer, well-worn, waterproof hiking boots, and unstyled, sweaty hair. I could understand her look of disapproval, but still. With another drag and an unconscious wave at her fumes, she dismissed me to resume focus on her tiles.

Ellen was sitting right next to the woman and was dressed nicely, in a black dress and boots. She was kidless, frozen, wide-eyed, and silent, as though she'd just realized the rules she'd neglected to tell me. Her whole face said "Oops."

"Oh, come on Barbara, stop being such a bitch," piped her friend from across the table. "Let the girl play awhile. She just scaled the building pulling some kind of pediatric SUV for heaven's sake. An' look at 'er, she's new!" She laughed at the obviousness of her statement. "How would she know not to wear jeans to mahjong?"

She turned to address me. "Your kids'll be good, won't they, love?"

I wouldn't bet on it, I thought as I nodded and said, "Definitely." I didn't want to go back down those damn stairs, not right away anyway. My lower back was throbbing.

"Go on then, sit at the far table," Barbara grumbled. "They need a fourth. Other three're fairly new, too, but they can show you how the game works. Next time have your ayi watch the kids, alright?"

Ellen started to stand up. "I can—"

"Oh no, Ellen, you're staying right here; there's nothing I love more than beating an Aussie. Well, except maybe beating an American, but I'll give this one a bye for now!" Barbara broke into hysterical laughter at her own joke.

Ellen may have neglected to mention the dress-code and that kids weren't allowed, but she had warned me at great length about the heckler, Barbara, who was also the President of the Ladies Mahjong Club of Shanghai. She'd been an expat for far too long, Ellen had said. She had seven ayis and treated them all like the dust bunnies she made them scour from the back corners of the linen closets on every floor of her giant art deco mansion down the road, which was often photographed for magazine covers featuring "the elegant side of Shanghai." She was well-known for ridiculing new people who showed up at Mahjong Monday and struck up conversations about nouveau expat problems.

"Don't let her hear you say you still get lost. Or that you don't speak Mandarin. One time I told her I'd never been to Beijing—big mistake," Ellen said.

"Please remind me—why'd you join this group?" I asked her.

"It's really fun once she ignores you, and that won't take long.

She's not fond of Americans, to put it nicely, but you're probably used to that."

"Uh—"

"Anyway, she won't want to play you while you're learning so she'll give you a spot at the new kid table, and then you're home-free." And just as she'd described, I found myself walking toward three women in the farthest booth. It had cracked red vinyl seats and was lit by a Tiffany-esque green glass orb hanging from the dusty wooden ceiling. Two of the women spoke quietly to each other in German, the other was a Chinese woman yet to look up from an intense examination of her tiles. *This is what home-free looks like*, I muttered to myself.

"Hello, uh, ni hao," I said slowly to the Chinese woman as she looked up at me. "My name is Tina, what is your name?" I enunciated carefully.

"I'm Wendy, and I don't speak Mandarin," she said grumpily in an American accent and looked back down at her tiles.

"Oh, I'm sorry—"

"Don't be, it happens all day long. The locals assume I speak Chinese and when they find out I don't, they treat me like a leper. The expats think I'm a local so they don't talk to me because they presume I won't understand them. It's just a giggle a minute being an American-born Chinese woman in Shanghai," she said, sounding like Eeyore. This gal was clearly also in need of some rainbows.

"I guess I could see how that would suck," I said, sitting down heavily across from her. I reached down to grab a giant mound of snacks from the stroller basket and heaped them onto the tray in front of the girls. *This should keep them quiet for a solid forty-five seconds*, I thought.

"Yeah," she sighed. "I'm addressing it, though—I just hired a tutor. She's coming to my apartment three times a week, so hopefully I can fulfill everyone's expectations and communicate in Mandarin soon. Probably right about the time we get sent home."

"You have a tutor? I desperately need one," I said.

"I'll give you her card," Wendy said. "This your first time at Mahjong?"

"Yeah, how about you?"

"It's my third," Wendy said. "I've been here almost a year. I started coming because I really needed something to fire up my brain. I was a project manager back in Ohio; I worked sixty-plus hours a week. And now that I'm the trailing spouse and full-time parent, I feel my intellect softening into oatmeal—"

"I have that problem too! Today I sat on my bed and put on one sock, and then looked up and thought, why did I sit here again? I still had the other sock in my hand."

Ellen walked up. "Hello," she said slowly to Wendy.

"I'm American," Wendy said flatly.

"Ah, okay, sorry. Hey Tina," Ellen squatted at the end of the table and looked at me. "Here's a rule sheet." She passed me a laminated 8.5 x 11 card. "It describes all the plays and how many points they're worth. Make sure to give it back to Barbara at the end or she'll have your head. And hey, sorry I forgot to tell you to leave the kids with the ayi—"

"I don't have an ayi."

"WHAT?" Wendy and Ellen screeched at the same time.

"You can't survive," Wendy said.

"Martyrs never prosper," Ellen said and then leaned over to whisper, "and Barbara does not suffer martyrs."

"I know, I know, I got the message," I said.

"No wonder you look so tired," Wendy said.

"How do you know I look tired? You just met me!"

"She's not saying that you look terrible necessarily, just tired," Ellen agreed. "That settles it; you need two things: number 1, an ayi, and number 2, nursery school."

"Actually, four things," said Wendy. "Number 3, a tutor, and number 4, brunch."

"Brunch? Why? What's that got to do with anything?"

"Because I'm sure we could all use a nice outing, and a good brunch is the best Shanghai outing there is." Wendy shrugged.

"She's right—the brunches here are outstanding," Ellen said.

"Where do you live?" Wendy asked.

"Century Club," I said.

"The place with the playground that's never open?"

I nodded.

"I'll bring my ayi's sister to your place tomorrow. She's supposed to come over to help me move a few things around the lane house, be an extra set of hands. But you need her more than me. That'll take care of your first problem," Wendy said. "And here's the card for my tutor."

"Thank you. Wait, your ayi has a sister? I thought no one but the retirees had siblings here?"

"Yeah, she's probably a distant cousin. Or maybe just a good friend."

"I'll book brunch and take you to see the school on Wednesday," Ellen said. She stood and came around behind me to squeeze my shoulders. "We'll get you all sorted, possum. No worries."

Dear Jennifer,

As of ten days ago, dramatic life improvement has arrived! I met a couple of women who took one look at me and came to a monumental, albeit obvious, conclusion: my situation was not sustainable. I thought I could push through, but the thing is, you can't pluck a ball-busting gal out of corporate America and plunk her in a sludgy metropolis with no toilet paper and an alphabet made of sticks and squiggles and expect success. Because, if it wasn't already clear, my exotic new life here is the polar opposite of my last Presidents Club trip to Turks and Caicos. For a while there I was stuck in shock and spinning, getting cooked on all sides like a hog on a spit.

Enter the magical new friends! They identified my issues and produced solutions! I now have half-day schooling for both kids, three days a week. It's not Harvard-for-Babies, but it also doesn't reek of pee, so both Daniel's and my wishes were granted.

I also now have an ayi, which is basically the combination of a maid and a personal assistant—someone who can do everything I can't do, plus everything I can do, except better. If I had an inferiority complex, this arrangement would never work. But I don't and thus, my life has been transformed—shot from the fecal quagmire like a seagull wedged in a whale's blowhole until, at long last, he sneezed from his back. Kapow!

I'm flying now, and finally I can breathe. And sleep. And eat! Because Ayi cooks, too—like a pro, in fact. Which means I have been relieved of all the jobs I suck at. And with Daniel gone so much, I finally have friends to help abate the loneliness. My glass is half-full, do you believe it?

-Tina

■ ■ ■

Dear Jennifer,

CHINESE NEW YEAR IS A TWO-WEEK FESTIVAL WHERE EVERYTHING IS CLOSED INCLUDING ALL BANKS AND RESTAURANTS AND AYI TOOK A FORTY-EIGHT HOUR TRAIN RIDE TO HER HOMETOWN FOR THREE WEEKS AND THE WINDOWS OF OUR APARTMENT NEARLY SHATTER EVERY NIGHT FROM EXCESSIVE FIREWORK REVERBERATION. I HAD NO CLUE.

I'm sure there's a rainbow in there somewhere.

Love,

Me

34.

"The purpose of tai chi is to open the channels for your energy to flow freely," Mr. Han said while standing next to Mt. Trashmore. He had allowed his cane to fall into the dirt and now his legs shook in his faded black sweatpants.

Even though the outside temperature was getting more bearable, it was now March which meant the arrival of the windy season, which in Shanghai translated to dust in every orifice. A thin film of gray cement lined the inside of my nose and collected in the corners of my mouth, and my eyes watered incessantly. Sunglasses didn't help. With all the gear the locals sported to avoid sun exposure, I was surprised that no one wore goggles. On top of this, the tai chi was not coming naturally.

"I have no idea what that means," I said, willing myself to stay patient.

"You don't know because you're blocked. It is very evident. Your energy does not flow freely."

"What do you mean by 'blocked,'" I curled my finger quotes at him like an angry cat. "Are you talking about my digestion? Because I don't see—"

"Perhaps I am talking about your digestion, how is your *dàbiàn*?"

"My what?"

"Your bowel movement."

I grimaced. "I honestly can't see—"

"I think I already know the answer. When your energy is stuck, everything is stuck." He put his hands on his belly and nodded.

I exhaled loudly and shook my head.

"When you're blocked you are also quick to anger. Because your mind," he held up one hand and made a small circle in the air, "it swirls, with no focus, and no release."

"I'm quick to anger because I need a spacesuit."

"Eh?"

"Isn't there an inside studio where we can practice? This wind is ridiculous."

"The wind is very cleansing. It reorganizes and realigns," he said.

"I'm not buying it," I mumbled.

"Eh?"

"Never mind. Let's just do the moves."

"*Hao de,*" he said and stepped next to me.

Thirty seconds later, I said, "I can't see how these motions could unblock anyone. How holding a leg at an unnatural angle while pushing one hand this way and hooking the other hand that way could possibly make a person less angry."

"It takes time to understand—"

"Time, which people may have had two thousand years ago, but no one has today." I continued to mimic his movements though, on the off-chance I was wrong. I positioned my hands like I was balancing a sphere between them the size of a large grapefruit. Or maybe a small watermelon.

"Try to empty your mind and breathe deeply," he said while leaning left.

I coughed.

"Is this hard for you?"

"If it weren't for the dirt in the air, it wouldn't be hard since this isn't even exercise. Where I come from, unless you're lunging or squatting, moving slowly like this does not burn calories. I'm going to have to go for a jog later."

"This is a different kind of exercise. It's exercise for your energy. You'll see."

I looked at my watch. "I still don't understand, but I have seventeen more minutes to exercise my energy until school gets out."

"But who's counting?" he smiled. "Collect a cloud now, Ting Ting. Focus on your breath. You'll feel a difference in time. In seventeen minutes, maybe your children will feel it too."

35.

It was tutor time. It had taken me a few weeks to call, but I'd finally talked myself into it. I still felt a little anxious as I sat down and stood up, sat down and stood up, waiting for the knock on my apartment door. I had brushed my hair more than once. Okay, more than twice. Fine, four times, but it was still windy outside, and my hair was a disaster.

Ayi was playing quietly with the girls in their room. *Why are the girls and Ayi so quiet?* I wondered several times, but every time I checked on them, they ignored me. They were engrossed in some sort of Farbie doll Olympics. Ayi was crouched between them, calling out occasionally in Mandarin. Keeping score? Cheering? I couldn't tell. *This would be part of the reason I've hired a tutor,* I thought. *So I know what people are communicating to my children.*

Mostly I observed that Ayi was great at playing with little kids, true butt-on-the-floor playing. *She's better at this role than me,* I admitted as my doorbell rang at precisely 4 p.m. I stood up straight and headed toward the front door while trying to finish this sentence: *Well, at least I'm good at _____.* I drew a blank. I wasn't sure anymore.

My new tutor was a full-sized Asian version of the Olympiads on Piper's floor. Red, fitted suit, red lips, red nails. Shiny black stilettos, shiny black ponytail, shiny black briefcase. "Hello, I'm Katie

Liu," she said as she raised her arm straight forward from her side, hinging at her shoulder.

I shook her hand. "I suck at French," I blurted as my anxiety assumed control of my mouth. "Eight years of French labs and I couldn't get myself off the airport curb in Paris."

"I speak fluent French," Katie said. "But I thought you hired me to teach you Mandarin?"

"I did! I definitely want to learn Mandarin. I was just giving you some background on my language acquisition. My track record is poor, but I'm determined to get it right this time, and the sooner the better."

"Well, there's no better way to learn a language than immersion, and there's no better tutor than me, so you're in the right place with the right person. Well actually, Beijing would be the best place since everyone speaks Shanghainese here, but," she shrugged, "at least you have me."

"Oh, should I learn Shanghainese instead?"

"Ha! No, that's only for kitchen talk. You must learn the national language."

"Do you speak Shanghainese?"

"Of course I do! All day long, to every local. I couldn't live here otherwise."

We paused to consider the implications of her statement.

"But you wouldn't learn Shanghainese in formal tutoring sessions, you'd learn it in a back alley, buying rice off a thug," she scoffed.

I shrugged. "Okay then, Mandarin it is. So how is your English so perfect?" I asked as she breezed past me. I turned to follow the sharp rhythm of her heels tapping on the linoleum.

"My dad's American, lives in LA," she said as she stopped at the dining room table.

"Oh—"

"But mostly it's the men," she said as she placed her bag carefully on a chair and smoothed her pencil skirt.

"The men?"

"I only date American men. I'll occasionally make an exception for the right Kiwi or South African," she said, and winked, "but I'm on a streak of Americans right now, and they're working quite well for me." She inhaled and her expression turned dreamy. Upon exhalation she regained composure and templed her fingers. "Shall we begin?" she asked.

"Ready when you are," I said.

Dear Jennifer,

As you are well-aware, I'm no sun worshipper. You'll never catch me in a tan bed or smearing myself with ill-scented creams. You'll nod in agreement as I say to you, dark orange leather is for saddles and smart casual handbags, not skin.

Sure, I may have occasionally swung by Tan Land before the odd high school dance. Perhaps in college I hit the university rec center pool sporting a jumbo bottle of baby oil a few times, a dozen tops. But that was last century! Now, with more birthdays under my belt, I know better (meanwhile you, my dear ginger, have always known better).

It doesn't matter how much I shun the sun, though, I'll always look a little tan. I can't help it that I'm olive! That if you say the word sun in the same room as me, I bronze!

But last week, my tutor, Katie, broke some less fortunate news—in China I have the skin tone of a peasant. Not wrinkled, not cancerous, just working class. My natural pigment? Not an excuse for my obvious and unfortunate social status. Only people who work in the sun look like me. She even suggested I visit a whitening cream counter, which wouldn't be hard because they're every ten feet.

"In China, you'd be considered attractive if you weren't so tan," Katie said while considering my arms. It was the first time she had seen them because the seasons just changed, and I no longer need layers between myself and the cold, rain, and/or dust.

"You're joking, right? I mean, this isn't even tan for me, but I'm still too tan to be pretty?"

"I think you're pretty, but you'd be prettier if you were more white."

I paused, wondering if it was a good time to launch into the myriad reasons her statement was offensive. "You should know, the opposite is true in America and other countries. Skin much darker than mine is beautiful there."

She looked at me like I was trying to explain how cyanide would extend my life.

"I think you're saying that in China I'm almost pretty?" I asked her.

She laughed and nodded. "You're funny, Tina," she said. "But I suppose you're also correct. If you were Chinese, you'd be almost pretty."

The white skin thing is an obsession here. I mean, our society has freaky obsessions, too, so I try not to judge, but seriously, these people are crazy for looking pasty! A skin lotion without the added benefit of bleaching doesn't exist here. What we want for teeth, they want for skin.

Chinese women cruise town in the most confounding get-ups, all to look void of color. Here are a few of the anti-tan devices I see daily:

1) Pants. This place is like a steam room on the sun four months a year. Yet I haven't set eyes on one pair of Chinese legs.

2) Arm condoms. This is the best way to describe these things. Chinese women wear short sleeved shirts, but when they go outside, they pull up bands of fabric with elastic at the top to hold them in place. They cover their entire arms and drape over their fingers at the bottom. Like a strapless dress for your arms. And that looks better than a tan.

3) Visors. Actually, 'visor' doesn't provide an adequate visual. Remember in *Flashdance* when Jennifer Beals wore that protective gear for her face because she worked as a welder at a steel mill? That's what I mean by visor. Chinese people wear them around town. They would rather wear welding gear than get a speck of vitamin D. In my mind, *Flashdance* was the first and last time welding gear looked remotely cool or sexy.

4) Parasols. I see more umbrellas in Shanghai on a sunny day than a rainy day. A lot more.

"I'm hot, Mom. Why can't we carry an umbrella like everyone else?" Piper asked me the other day. She's a fellow olive and already gets that it's not cool to be the tan kid in these parts. Poor thing doesn't want to be almost pretty.

"Because it's not raining and we don't live in Victorian England, that's why. And here's the other reason—you know that white stuff I smear all over your face and body in the morning before we step outside? That's your built-in parasol, buddy. So, lucky you, both of your hands are free to play! Now go run around on the cement! You can even try to climb that skinny tree over there when the guy with the whistle isn't looking."

Your friend,

The Ugly (I mean Tan) Duckling

37.

"**S**low down!" I screeched at Wendy's back as she deftly maneuvered potholes with her son, Charlie, strapped into her rear bike basket. I rode Lila in the front child seat, bouncing clumsily over the potholes Wendy seemed to be missing. I was steadily losing ground. Daniel rode Piper and trailed way behind us next to Wendy's husband, Tim, who had one hand on the handlebars, one hand pointing out architectural features on the street.

"I can't slow down!" Wendy squealed, stopping her bike briefly to explain. "I'm just so excited for brunch. I can't believe it took us this long to find a time that worked for everyone—I haven't had pancakes with syrup for six months. Do you know what they serve on pancakes at Malone's? Honey! Bleck. This should be a crime. Plus, the pancakes themselves are like rubber—I think they use rice flour or something. This brunch is going to be nothing like a normal day attempting to eat decent Western food in Shanghai."

"How do they know how to make Western food at hotel brunches but nowhere else in town?"

"Because the hotels hire foreigners to run their kitchens so tourists feel comfortable."

"Oh, then why don't you go to brunch more often?"

"Because it's outrageously expensive! And besides, I don't like to get drunk at breakfast more than a couple times a year—once a quarter at most. It makes Mondays too painful."

"Drunk at breakfast?"

"Unlimited Veuve Cliquot, Tina. Plus, a kids' club! Did you not read up on this? How long can you use, 'I'm new,' as an excuse anyway?" She smirked. "We will not be riding our bikes home, my darling."

"I'm not sure I—"

"They'll have to drag me outta there," Wendy muttered, pedaling faster.

"We're in the Ellen party, table for eight," I explained to the tuxedoed host. I wiped the sweat from above one eyebrow with my pinky.

"Rye dis way." He bowed and grabbed an armful of menus, leading us past the orchestra assembling in a clearing under a giant pink chandelier.

"Wow," Daniel said.

"There you are!" Ellen jumped up to hug me and Wendy. Ellen's husband, Jerry, was slight, with no. 2–razored red hair. He was a solid six inches shorter than Ellen if she weren't wearing heels, which she was—three-inchers. Wendy's husband, Ted, on the other hand, was also Asian and the exact same tallish height as Wendy, with the same cute set of dimples, and an almost identical haircut. I remember wondering if she'd married her twin and then dismissing that thought because *eew*.

Ellen's husband, Jerry, had never met Wendy's husband, Tim. "My name is Jerry. Do you speak English?" he asked slowly as he reached out to shake his hand.

"I'm Ted. I'm from Cleveland," he sighed as Ellen elbowed Jerry.

"I'm hitting the buffet before they run out of crab," Wendy stood and bee-lined to the seafood station.

The women eventually migrated to one side of the table, the men to the other. Champagne flowed and plates stacked.

"I'm having a hard time losing the baby weight," Ellen said, before slurping a crepe like a spaghetti noodle.

"Yesterday Tim complained about the entire meal category labeled 'brunch'," Wendy said. "He says these opulent meals are how restaurants repurpose leftover food from earlier in the week, all of which is mostly on the edge of rotten. To which I say, 'Bring me your tired, your poor, your huddled blintzes!'" She tossed back a deviled egg.

"The plate spinners are setting up, you guys, and the Sichuan masked dancers are queued up next. And all of this is happening right next to the chocolate fountain!" Wendy said as she walked up, balancing a full plate on each forearm and one in each hand.

All I heard was chocolate fountain.

It was glorious, like a dream inside of a dream. The food. The entertainment. The company. Even the restroom was immaculate and had toilet seats, toilet paper, sinks, even soap.

On my way out of the bathroom, I took a right before heading back to the table. I thought I should check on the kids; it had been awhile.

I hung a left into the large room at the end of the hall and almost walked into a cage. At least two dozen cages had appeared since we had dropped off the kids. They filled the center of the room. A white lab in a crate in front of me lifted his head to look at me, then set it back on his paws. Some kind of fluffy terrier in the adjacent cage barked and wagged his tail furiously. A large black-and-white cat in an enclosure against the right wall licked his paws and actively ignored me.

I looked around and spotted Piper and Lila—they were sitting together on a round pillow propped against the back wall, each hugging an orange-striped kitten.

A woman walked toward me with a clipboard. "I'm their mom." I pointed to the girls. "What's happening here?" I asked her.

"Didn't you know? It's Animal Adoption day," she said. "Every month, Animal Adoption Day falls on Expat Brunch Day. We target newer expat families to adopt the abandoned pets of those expats who recently moved home. Brunch is the optimal intersection of two lines that might otherwise never cross."

I looked at the girls holding the kittens, and my eyes welled up. I swayed a little bit, but I think that was from the champagne. Then I smiled. Because right then I knew, our family in China would finally feel complete.

In any Alfred Hitchcock film, there comes a moment right before a central character meets his or her demise via birds, Grandma impersonator, or other sinister being, when (s)he sets free a blood curdling scream. When you hear that shriek, you know the character is done for. It's not the sound of a survivor. It's not the holler of someone playing a prank, or the shout you hear on a roller coaster or in a haunted house. It's a notch or ten above those sounds. This immediate death scream is what Katie the tutor let fly when she next clicked her leopard print pencil heels into my apartment and laid her eyes on our new kittens. *Kittens.* Who were asleep in a cardboard box in my kitchen, not poised to leap up and rip her face off.

"*Wǒde mā ya!*" Katie wailed after her mighty death roar, and then covered her head with her forearms and sobbed.

This level of response to baby animals seemed unwarranted. It would have astounded me more had Ayi not reacted in much the same way the day before, upon her first sighting of the cats. After her end-of-life screech, she had proceeded to whimper loudly while standing on a dining room chair—treed by two tiny balls of fur. It took several cups of tea—in my bedroom with the door pulled closed—to get her to stop hyperventilating.

It was 10 a.m. when Katie arrived for our lesson, but it already felt like a long, rainbow-less day, as though the a.m. and p.m. had been switched somehow.

By 10 a.m. I had already almost lost my life to a truck driven by a man who couldn't see over his steering wheel while riding my bike in the gutter after dropping Piper and Lila at school. Then, when I got home, I'd caught the breaking news in the six-minute English segment on CCTV: a popular local baby formula had been tested and found to contain melamine, an industrial plastic, which was apparently a cheaper way to appear higher in protein. Six babies had already died from kidney stones. I hadn't bought the local formula for Lila, but what about Ayi? Sometimes she went to the store for me when I wasn't up for it. I'd asked her to only buy the imported formula, but had she understood me? Two days before, Ellen had told her ayi how much hair to have trimmed off her daughter's head. "Only this much," she'd said holding her fingers a half inch apart. Her ayi thought she meant that was how much hair should be left on her head. Now Rachel looked like Michael Jackson in 1969. And I didn't know if Lila had been slurping plastic.

This was my excuse for why annoyance showed up instead of empathy in response to Katie's kitten panic. "Seriously? Come on, they're tiny, infant cats!" I whined and smacked my hand against my forehead.

I closed my eyes so they wouldn't roll and waited; I heard nothing but whimpers. I exhaled loudly and pushed my chair back. "How about some tea?" I said.

"No." she sniffed, uncurling her arms. "Do you have any Bailey's?"

"Bailey's, as in Irish Cream?"

"Yes."

"I don't think so. I can get you a beer? Or chardonnay?"

"No, no thank you. I only drink Bailey's." She inhaled dramatically and then smiled stiffly, her lips pulling tightly over her teeth. "Shall we start?"

I shrugged and sat down.

She took several deep breaths and then pulled a slim stack of stapled papers from her briefcase and slid them toward me. "Mandarin has four tones," she said. "It is very important that you listen for them, Tina, because otherwise two words with very different meanings will sound the same to you."

She gave me a few examples.

"So depending on how I say the word *ma*, I am either saying mother, or horse?" I clarified.

"Or cart or question word. Yes, that's right," she said.

"That seems more confusing than it needs to be. Why wouldn't you use the context of the sentence to understand a word's meaning if, say, for some reason, you weren't sure of the tone?" I asked.

"In English you use context, in Mandarin we use tones," she said.

"I understand that as a culture, you don't admit to using context, but isn't it inevitable? I mean, how do you not use context when you hear an entire sentence?"

"Mandarin doesn't work that way. You must learn the tones."

"But I don't hear the tones."

"You don't hear them *yet*."

"No, I'm saying my ears don't hear them; they don't function that way. They aren't dog ears; they don't pick up distant sirens either."

The kittens mewed softly in the kitchen. Katie stiffened.

"You know they won't hurt you, right? I mean even if they wanted to hurt you, which they don't, they couldn't."

"Cats are not pets in China," she said.

"That I gathered, using context." I chuckled.

Her eyes flashed at me, then at her watch.

"Can I just bring them out here? To show you how weak and defenseless they are?"

Right then Lila toddled out, rubbing her eyes. "Mama?" she called.

I walked over and scooped her up. "It's your lucky day, Katie. You get to meet Lila instead." Lila nuzzled her head into my neck.

They hadn't met on Katie's first visit. "Katie, this is Lila, Lila, meet Katie."

Katie's eyes bugged out of her head. "What did you say her name is?"

"Uh, Lila?"

"Ayi!" Katie called in alarm. Ayi hustled in. Katie spoke to her firmly in Shanghainese. Ayi took Lila from my arms and walked down the hall making chicken noises while Lila giggled.

When Ayi was out of earshot Katie stood up and said, "Lila? You can't call her Lila! You must give her a nickname if she will live in China!"

I laughed. "Lila means 'come here,' right? I hear the ayis saying 'Lila' to the children at school all the time."

"No, it—"

"Don't get me wrong." I raised my palm. "'Come here' is definitely a strange name for a child in China, but we won't live here forever, so for now, it's okay if people think I'm asking my daughter to come here."

"Lila doesn't just mean come here, Tina. When you say it like you would say a name, it sounds like what we say on the first day of our menstruation."

I paused. "'Lila' means I just got my period?"

"Yes, that's what women from Shanghai say to each other." She sat down and clasped her hands together on the dining room table and then studied them.

I closed my eyes and put my face in my hands. "Wow. What an amazingly bad name," I said.

"Well," she said looking up and smiling brightly, "The good news is that if you use different tones, it won't mean that at all. If you say Li LA instead of LI la, it will sound much better. Call her Li LA."

"Katie, I just told you, I can't hear tones. I can barely tell the difference in what you just said."

"You must listen more, Tina. Now you have a reason to try."

39.

Dear Jennifer,

THE MOST AMAZING THING HAPPENED TODAY!

When I woke up this morning, something felt different. As I rode Piper to school, the feeling remained, but I couldn't pinpoint the origin.

I was almost all the way home when it hit me. I stopped, mid-gutter, and dialed Daniel.

"Doesn't it feel different, TODAY!" I sang to him in my best Ethel Merman voice.

"What? I don't know what you're—"

"Just STOP whatever you're doing and listen for a minute."

He said nothing.

"Do you hear it?" I whispered.

"Hear what? What should I hear?" he whispered back with only the tiniest hint of sarcasm.

"The incessant, maniacal horn-honking that never stops?" I screeched. "Do you hear it? Because I don't!" I bubbled in glee.

Jennifer, what you must understand is that since arriving in Shanghai, the traffic noise, especially the horn-honking, has been like breathing—so constant that you only notice when it changes. Like white noise but more awful. We could hear the horns everywhere—inside our apartment, at Daniel's office, in every restaurant, at the bank, at the massage parlor. Around the clock too, as in late late late and early early early. As I said, I hardly noticed it anymore, but still, there must be an underlying level of agitation when there is never a moment without a horn blasting.

But as I sat on the phone with Daniel, I felt almost serene. And until today, serene is a word I have never once used to describe myself. Especially not in Shanghai!

Daniel paused. "Holy shit! Cinderella!" he yelled to his assistant (Chinese people choose the darndest English names.), "Why are the horns not honking?" I heard a long, muffled reply.

"He said they made horn honking illegal starting today. From now on, if you honk, there's a 200 kuai fine."

"The whole city stopped honking today for twenty-five bucks?" I shrieked.

"Apparently."

"Can we declare this day a national holiday?" I cried.

He laughed. "Big change on a dime. That's China for you."

And then I danced right there, in the gutter, with the bike frame between my legs. I danced a love dance, with my arms over my head in honor of this crazy place. And no one honked at me! Because they couldn't!

40.

"**Y**ou are a white crane," Mr. Han proclaimed with conviction. He held one arm up, one arm down, his lower hand close to the handle of his cane. In the six weeks that had passed, someone had lit the city furnace. Yet, somehow, Mr. Han wasn't sweating.

"I'm a white crane," I repeated, sans conviction, feeling sweat roll into my socks. "Or maybe I'm a flamenco dancer in Southern Spain in August? I could be either, depending on my outfit."

He ignored me. "You are not rooted."

"That's because I'm a bird, not a plant."

"The white crane is always rooted, very strong, very balanced."

I dropped my arms. "Can I ask a question? It's not about the white crane."

"Why always questions? Never mind, it's your nature." He sighed. "After your question, will you focus on your roots?"

"I will," I lied.

"*Hǎo de*," he said.

"I know my Mandarin is still terrible."

"There is some space for improvement." He nodded.

"But, even at my novice level, I can tell that my comprehension has improved. I can finally understand what people are saying, both to me and to each other, unless they're speaking in a different dialect, but now I can tell when they're speaking in a different dialect. Mandarin doesn't sound like a jumble of angry sounds anymore."

"This is wonderful, Ting Ting! This is a huge step in your language acquisition."

"The problem is, now that I understand what they're saying, I don't like what I'm hearing. It seems like the only thing they talk about is money. How much did this cost? That's too expensive; I only paid this much. Over and over, all day long. Plus, any greeting or good wish I hear is related to acquiring wealth, for themselves, their friends, or whoever. I don't understand it. What about talking about current events? Or the weather? What about wishing for health, joy, or peace? In the US, when we send holiday cards to our friends every year, even on the cards we send to our customers, we would never write, 'May this year bring you a bucketful of cash,' because a wish like that would be crass; it would indicate that we'd lost track of what's important. I mean, even if we want success and wealth for ourselves and our family and friends, we would never wish for it over health or happiness, not out loud anyway."

Mr. Han cleared his throat. "An astute observation made from a position of privilege."

"What do you mean?"

"It means when you are affluent—"

"But I didn't notice it because I'm affluent. And, to be clear, I started with nothing but debt, and I've worked hard for everything I have. My point is that money does not equate to happiness or well-being. Sure, money reduces stress and makes things easier, but to achieve true happiness, we need something else. I'm not saying I know what that thing is—I don't. But I do know that a singular obsession with money will only create more societal problems down the road. Money should not be the only goal; it's not what life should be all about."

I felt proud of my speech, like I had shared profound wisdom.

As though I had come from a more enlightened place on the planet and was finally able to teach him something meaningful.

He templed his fingers. "It is true we must look inside ourselves. But, in your observation, is it also true that money affords security?"

"Sure it does."

"But you wouldn't wish security for your friends on your holiday cards, because they already have security, and they have had it for generations."

"Correct . . ."

"Would you wish food for your friends on your holiday card? Basic food, so they're not hungry?"

"Uh, no."

"But you see, in China, not long ago, we had nothing—no money, no food, no security. Today, we do have these things, and life is better. But we remember, you see. So when we wish wealth for someone, we aren't saying, 'My friend, my friend, I wish you can buy a TV for every room in your house.' It's not that at all. It is a wish for them to have security, and stability, a hope that their food won't disappear, their life won't be at risk, and they will never need to worry about having nothing, ever, ever again." He looked at me with kind eyes, deeply creased at the sides. "You see, sometimes our words say one thing but mean another."

I cringed in shame and dropped my face in my hands. I uttered the first thought that came to mind, "I'm such an asshole."

He smiled. "I do not know this word."

"It's, uh, hard to explain—Another word that says one thing but means another." I looked up at him. "It means that I feel unworthy of your kindness and your patience."

He grabbed my hands, squeezed them once, and then held onto them. "Of course you are worthy. Your thoughts are quite normal, Ting Ting. You have come to China to learn many things, both about the world and about yourself. The expats here, especially the

Americans, are ignorant of their abundance. This is because you have known no other way. Like we have known no other way than what we have seen, what we have lived. We do not share a common history, therefore it can be hard for us to understand each other. But we must continue to try."

With that he raised my left arm above my head, setting it at the correct white crane angle. Then, as he shuffled to adjust my right arm, he leaned in and whispered, "You are my most worthy student."

I laughed. "You are kind, but that's not true, and if it is, it doesn't say much about your other students."

"You are very strong, more powerful than you think, only lacking roots."

I looked at him and thought about how much I had already learned from him. He was so wise. How could he be so wrong about me? Or was it possible that he wasn't wrong? That I was both worthy and powerful? I stood up straight, inhaled, and breathed into my feet, trying to make Mr. Han's statement at least a little true. I yearned to know what having roots felt like, so I could imagine them for myself.

"You will be rooted one day, Ting Ting. Continue to try."

"I am a white crane," I said, wishing it were true now.

41.

"Yī, èr, sān, sì, wǔ, liù, qī, bā, jiǔ, shí. You know this already, right? One through ten," Katie said.

It was three weeks later, and we were sitting at my dining room table. I nodded even though I usually forgot how to say seven.

"Well today you will learn a Chinese truth that most of us take for granted: If you want to buy something at the local market, you must sign for it."

"Sign for it?"

"Yes, with your fingers. For clarity. To firmly quantify your want."

My brain matter felt particularly mud-like on this morning. I'd been up all night with Lila, who had cried and cried but couldn't tell me what hurt. Daniel was out of town inspecting a new factory. My bike had a flat. And I had run out of tea. I knew I had more gripes, but I was too tired to think of them.

"You're going to have to say that again, slowly. I don't understand," I said.

She held her hand in front of my face in a hang loose configuration. "This is liù. Six."

"This is six?" I stuck out my thumb and pinky and folded my middle three fingers.

"Yes, liù," she said.

I laughed. "Why on Earth would I use this to say six when I can just use my words, the ones you are teaching me, and say liu?"

"Because if you want six apples, six pears, six bananas, or six anything, you will show the man at the food stand the sign for six, and then he will make the same sign back at you. You will then nod, and he will tell you what you owe. It's very simple."

I paused. "What if I want eight apples? Because I really love apples."

Katie held up her hand like a gun, thumb up, index finger and pointed it at me, and then to her side. "Bā. Eight."

"How about nine?"

She balled up her hand, all except her forefinger, which she curled over. "Jiǔ. Nine."

I curled my forefinger like hers, then straightened it, pointed it straight at her, and wagged it. "I will never remember this, Katie!"

"Of course you will; I'm going to teach you a trick," she said with mischief in her eyes.

"A trick?"

"Yes." She smiled with excitement. "One through five are easy—the same as your American hand counting. But here's how you will remember the rest of them—Give me a call, which is liù, six, I know this Italian, which is qī, seven, and I want to shoot him, which is bā, eight, because his wanker is tiny, or jiǔ, nine, and he punched my mother, or shí, ten."

I made the signs, repeating, "Give me a call, liu, I know this Italian, qi, and I want to shoot him, ba, because his wanker is tiny, jiu, and he punched my mother, shi?"

"Exactly! But his wanker is more like this." She demonstrated again.

"And you can guarantee that if I use these hand signs, people won't ignore me when I'm trying to buy stuff at the wet market? Because that's a daily issue."

"I believe you will have a much higher probability of success."

"Then I can't wait to try it."

◎ ◎ ◎

Later, when she stood to leave, I said, "Do you want to hang out sometime, outside of lessons? Maybe we could go get a massage? I usually meet my friends on Thursday nights. There's a place right down the street that's great; we reserve a whole room. Maybe you could come with us and meet some potential clients? Wendy will be there, too. What do you say?"

"No thank you. I have my own masseuse. She comes to my apartment twice a week. Her brother brings her to me; she is blind."

"Blind?"

"All the best masseuses are blind."

"Oh, uh, okay, how about a run then? Meet me some morning. We can start at the park."

"A run?"

"Yes, a run. You know, for fitness."

She started laughing hysterically, guffawing louder than I would have thought she could. "That is your best joke by far, Tina," she said. "You want me to run!" She packed up her briefcase and walked to the door, still chuckling, and turned around. "You must understand—I'm a Chinese woman. I wouldn't even run from a tiger."

She opened the door and stepped out, then tipped her head back in. "I'd like to be friends with you too, Tina, but I'm very busy. I have another job that takes up a lot of my time. I'll tell you about it sometime when I don't have another client after you. Sorry."

"Another job? Seriously? This one isn't enough?"

"The other job is not about money. I'll explain later."

"You know what I think?" I asked Mr. Han the following Wednesday and then immediately took a bite of my large steamed bun. I couldn't wait. We were sitting on a bench under a tree in the neighborhood park. I got busy tucking into the meat section of my baozi, while he hadn't taken his out of the tiny plastic bag yet. We had just walked from a not-so-grueling tai chi session to our favorite baozi shack, then to the park to eat our purchases.

I put up a finger until I swallowed and began. "I think we should eat baozi on Wednesdays instead of practice tai chi. *Women yinggai yiqi qu chifan*." I nodded. "We should eat together. Instead."

Mr. Han looked at me and blinked.

"I mean I like tai chi, I do. I'm sure for some people it's a beautiful thing. However, it's possible I might be too high-strung for tai chi—I'm not sure it suits my personality."

"It will suit you. Once you're more rooted, it will feed you. Like baozi feeds you now."

"Nothing can feed me like baozi feeds me. Not in the East, not in the West."

"Tai chi will be even better for you someday," he said.

"That's not possible."

"More nourishing. To your energy." He nodded.

I sighed and looked at him. "I want to tell you something."

He nodded and took a bite.

"Is that a carrot baozi?" I asked.

"Mmm." He nodded. "And leek."

"I've never had that kind. Is it good? It looks really good."

"Mmm. Very good. Is this what you wanted to tell me?"

"No, sorry. I wanted to tell you that you remind me of my grandpa."

"I do?"

"Yes, very much. I didn't realize it right away, but lately I feel it more and more."

"Thank you."

"How do you know that's a compliment?"

He looked confused.

"I'm kidding, it is. I haven't told you before, but my grandpa was the only person who ever really loved me—a totally unself-ish, unconditional, uncomplicated love. He taught me things for no other reason than to make me better. Not for himself at all. How to make pancakes even though he couldn't eat them. How to play pool even though he had arthritis. How to play guitar but . . ."

Mr. Han waved his fingers, and I nodded.

"My grandpa was a great man and he loved me more than any-one ever has and probably ever will." I sad-smiled. "He's been dead for ten years, and I still miss him. Spending time with you feels like I'm spending time with him. That's why I come to see you every week," I said. "You're channeling my grandpa."

He thought for a moment, silently translating. "Ah. Okay," he finally said.

"I don't come to learn tai chi," I said.

"Eh?"

"I mean tai chi is nice, and your friends are there, and they're very patient with me."

"Because they want you to improve. To be a stronger team member."

"I know, and I appreciate that. Plus, your sister is much more pleasant now—she only occasionally yells at me, maybe because I've worn her down—I know I can do that. But I just want you to know, I go to see you, not to move slowly around in circles because, depending on the day, the practice of tai chi still makes me feel impatient. Like it serves no purpose. But for me, you're the purpose. And I wanted to tell you that. I am grateful for you and the way you make me feel, more than you'll ever know."

He looked away for a moment, toward the pond, then looked back and smiled. "My grandfather was also a wonderful man," he said.

"He was?"

"Yes. He was a teacher and a powerful leader. *Wǒ de zǔfù hěn yǒu quánwē.* He taught me tai chi."

"He did?"

"Mm. In Guìlín."

"Where is Guilin?"

"South and west. Twenty-four hours by train. I was born there, and I will die there."

"How do you know you'll die there?" I scoffed.

"Because, when it is my season, I will go there to join my ancestors."

"What do you mean? When will it be your season?"

He shrugged. "When it is. Probably three seasons from this season."

"Mr. Han, no. That isn't right. You are very healthy and vibrant. Three seasons is far too soon. I think you're forgetting the zero. Thirty seasons is more accurate."

He laughed. "Thirty!" he sighed and wiped his eyes. "Maybe you're right. Maybe I forget the *shí.*" He held his fist straight up, fingers curled toward me.

"That means ten!" I sputtered, pointing at his hand.

"Mm, ten," he said. "Shí."

"I know shi is ten, but last week I didn't know that this," I held up my fist like his, "means shi, which means ten."

He smiled, but I could see the significance was lost on him.

"I'm learning things, Mr. Han, about China. This is proof that I'm smarter today than I was last week."

"Ah," he said. "Ha ha. Good!" He patted my hand. "Grandchild. No, granddaughter. Good granddaughter."

I hugged him tight, then pulled back. "Now will you please give me a bite of your baozi? I don't know how many hints I have to drop."

"Eh? You want some?"

"Yes!"

"Okay okay," he said and pushed it toward me. "Please. Eat."

"Okay, Grandpa. Thank you. Here, have some of my pork and vegetable."

"Yes, okay, granddaughter."

"Favorite granddaughter," I said.

"Mm. Yes, favorite granddaughter. *Xiè xiè.*"

"*Xie xie ni,*" I said.

We chewed on each other's baozis for a bit, happy and quiet. Then he said, "Wednesdays will be for both baozi and tai chi."

I sighed.

43

A month later on a Friday night, Daniel announced, "I need a favor." He was perched on the glossy stool with his chin resting in one hand, a cold Qing Dao beer in the other. The bottom of the frosty bottle rested on his knee. The kids were asleep, and I had nabbed the love seat again. I rested my head on the hard, plastic arm and closed my eyes, wondering if I should let myself fall asleep there, even though it would mean I would wake up contorted, cramped, and with my cheek stuck to the fabric.

"What kind of favor?" I mumbled without raising my head.

"I have a potential buyer—a very big buyer—coming to China next week to meet with me and discuss rolling out the robot kits in stores across the US. Callie is flying in for it. It could be huge."

I raised my head, suddenly alert. "Wow, that's great. I can help you with that," I said. "I could be a customer liaison, or—"

"No, Tina. I don't need a work favor; I need an entertainment favor. The buyer is coming with his wife and two kids. While we're touring the factory, she and the kids want to tour 'the real Shanghai,'" Daniel said.

"'The real Shanghai?'" I asked. "I don't think they have much of a choice; it's pretty hard to water this place down."

"Right, well, I was going to have Cinderella take them around, but I need him for my meeting to help me communicate with the factory manager," he said.

"So you need a family-friendly tour guide for 'the real Shanghai?'"

"Yes. Their boys are eight and ten," he said. "They really want to see pandas."

"Pandas? But pandas don't live in Shanghai."

"I know, I know, but there has to be a panda around here somewhere. Listen, I want them to have a good time so their overall impression of China, and me, is positive. So please, if you can . . ."

I was surprised to see how stressed he looked. I was used to feeling like that, but anxiety wasn't Daniel's go-to emotion. I sat up straight and leaned toward him.

"Is everything okay?"

"As okay as it can be, I guess."

Right then Lila started crying. I groaned.

"I'll get her," he said. "But can you entertain them?"

"Of course I can. I'll take them on a tour, show them the highlights, and do everything in my power to skip the lowlights," I said. "Don't worry, honey, their time here will be more than positive. It will be unforgettable."

"What are the kids like?" Wendy asked the following Monday as she slid mahjong tiles toward herself from the center of the table.

"I have no idea; I've never met them. Why does it matter?" I asked, staring at my tiles, trying to make something out of nothing for my next turn.

"Because!" she said. "Are they brainiacs, in which case you should take them to the museum? Or are they sporty, in which case you could take them to the skateboard park?"

"All I know is they're eight and ten, they're from Texas, and they want an authentic Shanghainese experience. Oh, and they want to see pandas," I said.

"Would they prefer to see the feral pandas that roam the streets? Or the more domesticated breed?" Barbara chided from the neighboring table. I had recently graduated from the newbie area in the back, which meant that my mahjong was improving. It also meant that Barbara could hear and comment on my conversation topics.

"Take them to the Wild Animal Park," Ellen said. "They have pandas there and all kinds of other authentic Chinese animals."

"There's a Wild Animal Park here?" asked Wendy.

"Yeah, I haven't been, but I've heard about it. There's a bus tour that takes you through an 'open wilderness area' where animals roam freely; it's supposed to be pretty neat." Ellen shrugged.

"Free-roaming pandas? I'm all over it," I said.

"Mahjong!" Ellen called.

"Look, Mom!" Zack, the eight-year old, hollered. He was chubby and red-haired with a smattering of freckles across his nose. He held a chocolate covered pretzel stick through the bars at the llama enclosure in the Shanghai Wild Animal Park. A dirty, matted llama gobbled it and trotted off. There was no sign prohibiting it, and no security guard in view.

It was touring day, and I wasn't feeling well, a little pukey, like I had eaten something rotten or unclean the night before. I was determined to shake it off. I had decided to leave Lila at home with Ayi so I could focus my flickering light on our guests and hopefully show Piper a good time, too. But for the life of me, I couldn't stop sweating. And not just because it was July. I felt like the heat was also coming from the center of my body, like I was also sweating on the inside.

"I'm not sure you should be—" I started.

"Zacky, do that again so I can get a picture!" his mom, Darla, said. Darla was small in stature but big in personality. And hair. And voice.

"The chocolate might be bad for the animals," I gulped.

"Oh, don't be silly, only dogs have that problem." She chuckled.

I cocked my head. "Are you sure?" I asked.

She shrugged.

There was a small enclosure of underfed orangutans, and just past it stood a baby bear and a baby tiger, each in the center of a circle of concrete, under a faded blue pop-up tent. They were chained to the ground by the neck. The chain was short enough to keep them from moving, turning their heads, or standing up straight.

"Hurry boys! This could be our Christmas card!" Darla hollered and then turned to me. "Do you have a brush? I left mine at the hotel."

"No, sorry," I said.

"Never mind," she said and patted her hair, pushing it back an inch on the left side, pulling it forward an inch on the right. "I'll take your family shot if you take mine." She reached into her bag and handed me her camera.

"This bear's fur isn't even soft, Mom!" Zacky shouted. "It's kinda sticky!"

"Maybe that's because you just ate a bag of caramel corn, honey." She winked at me. "I don't think he made that connection. Not the brightest bulb in the drawer, that one," she said under her breath, then yelled, "Get with the tiger, boys! Grandma's gonna love this shot."

"Can I pet the tiger, Mommy?" Piper asked.

"I don't think that's a good idea," I said.

"Well of course it's a good idea! That's what the chains are for!" Darla said.

I took a few pictures of their family with the tiger.

"Why isn't our zoo at home like this?" Zacky stomped his foot.

"I'm hungry." Hunter, the dark haired, chubbier ten-year old pulled on his mom's tank top and whined.

"Should we go to lunch? I saw a Chinese restaurant on the park map," I said, hopeful that a bowl of white rice would settle my stomach.

"Oh no, we don't do Chinese food. We tried some last night and it was all wrong. Not even slightly like Panda Inn back home. There were bones in the meat, and they forgot to take the head off the fish."

"It was disgusting!" yelled Hunter.

"But the fish heads are yummy! Even the big ones, mmm!" Piper said, rubbing a big circle on her tummy.

"Well, aren't you a funny one." Darla chuckled and gave me a look that said, *you may want to have a word with your offspring.* "Is there a McDonald's here?"

"Not here, but there's one near your hotel," I said.

"Yeah! Mommy, Mommy, I want a Big Mac, Mommy!" said Zack.

"Alright, eat this candy bar to tide you over. We'll hit McDonald's when we get back to town," she said, tossing them each a Snickers from the bottom of her purse. "You want one?" she asked me.

"No thank you," I said.

"This is boring," Hunter said, working his jaw on the caramel.

My head snapped to attention. Boring? We could not have boring. "One sec," I said. I walked up to a man with a broom. "Panda *zai na li?*"

He looked confused.

"Panda, panda," I repeated, slowly, loudly, to no avail.

"Mommy! Is that the bus you were looking for?" Piper pulled on my hand and pointed. "For the foaming animals?"

"Free-roaming animals." I looked up and smiled. "It is indeed, buddy," I said and felt a little better. This would set our day back on the unforgettable track.

Piper and I sat in a row toward the back of the yellow school bus. The boys sat in the aisle across from us and alternated punching each other in the shoulder. Darla settled in the seat in front of them and started an intricate routine of lip gloss application. As soon as everyone was seated, the driver started the engine.

We followed a dirt path running along the perimeter of the park. At the first corner, we turned left and stopped at a gate in a twenty-foot chain link fence with electric wires trimming the top of it.

A dozen park workers who sat on the ground under a tree stood slowly and dusted off their pants. They meandered to the gate and pulled it open. Our bus entered and immediately stopped. Directly in front of us sat another electrified twenty-foot fence which was closed. The workers pulled the gate behind us shut, then ran to open the gate in front.

"Look Mommy, giraffes!" Piper called out, bouncing on her seat and pointing as we pulled into a large grassy enclosure where about twenty spotty necks bobbed around in a cluster. They were only a few yards from the bus and looked unperturbed. A sign nailed to a stake next to the road indicated in both Mandarin and English that this was the "herbivore area."

We pulled slowly past the camels, zebras, and elephants, all in large numbers, all unfazed by our bus. The boys had stopped fighting and were furiously snapping photos with their mom's camera.

I was happy with my tour guide skills. This felt like a National Geographic moment that would be hard to recreate in the US. I hugged Piper to me. "Isn't this great?" I asked as we pulled up to another set of twenty-foot gates and stopped. "Carnivore area," the sign read.

We followed the gate drill again but this time, when the workers closed the first gate behind us, the driver cut the engine. The fence in front of us remained closed.

After a few minutes with no foreseeable change, I stood up, pushing myself taller on the back of the bus seat in front of me for a view out the windshield into the next enclosure.

"What's taking so long?" I said.

I jumped as the bus driver barked something into the microphone.

"What's he saying?" Darla turned to me.

I squinted. "Something about something costing 50 kuai, but I don't know what. Maybe snacks? A photo? I can't understand that part."

The bus door opened. Five Chinese men scurried down the stairs, led by a man in a tan polyester safari suit to a large wooden box with slatted sides. The leader reached into the box and pulled out a live chicken.

Zack and Hunter looked at me. "Is this the chicken exhibit?" Hunter asked. "'Cause I already know what a chicken looks like."

I shrugged and looked at Darla, who was filing her nails.

The man in the safari suit held the chicken with one hand and grabbed a skinny brown rope about fifteen feet long. He looped the rope around the top of one wing and handed it to the closest man from our bus, who grabbed it, awkwardly juggling the flapping, squawking chicken-on-a-rope back toward our bus.

"Hold it! What's happening?" I said. "Is he? He can't be. Oh my gosh, he is. He's getting on our bus with that chicken."

I thought of the article I had just read in the Herald Tribune detailing the potential global pandemic predicted to start in Asia, probably with chickens. Bird flu. But what could I do? I didn't want to get off the bus for fear I'd be trapped there, stuck between two enclosures, surrounded by poultry. So instead, I sat on the bus in stunned silence and looked at Piper, contemplating our inevitable feathery death.

The four other men collected their tethered chickens and brought them onto the bus. They returned to their seats as the chickens squawked and flapped next to them, filling the air with floating fluff.

The driver started the engine and spoke into his microphone as the men stood and opened their windows. They pushed their chickens out the windows and held onto the ends of their ropes. The chickens dangled outside, flapping and screeching.

The gate in front of us opened. Our bus inched forward.

Piper looked at me curiously. "Do you think that hurts the chickens, Mommy?" she asked.

"Well," I started to answer.

And then I saw the lions.

"HOLY SHIT!" I yelled.

There were dozens of them, trotting toward our bus from every direction. The first one to catch the scent began running at full speed. His front legs left the ground about ten feet out. SLAM! He hit the bus on Darla's side. We rocked. He trotted away carrying a chicken, rope dragging behind him. The man who'd been holding that chicken laughed gleefully.

Piper and I looked at each other. I realized my mouth was open and a scream was coming out of it. I needed to make an immediate decision. What does one do when faced with imminent mortality alongside their child? Would I have fallen to the ground in a blubbering mess as the Titanic sank? Or would I have picked up a cow bell and joined the band as the water level inched higher?

I reconfigured my scream into a strange throaty laugh. "Oh my goodness, Piper! Look at these hungry lions!" I hugged her so she wouldn't see my face. "Hold on tight 'cause here comes another one!" Chicken number two dangled high on our side of the bus. The corresponding lion slammed into the window, catching the body of the chicken between his giant teeth. He tossed his head to the side, ripping the rope from the man's hand, who shook off his rope burn, laughing.

"Wow," I said, feeling strangely detached from my body. "That lion has some serious vertical leap. He must be the Michael Jordan of his pride!"

"They're coming so fast, I can't get a picture!" Darla said. "Boys! Stand closer to the man with the rope!"

They scrambled down the aisle toward the final chicken as Darla hopped after them. "Take hold of the rope, boys!" she hollered as the lion slammed into the bus. It rocked so hard that Zack fell over.

"Zack! Are you okay?" I shrieked.

Darla looked at me and cocked her head. "Zack's fine, but I'm not sure the same goes for you. Why were you screaming?"

I looked at Piper—she was pressed against the window, so I leaned toward Darla, deciding to share my greatest fear. "This is a school bus, Darla. These windows pop out easily so kids can evacuate. If one leaping lion gets one powerful claw on the top edge of one open window, they could open this bus like a can of sardines! And, in case it's not clear, we'd be the sardines!"

She smiled and smoothed her hair. "You're right," she said. "That could happen, and we could all sit here and expect it. Or we could not worry about things that might or might not happen and have a good ole time watching lions eat chickens." She shrugged and turned back to her camera. "I'm going with option two."

I dropped onto my seat and squeegeed sweat from my brow with my pinky. I exhaled loudly and said, "I respect that, I do. But I don't have access to option two, Darla."

We pulled into another chicken enclosure. As the bus doors opened, Darla and the boys careened off the bus. They returned a few minutes later, each with an angry chicken.

We entered the tiger area like a rolling yellowed Christmas tree festooned with living ornaments. "What song should we sing?" I asked Piper as the tigers slammed into our quivering bus, chicken blood spraying in an arc on the windows.

"Now this is Christmas card material!" Darla whooped.

As the last gate closed behind us, I mopped the sweat off my face with a baby wipe I'd discovered in the bottom of my purse. I couldn't believe we'd survived.

"Mom, can we go again, please? Mom, please?" The boys begged as we stepped off the bus.

Darla looked at her watch. "I have a better idea—let's make like a McLion and go eat us some McNuggets!" she winked at me and laughed.

"Yeah! Yeah!" the boys yelled.

She walked over and squeezed my shoulder. "Thank you for bringing us here, sweetheart. This was a highlight, for sure." She paused. "Are you sure you're not car sick? You're looking greeeen."

"No, I'm okay. Thanks, Darla," I said, but my limbs hung heavy and my tongue felt dry.

"Mommy!" Piper pulled on my shirt as Darla walked away. "We need to take them for fish heads and duck skin! Please? They'll love it!" She jumped up and down.

"Oh, Piper, it's a great idea, but I think they're set on McDonald's."

She was quiet for a minute, watching the boys run off. "But they can get McDonald's anywhere."

I patted her shoulder. "You're right. But sometimes it's hard for people to try new things. It's easier to eat things they already know."

"But I try new things, and they're good."

I crouched down so we were face to face. "And that's part of what I love about you, Pipes. You're my fearless explorer." I hugged her.

She pulled away. "Why are you proud of me for eating fish heads?"

"I just am, okay?"

"Okay, Mommy. Then can we go get fish heads today? After we drop them off at McDonald's?"

"Not today, buddy. I'm feeling a little yucky," I said as my butt dropped to the ground. My vision was suddenly smeared. I wiped my face with the other side of the wet wipe, but my pores would not let up. *Maybe my bird flu is already symptomatic*, I thought. I'd forgotten all about it during the large cat feeding. Then I scrambled to my feet, ran to the nearest trash can, and retched.

44.

"**D**aniel? Daniel! Are you awake?" It was early the following morning. I dug my elbow into the flesh of his forearm at an ungodly hour to ensure that my question was rhetorical.

"Ow, Tina. What?"

"I think my period is late," I whispered. I couldn't say such a thing in a larger voice for fear it would make it more true. But the mere possibility had woken me up like an air horn blasting in my ear.

"Mm. Okay," he mumbled and rolled over.

"Daniel, I mean, it's really late. Maybe two weeks. Or more! I think I might be pregnant." I sat up, fully alert.

"Not a chance," he said into his pillow.

"Yes a chance! My cycle's been more regular here. This is—"

"I don't believe it," he mumbled.

"I know, it's crazy. I think I have an extra pee stick under the sink. I'm going to look for it."

"I don't know why you would. You're just going to drive yourself nuts."

I scrambled out of bed, scurried into the bathroom, and yanked open the cupboard under the sink. I flipped on the light and began rummaging through the-box-of-stuff-I-kept-for-no-reason.

"Found it," I called out. "I'm going to pee on it now!"

Three minutes later I walked into the room in complete shock. "It's positive."

"It's also wrong."

"Daniel, the stick doesn't lie. You know that. These things are never wrong."

"Tina, it's a Chinese pregnancy test, of course it lies. It's probably defective, or expired, or a poor excuse for a knock-off. It's definitely wrong. Of all people, *you* don't just get pregnant without trying."

"I know! But I think I am this time."

"Well, you should go see a doctor because that stick's wrong." He pulled the sheet over his head. Conversation, over.

I knew why he didn't want to talk about it. Getting pregnant with Piper and Lila had been monumentally difficult, a feat we hadn't wanted to relive. We'd agreed after Lila was born—never again would we embark on the endless tests, scads of shots, rivers of tears, and lifetimes of waiting that are the same-old-same-old of the fertility challenged. I had spent six of my thirty-five years clocking my cycle like an OCD referee with a Timex clutched in each hand. I knew when my period was one second late and exactly how long to wait before ripping open the top box in our mountain of early pregnancy tests, extracting the shiny white stick, and then showering it, along with my hand, with highly concentrated first morning pee. Six years bug-eyed and desperate for any indication that a baby was growing inside of me instead of some flukey blip in my cycle.

There were a lot of flukey blips. Numerous retests. An overabundance of time questioning the validity of the almighty stick.

The dream of having three children had been revised to two once Lila was born. And on many, if not most, days, two had been more than enough. We had mutually decided to matriculate to the stage in life where we would focus our energies on nurturing what we had instead of wishing for what we didn't.

"I'm pregnant," I told him on the phone later that afternoon, in a taxi on the way home from the doctor's office. I couldn't believe it was my voice saying the words. "I took a blood test. You have to believe it now."

He paused. "Tina, I can't talk about this right now. Let's discuss this when I get home."

When he walked in that night, I would have known he'd stopped at a bar even if my nose hadn't been working. However, since I was pregnant, my nose was bionic. He reeked.

The kids were asleep, and I was sitting at the dining room table staring at my blank laptop screen, about to compose a "Holy Shit" letter to Jennifer when he stumbled in, light socket hair, shirt untucked, streaks of dirt on his forehead.

I was determined to remain calm, to not be angered by his reaction. I thought of Mr. Han and breathed into my belly, attempting to feel rooted. I reminded myself that we were both caught off-guard, stunned by this news instead of ecstatic. We needed time to digest. He would come around and, like me, start to feel a small but recognizable spark of excitement growing alongside our newest family member-to-be.

"Are you hungry?" I asked.

"Not so much." He shrugged.

"That's good because I ate enough for both of us and the remnants in the take-away box look like the nuclear test site in the Nevada desert. Ground zero. Utter devastation," I said and then with a small smile added, "I'm due in December."

He sat down and, with a let's-get-real expression on his face, said, "Do you really want another baby?"

I laughed with a bitter undertone. "I think you know this isn't a matter of wanting. It just happened. Unplanned. Unexpected."

"So if you don't want it, why are you having it?" he asked, tilting his head.

"What do you mean?"

"It means that we live in China; it's common to terminate a pregnancy here. It's fast, it's cheap, and it can happen tomorrow," he said, putting his hands on mine on top of the table. They were heavy, sweaty.

"I said it was unplanned, not unwanted!" I pulled my hands away and pushed my chair back.

"You don't have to tell yourself you want this. You're pro-choice, remember?" he said.

"Of course I remember I'm pro-choice! Pro-choice for other people, Danny! I don't need to make a choice about a baby I want to have with my husband!"

Daniel was quiet. "Yeah, okay then."

"Okay then what?"

"Okay then, if you want it, you should have it."

"I should have it, or we should have it?" I asked, the pitch of my voice was near-hysterical.

"We! You know what I meant. But I think you should still think about—"

"I should still think about the choice that's not an option?" I shrieked, then stood up and crossed my arms.

"Just think about it, okay? Don't be so close-minded." He stood up and walked into our room, slamming the door behind him.

45

"**I** can't believe they opened an outdoor patio at Starbucks," I said the next day as I plopped myself onto a wrought-iron chair. My eyes were still puffy and stinging from crying myself to sleep the night before. Even though Daniel and I were barely speaking, we had agreed to push our issues to the back burner and not cancel our outing of the day—a coffee date with Kristy, Andrew, and Jeremy. Daniel was leaving later that day for a week of meetings and shipment inspections near Beijing. We both wanted to be distracted and end our time together on something positive.

"I would label this area less 'patio' and more 'cement-slab-surrounded-by-chain-link-fence,'" said Kristy.

"On the 'patio' spectrum, it's more 'prison yard' than 'comfortable area intended for fraternizing with peers'," added Andrew. "And they've only erected it temporarily, until they bulldoze this whole building for the new train station."

"I don't care why it's here or what its intended purpose is. I'm sitting here and the kids are over there playing happily which, for me, designates this spot as a 'heavenly patio.' I give it five out of five stars," I said.

"They should lose at least half a star for the occasional whiff of rancid meat drifting over from there," Daniel said nodding at the entrance to the wet market across the alley.

"The smell isn't bothering me; I've learned to breathe through my mouth," I said.

"It's not bothering you that we're 100 feet from the square block housing more flies than Shanghai has people?" Andrew laughed.

"It's not. I'm content right here, right now, in this chair on this patio with this warm beverage. And I don't want to talk about the flies," I said.

"Wow, Tina's changing," Kristy sang.

"I wouldn't go that far," I said.

"I see a glimmer of it, too," said Andrew. "You're accepting some unpleasant truths about this place."

"Accepting or disregarding?" I asked.

"Either way, you're evolving," he said.

I paused, then slowly nodded. "You're right," I finally said. "I may be coming to terms with some of the less savory elements of this place."

"You are! You said it!" Kristy said.

I shrugged. "One does what one must to survive."

"First survive, then thrive, I say." Andrew nodded and bit into a chicken foot.

"Did you just pull that claw out of your pocket?" Daniel laughed.

"Mm. Yeah, I got a whole bag of them in my jacket."

"Seriously?" Daniel asked.

"Yeah, we walked through the wet market to get here."

I coughed. "I'm pretty sure I'll never thrive at your level."

Andrew sighed and looked over at the throngs of locals pushing their way into the wet market to buy their daily vegetables. "How about you Daniel, are you thriving?"

Daniel hesitated and looked at me, then looked down and said, "Eh. Mostly I'm thriving."

"How long have you been here now?" Andrew asked.

"Eighteen months," Daniel said.

"Ah, okay, you're right at that spot. From here it gets harder, but then it gets easier. Before you know it, you'll barely notice all the things that shock and horrify you now."

"I can't even imagine not noticing some of this," Daniel said.

"Oh, you will. Trust me."

"You've been here over a year? It seems like nine months, tops, since I found you, quivering in Starbucks, unable to order yourselves a coffee," Kristy said.

"I remember well," I said.

"Now Tina'll push herself to the counter and holler out an order in two seconds flat," Daniel said, almost sounding proud. "She's really sharpened her elbows."

"Let's just say I'm learning how to get the job done," I admitted.

"How's your Mandarin then, Daniel? Tell us," Andrew said.

"My Mandarin? It's non-existent. Tina's the one hitting the flash cards in our house. And she's got nothing on Piper."

"Oh, come on," I said. "You can speak a little."

"You're right," Daniel said without looking at me. "I speak taxi."

"And restaurant," I reminded him.

"Yes, that's true. I speak taxi, restaurant, and bar. That's pretty much all I need."

I looked at Kristy. "He's either at work all day in an office full of English-speaking locals or traveling to visit factories who employ English translators. He occasionally goes out to dinner with me so Ayi can work late to make a little extra money," I said.

"You pay her to stay late?" Kristy asked.

"Yep," I said.

Kristy and Andrew looked at each other.

"I don't care if it's not customary here to pay overtime; she's happy, and we're happy."

"You're the reason the locals love working for new expats— better pay for fewer hours. Do you offer benefits?" Andrew asked.

I shrugged. "I paid for her tooth to get pulled last week. From a guy with a chair on the street corner."

"You didn't," Daniel said.

"I did."

"You do offer benefits!" Kristy cackled. "How much did that set you back?"

"50 kuai."

"Six dollars?"

"Yep."

"Hey, is this the wet market that's connected to the fake market?" Daniel craned his head to see beyond the front stalls.

"The very one," Andrew said.

"Great—I'm thriving so much that I need a new belt."

"Too much puffer fish and bai jiu on your factory visits?" Andrew laughed.

"Mm hmm." Daniel leaned back and patted his belly like Santa.

"And pizza. We still eat a lot of bar pizza," I confessed.

Daniel stood up. "I'm going to duck over there for a couple minutes."

"Do you know where to go?" Kristy asked.

"Not really, but I'll find my way."

"I know exactly where the belt stalls are. I'll take you there and then let you find your way back here on your own if that's okay—I need to hit the sock aisle for Jeremy." Kristy stood up.

"You two hit the shops," I said. "I'll stay here and keep an eye on the smalls. Andrew, you can go too if you want. I hear the wet market just got a fresh delivery of pig faces and goat hearts." I smiled.

"I'll stay back with you, thanks," he said.

"All right." I shrugged.

As Daniel and Kristy Frogger-jumped across the alley, Andrew leaned toward me. "Truth is I've already got my snack for the day and I'm not crazy for the non-food side of the market—too many pick-pockets for my liking."

"I know what you mean," I said.

It got quiet for a couple minutes. I wasn't sure if it was awkwardly quiet, but I figured it was probably less uncomfortable than a forced conversation.

"So tell me, is Daniel enjoying his job?" Andrew finally asked.

I snorted. "Of course! It's his dream job."

Andrew laughed.

"What's funny about that?" I asked.

"Dream job. In China. It's oxymoronic, that's what's funny."

"How do you figure?"

"Working in China as an expat is no one's dream. It's infinitely challenging! No matter what your job is, you spend more time managing the unanticipated than anything you're meant to be doing. The unpredictability is hard to plan around. That's why the expat community is so fluid, so transitory. People can't hack it for too long. The pressure, the cultural misunderstandings, the people constantly ripping you off . . . then there are the hours it takes to complete simple tasks and then redo them when circumstances change—and they always change—it wears people down. I see it all the time with the families of the kids I teach. The corporate burnout rate is extremely high, no matter how much the execs get paid. Most people can't handle more than two to three years, I'd say."

"How've you been able to stay here so long?"

He tapped his fingers on the arm rests of his chair. "Not sure, really. The opportunities kept growing, so we hunkered down to witness this incredible transformation. Then at some point it felt better to stay than to leave."

"Wow. That's something."

"Something you think you and Daniel are up for?"

"It's not completely up to us. Daniel has to renegotiate his contract soon; we haven't really talked about it for a while—"

"Have you asked him if he likes the job?"

I shrugged. "Not recently."

"You should ask him again," Andrew said while stretching his arms over his head. "Now that he's no longer new, I'd be surprised if he loves it as much as you think he does."

"I think he would tell me if he was unhappy," I said. "I don't always have to dig for information."

"True, and I meant no offense; he just doesn't seem the type to complain without prompting."

I thought about this without answering.

He smiled at me. "So how about you? You're enjoying your life here, I presume?"

"Some aspects of our life here are great," I said. "But there are days when I think I need to get out of here before I lose my mind. But when I consider the bigger picture," I paused and looked down at my belly, "I think maybe it would be better to stay for a while, postpone the real world a little longer, watch the kids grow up . . ."

Andrew sat up straight and looked at me with wide eyes.

I thought he'd guessed I was pregnant, so I smiled, feeling excited to share the news for the first time.

Then he said, "Did you hear that?"

"Hear what?"

He stood up. "Your name, I thought I heard someone yelling your name." He looked toward the market holding his hands over his eyes like a visor. I glanced at the kids happily playing on the corner of the slab.

"I don't think . . ." and then I heard it—someone screaming my name—a distant, extended holler coming from the center of the market.

"TEEEEEEEEEEEENAAAAAAAAAAAAAAAAAH!"

"Oh my God. It's Daniel! What do I—"

Andrew was already scaling the fence. "Stay here with the kids. I'll find him," he yelled as he launched himself into the center of the alley, stumbled once, and then took off running toward the entrance to the market.

46.

"You're not in trouble," Andrew said to Daniel twenty minutes later as I sat furiously chewing my nails. "Just describe what happened and I'll translate it to the *jingcha*."

"Who's the jingcha?" Daniel sniffed.

"That guy," he said, jerking his head in the direction of the policeman.

We sat in a small, square, gray room lit by one long, bare, fluorescent bulb. Andrew, Daniel, and I sat on one side of a rusty folding table in the middle of the interrogation room of the underground police station next to the fake market. Daniel held sheets of toilet paper to the gouges down the center of both cheeks. Thankfully, the bleeding from his face had slowed. His t-shirt was ripped and bloodied around the neck.

The policeman sat on the other side of the table smoking a cigarette, a pen and paper in front of him. A skinny, swarthy man sat moaning on a chair in the corner, his head resting against the wall, blood trickling from his nose. Every few minutes the policeman would turn and holler at him, then turn back to face us and suck his cigarette. Kristy, thankfully, had wrangled the kids into a taxi to her apartment.

"Kristy had just left, and I was standing in front of stall 453, reaching in my jacket for my wallet to pay for the belt I'd just tried on, when I felt someone kick my right shoe. I pulled my hand out and saw a boy run away from me into the crowd. Meanwhile, this clown," Daniel jerked his thumb toward the man in the corner, "was reaching inside my jacket from the left. I grabbed his hand. He tried to jerk it away, so I held him and punched him—I wanted to stop him, but I'm pretty sure I broke his nose. Then he went crazy! He reached up with both hands and scratched my face, so I pushed him as hard as I could. He fell and then scrambled into the neighboring stall where he grabbed a fire extinguisher and started swinging it at me."

"What did you do?" Andrew asked.

"I covered my head and kicked him when he got close to me. I was trying to get him off balance so I could grab him from behind to take the fire extinguisher."

"Wait—you broke his nose?" I said looking at the man. He moaned on cue.

"Yeah, I'm pretty sure. Then the crowd separated us; a group of people pushed him to the ground and fell on him and a giant mob picked me up and brought me here. They were holding me by my arms and legs; I had no idea where they were taking me. Kristy was gone; I was terrified. Then Andrew found me in the lobby, thank God."

The police officer hollered at the man and spit on him.

"What's going on?" I asked Andrew.

"I don't know, but I can guess. This guy is from Xinjiang, one of the autonomous regions in Western China."

"He's Chinese?" I asked. "He doesn't look it."

"He's not ethnically Han Chinese, he's more Middle-Eastern, but now his homeland is part of the People's Republic of China and, suffice it to say, his people aren't well-liked around here. His guilt is already presumed. This whole procedure is just a formality." He looked at Daniel. "They'll take your statement and let you go."

Daniel nodded and gingerly extricated his tissue from one wound, transferring it to a different oozing area on his chin.

I folded my hands on the table. "What will happen to him?" I nodded at the man in the corner.

Andrew exhaled. "I don't know."

"Yes you do," I said.

He drummed his fingers on the table several times, then tapped just his index finger, then stopped and lay his hand flat. "The punishments are quite harsh here, Tina."

"So I've heard."

He nodded. "There's no 'trial by a jury of your peers.' There's only a local judge, and he won't be lenient. His guilt will be presumed, and stealing from a foreigner is, to understate, frowned upon. Plus, he's not from Shanghai so he already has that going against him. His punishment is out of our hands. Remember, this is his fault. We didn't ask him to steal."

I closed my eyes and tried to breathe, to beckon my roots again.

"He's made a fateful error; I don't know what else to tell you," Andrew said.

"But what if he's desperate? What if he has a family?" I asked, my voice quivering. No one answered. I grabbed Daniel's arm. He winced. "I know you're hurt, but this, it's too harsh a punishment, right? You have to agree with me."

He pulled his arm away. "He was trying to rob me, to harm me," Daniel said.

"But he failed!" I said. "And how much would it have stung, really, if he'd grabbed your wallet?"

He snorted. "The fire extinguisher would have stung a lot."

I looked at Andrew. "Would it be possible to drop the charges?"

"It doesn't work that way."

Daniel dropped his elbows on the table and rubbed above his eye with one hand, then winced again.

I looked back at Andrew. "What if we said it was my fault?"

Andrew looked confused. "But you weren't even there."

"No one knows that but us."

Andrew blinked a few times, then nodded at me with sad eyes. "I see what you're trying to do, and I commend you for it, but it's not worth—"

Daniel looked up. "She's not going to let it go."

"Daniel, please, I—" I started.

"Excuse me?" Andrew said.

"You don't know my wife when she's convinced that she's right. You can go ahead and tell the jingcha—he was right, and I was wrong." He rubbed his thigh with his knuckles.

"It's not about who was right, Daniel!" I said, my voice getting high and screechy. "I just don't think we should try to exact justice from this, from an unjust system!"

Daniel pushed his chair back and stood up. "So, he goes free and tries this trick on the next foreigner?" How is that better?" He threw a ball of crinkled up TP on the table. "Never mind. Just tell him I hit the wrong guy so we can get out of here."

Andrew looked at us both and said nothing, then looked at the officer and spoke quietly, too quickly for me to understand.

The officer threw his hands into the air, shouting, gesturing wildly, first at Daniel and then at the man in the corner. Andrew spoke calmly again. The officer bellowed back. Andrew spoke again at almost a whisper, this time gesturing at Daniel. The officer finally stood, his chair legs scratching the cement in a high-pitched screech as he pushed back. He stormed from the room and slammed the door behind him.

Andrew sighed. "He said to write your confession on this paper and then sign it."

"Confession?" I asked.

"Another formality. You also must pay 500 kuai directly to him or he can revoke your work visa."

"That's fine, I can pay the fine since I still have my wallet." Daniel glared at me.

"Daniel, I'm sorry—"

"You're always sorry."

I paused and closed my eyes. "I'm just trying to get to the least-bad resolution. To make sense of things the best I can."

Daniel was silent as he scribbled his confession.

"It's not worth his life," I said.

"I hate to tell you this, but he may lose his life anyway," Andrew said.

"What?" I looked at him, startled.

"Look, I'm just being honest with you. You've done what you can to save him; there's nothing else to do that won't jeopardize your visa, or worse."

I turned to Daniel, tears welling in my eyes.

"But," I started.

Daniel dropped the pen on the table. "Here's my money." He slammed five 100rmb notes on the table. "I'm getting out of here. I've got a plane to catch."

Once outside Daniel speed-walked down the road, frantically waving his arm for a cab.

"Go talk to him, Tina. Hurry," said Andrew.

"Yes, I will," I said and gave him a hug. Then I took off after Daniel.

When I caught up to him, I said, "Daniel, please stop!" But he wouldn't stop, so I strode next to him and hollered, "Why won't you talk to me? What are you so mad about?"

He wouldn't even look at me. "It's always the same with you, Tina. You're not on my team. Not ever. Not at home, not here. You'll always find some lame excuse for me to be wrong."

"A man's life is not a lame excuse!"

He stopped to glare at me. "A man's life that he chose to throw away for a wallet! He knew the consequences! You forget that life is cheap here, Tina. And there's literally nothing we can do to fix that large of a societal flaw."

"But we can't just stand by and watch it! We have to try!"

He started walking again, as did I. "Go ahead and attempt to fix this place. And while you're at it, try making Jello in a sieve—you'll have about the same rate of success!" Then he stepped toward me and leaned in with cold eyes. He wasn't yelling anymore, but his words bit. "You can try and try and try, but at what cost, Tina? What price do you pay to be self-righteous, to assert control and uphold your vision of how everything should be, even when this vision undermines the ones you love? You don't hesitate to protect people you don't even know, but it's an altogether different story when it comes to me. I get hijacked. And I'm sick and tired of it!" He backed away to flag a cab again.

I was a fireball of emotions, regret and remorse among them, but fury and fear were dominant. I marched up to him again. "Oh yeah? Are you on my team right now? Or the team of our unborn child? Have you asked yourself that?"

He left his cab-flagging arm up but looked at me and spoke calmly. "You can be right about that, too, if you need to be. But we didn't agree to another child. That's on you."

He squinted into traffic as I wiped burning tears away with my right forearm and then with my left forearm, like Wonder Woman batting away arrows. My outrage grew until I jumped up and down and seethed, "How can you say I'm not on your team? If I'm not on your team, then why did I come here?"

He shrugged. "That's a question between you and your astrologist, Nancy Reagan."

There were so many things I wanted to say, such as "She wasn't an astrologist!" and "How dare you call me Nancy Reagan!" and "I know the career pressure was getting to me just like it's getting to you, but I also knew I had a good thing!" Plus so many more things. But the only words that floated to the top of my lungs and then flung themselves out into the world to Daniel and the city where we lived and anyone else that could hear them were: "I HATE YOU!"

That was the last I saw of Daniel before he left for Beijing, and I didn't answer his "I arrived safely" call that night. I wondered how his appointments would go with his face so scratched, and I worried that he could get an infection, but I refused to take his calls for the whole week because I was still mad and unable to see how our conversation could be anything but a continuation of our argument, and I didn't want to say something else I might regret.

47.

That Wednesday I went to Mt. Trashmore to see if a shred of peace could be found there.

"Something is different about you today." Mr. Han paced slowly by his friends and stopped in front of me as we practiced our tai chi sequence in a line.

"Don't distract me, I'm focusing," I said.

"Really?" he asked.

"Really."

"*Zhēn de ma?*" he smiled and turned his head to get in front of my line of sight.

"Zhēn de," I grunted and swooped my arms in a dramatic turn to face another direction.

He observed me for a few moments. "This is new then. Maybe you are present today, Ting Ting. What changed?"

"I read online that tai chi is good for anxiety," I said and scrunched my face in concentration, inhaling loudly through my nose.

"Ah, *jiāo lú. Dāng rán*," he said. "Of course."

"Well then right now I need it by the truckload."

"Eh?"

"I'm frustrated by this place, Mr. Han. And on top of that, I'm anxious for other reasons, and I can't sleep. Normally I would take

247

medication or drink wine, but right now I can't. I need to find other ways to feel better about everything."

"Ah," he said. "So now you listen."

"Yes."

"Step from the line, Ting Ting."

I dropped my arms and walked toward him.

He took my hand and led me slowly behind the hairy hill, then stopped and turned to face me. "Our regular sequence is eighteen minutes," he said.

"Maybe here it's eighteen minutes, but if I'm practicing by myself, away from the team, it takes me about twelve," I said.

"*Zhēn de ma?* Because it is too difficult for you to go slow?"

"Zhēn de. Bingo."

"Eh?"

"Yes, slow is hard for me."

"Then you won't like what I'm about to tell you." He closed his eyes and inhaled. He raised his arms straight overhead and then, almost imperceptibly, began to lower them. "For ultimate relaxation, you must go slower. The tai chi master will take one hour for this same sequence. His breath will be shallow; he will be in a perfect meditative state. Tranquil on the inside, his mind is peaceful."

I watched him as his arms slowly dropped. His shirt peeked out from the bottom of his faded black jacket which was thin and had a hole in one armpit. He wavered a little bit and I stepped closer in case he lost his balance.

He opened his eyes and brought his arms back to his sides at regular speed. "For power, you must go faster; for relaxation, slower."

I exhaled loudly. "I must have super-human power then."

"Indeed," he said and patted me on the shoulder. "But more power comes to those who are also peaceful. Just imagine your strength if you could relax. Why you worry so much, Ting Ting? Why you *jiāo lú?*"

I shook my head, blinking, trying not to cry. "For a complicated confluence of reasons, Mr. Han."

He paused. "If you breathe and go very slowly, the complexity of your problem may reveal itself to be very simple."

I laughed. "Very simple?"

"Exactly," he said. "When we meet here next Wednesday, we will practice going slow."

I scowled. "I find it ironic that I've spent a lifetime practicing to go faster, to do more in less time, and now you're telling me I should have done the opposite."

"That is not what I said."

"But—"

"You have lived your life in exactly the way you were meant to, until now. I am saying that it may be time for you to consider another way, because only now are you ready."

I covered my eyes with my hands for a moment, trying to block out the light, but it filtered through my fingers. "Okay," I said.

"I see you Wednesday, Ting Ting. Until then you must rest. Right now, you need it more than ever."

He walked away from me then and, not for the first time, left me wondering if he already knew what I hadn't told him.

48.

"When's your first prenatal appointment?" Kristy asked over dumplings the next day. I'd unloaded everything on her when I'd gone to pick up the kids after the incident. I hadn't wanted to get emotional then or talk about the baby, so I'd asked her to meet me in a few days, after I'd settled down.

"Friday morning," I said, pushing my plate away. "I can't eat these; they smell like arm pits."

"Is Daniel coming with you?" she asked.

"No, he'll be in Beijing until Friday afternoon. But I wouldn't invite him even if he were here. I haven't even told him I'm going," I said.

"At least you're handling this like an adult," she said.

"You know what? I'll be an adult later, when he makes the tiniest effort to be supportive," I said. "Until then, if I'm the only one trying to be remotely positive about this, I'll go by myself."

"Do you want me to come? I'm supposed to work, but I can try to reschedule."

"No, no, I'll be fine alone. I'm seeing your gynecologist, right?"

"Yeah. She doesn't have a lot of expat clients, but she's definitely your most affordable option. She's local but she trained in Hong Kong so her English is pretty strong. Don't worry, you'll be in good hands."

"If she's your doctor I'm sure I'll be fine," I said.

49.

Dear Jennifer,

I can't believe it—I'm having someone else examine my crotch tomorrow to identify intra-terrestrial (Intra-womb-estrial?) life. It's always been you down there, and now I feel like I'm cheating. I can only hope she's half as good as you.

-Tina

■ ■ ■

Tina,

I'm sure she'll be a fine stand-in. Just don't be nervous, and don't clench. Let me know what she says about Jennifer Jr.

-Jennifer Sr.

50.

"This fetus is too small," the doctor said as she squinted at the screen behind coke bottle glasses. We were in a poorly lit, poorly ventilated room in the basement of the local hospital. She blinked at me with magnified eyes and then turned back to the screen. She was tiny, swimming in dingy blue scrubs sized for someone in the NFL.

"What do you mean too small?" I asked as I scrambled to sit up. "I thought it was supposed to be the size of a peanut."

"No. According to your cycle, you eight weeks. This fetus five weeks. Not growing. No heartbeat. This fetus dead," she said, snapping off her gloves and pushing her chair back. "You need make appointment for D&C."

"No I don't! That's not right! You are wrong. You must be wrong," I scoffed. "I may have trouble getting pregnant, but I don't have trouble staying that way." I swung my legs around so they hung off the side of the table. "I'm going to find another doctor." I slid down and rushed to button my pants and pull down my shirt. I stepped the front half of my feet into my black "Converse," tripped to the door, then stopped and turned around. "You know, in the future, you really shouldn't just make statements like that when, when, when you don't even know what you're talking about!" I stormed down the hall.

I called Kristy sobbing from the taxi stand.

"Here, call this midwife," she said and read me the number. "She's at the expat hospital and comes highly recommended by some of my clients. Apparently, she's excellent; she trained in the US. She'll give you a trustworthy second opinion," she said.

"Okay." I sniffed. "Thanks, Kristy." I paused. "You don't think she's right, do you?"

"Oh Tina, I wish I knew that answer." She paused. "I'm so sorry. I had a miscarriage here a few years ago, it was so awful."

"But I'm not having a miscarriage yet, okay? She's wrong; she could barely see the screen," I cough-sniffed. "Plus, her bedside manner was absolute SHIT."

The Chinese midwife wiped her forehead on the arm of her white lab coat. It was later that afternoon, and we were in a clean, modern room on the third floor of the expat hospital, which felt more like a high-end shopping mall.

"I'm sorry," she said. She put down the ultrasound wand and took off her gloves. "I know this is hard to hear, okay? I wish I could tell you the doctor was wrong. But I can't tell you that, Tina. She's right—this fetus is not viable. I'm very sorry."

I turned away from her sympathetic expression and closed my eyes. "You're 100 percent positive?" I asked.

"I'm positive. I checked everything. You've miscarried; you need a D&C."

I called Daniel from a taxi before turning off my phone. He was at the Beijing airport; I could hear the flight announcements in the background.

"We aren't going to have a baby after all," I said when he answered.

"What? You, you changed your mind?" he said.

"No, I miscarried," I said. I spoke calmly and quietly, without tears.

"You, you what? When? When did you—"

"It's still stuck inside of me, but it's dead."

"Oh shit, Tina. Are you okay? Where are you?"

"You must be so relieved," I said.

"Tina, don't say that. Where are you? I'm on my way back. Are you home?"

"No, and I'm not going home," I said. "I don't want to see you. I don't want to see anyone. I want to be alone." I hung up.

I spun around on my barstool when I heard the door to Malone's bang open, and there was Kristy, running toward me.

She hugged me hard, and I slurred into her shoulder, "How'd you know I was here?"

"Because you finally texted me, dip shit. Daniel's freaking out. He's spent hours looking everywhere for you. Did you text him too?" she asked.

"I don't know." I shrugged, then waved my arms around. "But you know what I do know? I know that Malone's is the only bar in this godforsaken hole of a city that has tequila, the liquor of my homeland!" I held up the bottle. "I'm going to drink this whole bottle, and my friend, here," I waved at the bartender, "Wait, what's your name again?"

"Buzz," he said, continuing to wipe beer glasses and avoid eye contact.

"Buzz Lightyear has been kindly serving it to me, one shot at a time, like the fine astronaut he is."

"Let's call Daniel," Kristy said.

"Let's not call Daniel, okay, Kristy? Since you're my friend, and I don't need him right now, I need you."

Kristy sighed. "I think—"

"Do you know where I was born, Kristy?" I interrupted, lightly spraying her face. I wiped my mouth. "Sorry."

"Arizona," she said, wiping her cheek.

"Ari-fucking-zona, Kristy, you're damn straight. I lived there from birth 'til I was twenty-one years old, and then I got the hell out of that place, because it was always stinking, bloody hot, and I didn't want to be hot anymore. Hot golf courses and hot drive-through ammunition stores; there's only so much heat a person can handle in one lifetime," I explained.

Kristy poured herself a shot.

I slapped my palm on the rim of the bar. "But I have to tell you—today, when I think about my homeland, I realize that Arizona is pretty fucking great. You wanna know why?"

"Sure," Kristy said with sad eyes.

"Because in Arizona, people care about hygiene. You don't just spit loogies anywhere you want! Not in Arizona, you don't!"

"No loogies in Arizona." Kristy shook her head.

I scrunched my face in fury. "And you don't just cop a squat and poop on the sidewalk in Arizona either! No way would you do that!"

"No way," she said, resting her chin on her hands.

"And you know what we do do in Arizona? We wait in line. Because we understand the concept that just because I *want* to go first doesn't mean I *get* to go first. Because there's no I in team, Kristy, and in Arizona, we're a team."

"Team Arizona," she said and sighed.

"Exactly! And you know what else? In Arizona, we don't rush people as they step out of an elevator. We wait until they're all the way out, and then and only then do we calmly, enter, that, elevator," I said.

"Of course that's what you do." Kristy nodded slowly.

"Because in Arizona we know that you aren't getting where you need to go faster by acting like a lunatic! Because Arizonans are fucking smart!" I said.

"So smart," Kristy said.

I scooted my barstool closer to hers. "And another thing—in Arizona, we're kind. Like when we have bad news to share, because bad things happen everywhere, we're nice about it. We break news gently, because the fact is, Arizonans believe in kindness," I said, my voice cracking.

Kristy's eyes went wet and glossy. She grabbed my hand. "Of course you do."

"The doctors in Arizona would never say, 'The fetus is dead, Tina,' after I accidentally find myself pregnant even though it's next to impossible for me to accidentally get pregnant." I inhaled sharply and looked at Kristy through newly forming tears. "And then this baby, who wasn't even supposed to be here but who somehow had already found a space in my dark, shriveled heart, just dies, for no fucking reason."

She wiped her eyes and reached out to hug me again. "Tina, I'm so, so sorry. I wish I could make this easier for you."

I pushed her away. "That's not your job! That's what the bottle's for! You don't need to assume my misery," I said, looking down. I tapped my empty shot glass slowly on the wet, shiny wood, contemplating a refill, but suddenly feeling blecky.

"I'm your friend, Tina. Your misery is my misery."

I looked at her and wiped my eyes with the back of my hands. "You must have some Arizona in you, Kristy, because that's the kindest thing anyone has ever said to me, or at least in a long, long time."

She raised her eyebrows. "It may just be an Alaskan kindness thing since I'm pretty sure I've never been to Arizona," she said and handed me a clean napkin.

I took it, balled it up in my fist, and then lay my cheek on the wet bar while still looking at her. I briefly wondered if the mysterious liquid my face was resting in would splash into my eyeballs, and if it would sting when it did. "I want to go home," I whispered.

"Great idea, I'll call us a cab."

"No, not home in Shanghai. Home home."

"Back to Arizona?"

"No." I hiccupped. "It's still too hot there. I guess I don't really have a home anymore; all I know is I need to be somewhere far away from here. Maybe I'll just go to the airport and buy a ticket to the first place on the departures sign. I can make that place my home."

"Tina—"

"But first I need to sneak into my apartment and get my passport and some money."

"You've just been through a traumatic experience and you aren't making sense right now."

"Really?" I lifted my head. "Because I feel like I have more clarity in this moment than I've had in the last year and a half, since crash-landing on this terrible planet!" I laughed. "I can now see that I can't do this anymore, Kristy, not for another minute. I thought I could find myself here, be a better wife, a better mother, a better Tina. But instead I've become the worst version of me I can possibly be." I raised my head. "And furthermore, I think I need to go to the bathroom."

"Do you need help?"

"No." I hopped off the barstool. "I mean yes."

As I weaved out of the bathroom, the floor slid beneath my feet like black ice. Kristy kept her arm firmly around my shoulder. "I'm pretty tired all of a sudden," I said.

"Why don't I take you to your home in Shanghai now? You can sleep this off and then figure out how to get to your new home tomorrow."

"No." I shook my head and then regretted it. "I can't go home."

"Sure you can."

"How about we go to your place and talk about it?"

"Tina—"

"But, before you wave down a cab, I need to show you something,

something I learned in Arizona." I flung her arm off my shoulder and stumbled out the door onto the curb, nearly face-planting. I caught myself and stood up, swaying under the streetlight.

"Tina, I—"

I backed away from her, holding up a pointy finger. "Line dancing is a big thing in Arizona, HUGE," I called and clapped my hands twice. "Heel, toe, do-si-do, come on baby, let's go boot scoot!" I stomped my foot and quarter-turned to the right. "Cadillac, black jack, baby take me out back, we gonna boogie!" I sang louder and prouder as locals waiting for taxis on the sidewalk turned to stare. "Oh, get down, turn around, go to town, boot scoot boogie!" I sang and then shouted, "Line dancing is Arizona-style tai chi!"

"Wait, what?" Kristy said.

"Watch this!" I said and attempted a combo twist twirl-stomp with an exaggerated arm sweep, but my twist got wonky and my twirl spun off balance and my stomp went sideways, and I hurled myself into the gutter instead, landing in a large, murky puddle. On my back. In white jeans.

I moaned. I couldn't move. My ribs felt like they'd been lit on fire. My breath came in puffs. I closed my eyes. That's the last thing I remember.

51.

Sometimes I think I've woken up from a nightmare when I'm still actively experiencing the nightmare. I may trick myself into thinking the danger is behind me and the scary-awful part is over, but I'm not actually out of the woods yet. This felt like one of those moments.

I heard voices speaking before I opened my eyes the next morning. Voices I didn't want to hear from people I didn't want to see. And then I remembered—the miscarriage, Malone's, the tequila, the puddle.

The miscarriage.

The miscarriage.

I sealed my eyes tightly, but tears still leaked out. I ached everywhere, inside and out, heart, body, and soul. My tongue was a small section of beef jerky, drier than carne seca.

The miscarriage.

Someone with a snarky British accent a lot like Barbara's said, "Well, go on, what'd he say then?"

Someone with a mild Chinese-American accent a lot like Katie's said, "He's coming, he's waiting for Ayi to show up to watch the kids."

My heart began thumping double-time. *What if this is real, and they're talking about Daniel?* I thought. *I have to get out of here before he sees me. But I don't know where I am. I should hide. But I'm too ill to move.*

I should pretend I'm in a coma. Yes, that's the most sensible thing to do. Wait—how would Barbara and Katie know each other?

I opened one eye.

"Well, good morning, Tina! How are we feeling?" Barbara said, far too loud. She sat on a poofy, luxurious single bed parallel to the one where I lay sweating. She was surrounded by a fluffy white duvet and perfectly placed, embroidered, white on white pillows, staring at me from a simple cream-colored caftan and matching cashmere pashmina.

"Been better," I croaked.

"Have some water," she said and pointed to the crystal goblet on the antique bedside table between us.

"I can't, it might make me puke."

"Ha!" she laughed. "I doubt that, there is nothing left in you to puke. No bile in your gallbladder, either. You are gloriously empty."

I swallowed painfully. "Is this your house?"

She nodded with a closed-mouth grin.

"How did I end up here?"

"You were causing quite a ruckus in front of my bar, and I couldn't have that now, could I? So I whisked you up and brought you home, like a little lost puppy."

I lifted my head slightly. "You own Malone's?"

She tossed her head. "The land, no, the bar, yes. I've owned it for seven years. It's quite a cash cow, really, very popular with the expats, especially the Singaporeans." She laughed. "And last night one of my American patrons drank a significant amount of my best tequila—a bottle I'd hand-carried in my luggage from New York City, I might add. A fine vintage like that is meant for sipping." She smirked. "Not for disgorging in two separate taxis."

I looked down, unable to argue or agree.

"I'll assume you'd had a rough day."

I nodded.

"How long have you been in Shanghai?"

"Eighteen months."

"Ah yes. That's about the time when everything gets turned inside out. The adrenaline has worn off, and you start to experience some of the, shall we say, less savory aspects of this culture—things you might have missed earlier, or been too bowled over by the rest of it to notice."

I blinked in assent because nodding my head hurt too much.

"Where's Kristy?" I whispered. I noticed I was wearing a sand-colored silk negligee, the likes of which had never touched my skin before. I touched it gingerly with one index finger. Painfully soft.

"She went home after I offered to bring you here. She needed to clean up, wash the vomit out of her hair—"

"Oh no." I winced.

"Where do you keep the tea again?" Katie, my tutor, tapped into the room wearing a skin-tight off-white cable knit sweater dress that pulled open in all the right places and matching thigh-high stiletto boots. She smiled when she saw I was awake. "*Nǐ hǎo wǒ de péng yǒu.*" She bowed slightly in my direction.

"It's not ni hao, it's ni OW," I said.

"*Zuótiān wǎnshàng ni où tu le. Jīn tiān nǐ tóu téng, duì bù duì?*"

"Yes, I barfed, and now I have a headache. Are you charging me for this lesson?"

She smiled, then sat on the bed next to Barbara.

I squinted at the two of them in their monochrome splendor and caught a whiff of my hair, which smelled maybe better than it ever had, like some exotic flower, probably a white one. It struck me that someone in this house must have bathed me last night because I smelled nothing like the fecal puddle I'd ended the night in. Plus, the nightgown. I looked around the room at the warm dark wood-paneled walls, the rich, earth-toned, non-Ikea area rug. "Wait, am I dead?" I asked. "I must be dead. Is this heaven or hell? It appears to have elements of both."

Barbara laughed. "You aren't dead. More lucky I'd say."

I snorted. "Trust me, luck hasn't made an appearance in my world for a while. I think she's mad at me." I flopped a hand in their direction. "How do you two know each other?"

"I'm her biggest client," Barbara said.

Katie laughed. "Yes, we work together now, but many years ago, Barbara helped me and my family."

"You're kidding," I snorted. "You helped someone? On purpose? What was your upside on that?" I looked at Barbara.

She smiled and looked at Katie.

"She helps a lot of people," Katie said. "It's her, what do you call it, favorite past-time. When she found me, I was selling vegetables off the back of my bike, trying to earn money for my parents who were both ill. It was very difficult."

"And now look at her." Barbara beamed. "She's like the child I could never have."

I dropped my head back onto the perfectly stuffed pillow and closed my eyes. Suddenly I heard a baby crying. My eyes snapped open, and I inhaled sharply.

"Ayi!" Katie hollered.

A young Chinese woman in a tidy white nurse uniform hustled into the room holding what could only be described, without exaggeration, as the most adorable baby to inhabit our planet. She looked about five months old with an explosion of black hair, perfect pink cheeks and lips, and ensconced in what looked like a christening gown from a previous century.

I gasped and my eyes filled with tears.

"*Wha! Xiǎo bǎo bǎo!*" Katie exclaimed, leaping to her feet.

"*Zhēn piào liang de xiǎo bǎo bǎo,*" Barbara crooned at her.

The baby bounced and giggled. Katie took her carefully from the nurse.

"May I see her?" I said softly, feeling the dull ache of my loss even as I propped myself on one elbow and reached my other hand out to her.

She stepped next to me and bent at her knees so I was face to face with the baby.

"This is Xiǎo Yù," she said. "She's a perfect example of the work Barbara and I do. Xiao Yu was born with her organs mostly outside of her body, which is surprisingly not a fatal affliction, as you can see. The fix is actually quite a simple and inexpensive surgery. However, when a poor family gets one chance at progeny, well, it's bad enough to have a girl, let alone a girl with birth defects."

"So what happens?" I asked, smiling as Xiǎo Yù grasped my finger and thinking back to the baby in the gurney when Daniel broke his arm, all alone on the hospital gurney.

"Let's just say Chinese families often don't keep children like this, so Barbara finds them, makes arrangements for their surgeries, and then locates a family to adopt them. It's called the Bǎo Bǎo Foundation. Barbara's the Executive Director."

"You save these babies?" I looked at Barbara, stupefied.

She nodded. "We zip up bundles of cleft palates, too. Been at it for about a decade."

"Seriously? Why haven't I heard about this before? Do people know this side of you exists?"

"Only a select few. The more it gets out, the more likely my special favors will no longer be granted by the government. And it takes a lot of favors for this organization to work."

"That's why I'm her partner; she needs my *guānxì*," Katie said.

"Guanxi?"

She sighed. "This is vocabulary from our second lesson, Tina. Guānxì is a relationship where you can trade special favors, often from high level officials."

"Like the Godfather?"

Katie shrugged. "Yes and no."

"Why wouldn't the government want to highlight your work and how they help you help people? That would be great PR," I said.

"Because fixing a problem means first acknowledging there is a problem. We, as a culture, don't like to admit there's anything wrong to start with. That's how we lose face," Katie said.

"Let me get this straight," I sputtered, leaning forward. "Your people will stand before a thousand strangers in a hot karaoke box bellowing an off-tune rendition of a B-side Richard Marx ballad, but only lose face when admitting one of the most universal and undeniable truths of humanity—that the world and all of its inhabitants have problems?" I set free a salt-and-vinegar laugh. "No wonder I can't get this place to work for me—its basic tenet is denial, and I can't relate! I mean, what would I even talk about if it weren't for my problems? What would I do if I weren't always on a quest to fix myself?"

Katie and Barbara looked at each other, then Barbara leaned toward me and smiled. "There are many things you could do actually, for us and for the children," Barbara said. "Which is why it's serendipitous that you landed, quite literally, at our feet."

"We could use your help," Katie said.

I turned away from her. "My help? Very funny."

"I'm serious. So is Barbara. We'd spoken about you before last night happened. We need more strong volunteers at Bǎo Bǎo. The expats here are transitory, and lately we've lost more volunteers than we've gained. But it's not a good fit for everyone we meet. There are lives at stake here. We need people who will work hard and fight for what's right and refuse to back down; people who would not, could not, take no for an answer. It's hard to find people like that in this environment—people who don't already have a career—"

"I had a career."

"I know that, Barbara knows that, anyone who's ever had a conversation with you knows that." She smiled. "We need stubborn, headstrong women like you to keep this foundation going. You fit the profile perfectly. You're a, what's your word for it? A ballbuster."

"A ballbuster," I repeated softly, turning back to her, feeling like anything but that. I gently extracted my finger from Xiǎo Yù's grasp and Katie stood up. Her little feet kicked underneath her gown.

"What do you think?" Barbara said.

I shook my head. "I don't, I'm not, I mean, I'm flattered that you see value in how I am, but I—"

She put her hand up to shush me. "Please, don't answer now. Why don't you think on it once you feel better? You'll probably have some questions at that point. Let's discuss it after mahjong on Monday."

As much as I hated agreeing with Barbara, I knew she was probably right. I wasn't clear-headed. I couldn't speak anymore either; I could feel myself starting to crumble again. I nodded my head and blinked several times.

"Monday it is, then," she said. "We'll leave you to get some rest." They filed out, and I gazed at the doorway after they left, considering the void they had left where there had been none before. I sighed and my eyes lost focus. Right then a dark, menacing form appeared in the same space, someone like Darth Vader, except more sinister and terrible. I closed my eyes.

"Tina?" Daniel said.

52.

A n unusually quiet taxi ride home ensued. Not on the outside of the taxi, of course, but on the inside, the silence was palpable and the animosity, thick. From both of us, it seemed. No apologies were forthcoming.

I did regret a few things, and I wished I could issue a selective apology for them—for my disappearance and lack of communication. The rest of it was an opaque area where both of us were at fault to some degree. No one was to blame for the miscarriage— not Daniel, not me, not China. Even in my highly emotional state, I knew that. But I definitely should not have disappeared. However, when I dug a little deeper, I realized that my disappearance was in response to his insensitivity and overall asshole-ness, which, because it was so poorly timed, caused a chain reaction which led to my disappearance. So, in a sense, the whole thing was his fault. But I didn't have the energy to explain this to him. And I didn't want a simple apology to be misconstrued to include all the things I was most definitely not sorry about. This was why I stayed silent. I wasn't sure of the reasons for his silence, but unless they were remorse-laden, I had already deemed them in my mind to be unacceptable. Wordlessness on his part may not have been his worst idea.

He turned the key in the knob and pushed our apartment door

open, stepping aside so I could walk through first. And my heart melted.

Because colorful construction paper signs hung everywhere, from every surface, by scraps of yarn.

"Welcome home, Mommy!" one sign said.

"Get well soon!" said another one.

"I love you soooooooooooooooooooo much," said another.

Several signs were written in Mandarin characters that I couldn't read. I looked at Daniel and shrugged.

"I think they convey a similar sentiment," he said, waving at the others.

I giggled, almost appreciating him.

There was a lot of lovely, adorable scribble scrabble art, compliments of Lila, and some additional hand-drawn family portraits, compliments of Piper. Each included a yellow circle sun in the top right corner, a few M-shaped birds in the sky, and Daniel and I float-standing on green grass, holding hands. Me with big hair, Daniel with not so much. In every picture, Piper stood in between us, and Lila was depicted in a dark corner and so miniscule, she was tucked between two of the shorter blades of grass, like an ant.

I looked at Daniel. "She's never been one for siblings." I shrugged. "Which right now, could be either gut-wrenching or comforting, but since I feel only numb, I can only laugh."

Daniel furrowed his brow and then dropped his head, perhaps wisely choosing, once again, not to speak.

I sighed. "Where are the artists?"

He looked up. "At the park with Ayi."

"Oh," I said, feeling disappointed that I couldn't thank them and kiss their fuzzy heads.

Daniel grabbed my hand and walked me into the kitchen. "And speaking of Ayi, she prepared quite a treat for you last night. I told her you were sick and that's why you hadn't come home, and boy, did she whip up a vat of something special. She was chopping in here for quite some time and the apartment started to smell amazing. When she finally left, I grabbed the ladle to sample her concoction, but when I gave it a stir, a chicken head came floating up at me, like this, and then two chicken feet bobbed to the surface, like this." He made a chicken face and moved his hands around like floating chicken feet.

"Is that your impression of Chinese chicken soup?" I asked.

"Yeah." He screwed up his face and waved his claws again.

I smiled, then sighed and looked down. "I'm a little bit sorry," I whispered.

He brushed my hair back from my face. "I'm a little bit sorry, too."

I looked away and then back at him. "I'm, I just think you should know—I'll never be the same," I said, my lips quivering.

He grabbed my shoulders. "I know. You won't. And I won't expect you to." He took a deep breath and continued. "I'm sorry for what happened, and for letting you down. And I'm sorry for blaming you for things that weren't completely your fault."

"I'm sorry for doing all the same things."

He shook his head. "But you're not to blame this time; it's me—I've been so focused on my job that I've lost sight of what really matters: you, and them." He waved at the decorations.

"I remember feeling like that," I said softly.

"I'm pulled in so many directions that I'm doing everything badly."

"When I was in your shoes, I sucked at everything. Regular human interaction exhausted me. It all felt like too much."

He nodded. "Try it with a language barrier! And then, I don't know, I couldn't even get my head around the idea of more kids. But now that . . ." his voice quivered. He gulped and shook his head. "This was our dream, remember? And not that long ago, another baby was part of it. But then our focus changed and . . . I don't know. I never should have taken this job; I should have accepted a position I was less excited about back home. I brought us here thinking things would be different. That our lives would be more fulfilling. That I could somehow redeem myself. But I can't do that because I'm the same person in a different place, making the same mistakes but bigger. I wanted to become the man I was meant to be, but the man I was is the only one looking back from the mirror. And he's nothing like the one you deserve." He let go of my shoulders and looked away from me, blinking in the direction of the soup.

"He's exactly the one I deserve!"

"No, he's not."

I grabbed his hands and held them up between us. "He's a great dad and an honorable man. He has incredible vision and patience, and he's so, so smart. He tries his best, and he puts up with a lot. And no, he's not perfect, and his plans don't always work out, but at least he's trying, and that's enough. He is enough. You are enough."

Daniel shook his head, avoiding eye contact. "No, I'm not. I'm terrible at being human; I can't figure it out."

"I can't figure it out either!" I squeezed his hands harder. "But did you ever think that maybe that's because we're kids trapped in adult bodies? Trying to understand our place in this world and what it should look like and what our role in it should be? Daniel, look at me." I touched his chin and lifted it. He wore the expression of a confused little boy; his blue eyes blinked. "If we're horrible at being human, isn't it better that we're horrible humans together? I think so. We just need to have each other's backs. And we can do that." I shuffled close to him and nuzzled my nose above his clavicle.

He tensed. "That tickles!" he said. Then he wrapped his arms around me and held me close. I closed my eyes and turned into the crook of his shoulder. I felt the evenness of his breath and admired his stillness. *How does he do that so easily?* I wondered.

After a few minutes he pulled me away but held onto my shoulders with a soft touch. "Next month I need to renegotiate my contract. I don't want to renew it; I want to move home," he said. "I want us to do this right, in a place that's easier to manage."

"But it's not easier back home! The challenges are different, but this life thing is hard everywhere."

He exhaled and shook his head. "Not this hard."

I paused, looking at the signs the girls made in the living room and thinking it finally looked like home. Then I thought about Barbara and the babies.

"But what if we're in the deepest, darkest, hardest part and we're just about to clear it and the forecast predicts blue skies ahead?"

He shook his head. "I'm not feeling it, Tina. I'm ready to chalk up our time in Shanghai to a lesson learned."

I looked down and sighed. I wanted both to go and to stay. To make peace with this place and myself in it, and also to support Daniel like I'd promised. But I didn't want to dwell in uncertainty and indecision, to agonize for another second over where we should live, what I should do, and who I should be. Tears flowed down my cheeks.

"Yeah, okay," I said. "Let's go home."

53.

AD&C, two weeks of self-pity in adult diapers, and *xiuxi yi xia*, which means to rest a bit. This can also be a command, as in, "Xiuxi yi xia! Take a load off!" These were my midwife's exact orders.

Because of my mandated rest, I missed mahjong and the conversation with Barbara about the opportunity to help babies, which I had decided to decline with regret. I also cancelled my Mandarin lessons and didn't respond to one of Jennifer's seventy-five emails. Email felt like the wrong forum to break the news. Finally, I called her. At four dollars a minute and with significant delays, I meant to keep it quick.

"I had a miscarriage," I blurted as soon as she answered.

No response.

"Hello? Jennifer?" I started to wonder if we had a bad connection. Then it struck me—maybe she was angry that I'd left her in the dark. I didn't blame her; in a sense, I'd disappeared on her, too.

The sobs finally traveled through space. And finally, this single sentence arrived in my ear. "I'M SO SORRY I THOUGHT THAT MAY HAVE BEEN WHAT HAPPENED WHEN I DIDN'T HEAR FROM YOU BECAUSE YOU TEND TO RETREAT INTO YOURSELF AND I KNEW YOU WOULD TELL ME WHEN YOU WERE READY AND (INHALE) I SEE WOMEN WHO

271

MISCARRY EVERYDAY AND IT'S (INHALE) SO AWFUL AND THERE'S NO REAL RECOGNITION FOR THIS IN OUR SOCIETY AND (INHALE) I'M SO SAD THAT YOU'RE THERE AND I'M HERE AND I CAN'T HUG YOU AND I HOPE DANIEL IS OKAY ARE YOU OKAY?"

"I'm okay, I mean I'm not okay, but I'm okay, if that makes any sense," I said.

"It makes perfect sense." She whimpered and blew her nose. "Are you getting hugged? You need to be hugged, Tina, a lot. Don't push people away right now. That's your tendency, we know this."

I smiled. "Believe it or not, I have a whole committee of huggers over here."

"I'm very relieved to hear that." This time I could hear her breathing as we both sat quietly, unable to assign more words to the moment.

"I'm coming home," I finally said softly.

"Really? To visit?"

"No, for good, in about six months," I said with a quivering voice and then gulped down the rising knot.

"You're, you sound like you're breaking the second piece of bad news."

"No, this is good news. It will be good. It has to be."

"But what about Daniel's job?"

"He hasn't told them yet. I doubt they'll have a spot for him back in the US since he's working for a cash-strapped start-up. He's going to start talking to headhunters, but I think I can get my old job back, so we'll be fine." I took a deep breath and tried to sound perky. "I can hop back on that ole corporate ladder! I'll be a couple rungs down from the position I left, but I'm sure I can climb back to where I was pretty fast. The rat race is probably the best place for someone like me, anyway. I'm a, you know, a ballbuster." I wiped my eyes.

"Are you sure about this, Tina? Your emails have sounded so much happier lately, like you were really getting the hang of it over there."

I sighed. "Maybe I was. My head is so jumbled right now, I don't know how I feel anymore, but I do know that this place has been intense and difficult. And wonderful, too, but in different ways than home is wonderful. I'll miss all the time with my girls, but it would need to come to an end eventually anyway. This was never supposed to be forever."

"So what do you do now?"

"I need to wrap up a few things, tell my tai chi coach, and before you know it, I'll be home, filling you in on the latest motivational speaker, which you will soundly ignore until I pester you so much that you cave and go to a workshop with me. It'll be great! Just like the old days."

I could hear her sigh. Almost see her head droop.

"Hey, I gotta go, this chat is costing me half a semester of Piper's preschool tuition. I'll email you soon, okay?"

"Please take care of yourself, Tina. Take some time to honor—"

"Of course! Don't be silly. I'll be very nice to me, almost as nice as you are. Signing off from Ork now, Jennifer. Nanoo nanoo."

54.

The following Wednesday, I went looking for Mr. Han to break the news. He wasn't in the alley. He wasn't at Mt. Trashmore. He wasn't at our favorite baozi shack or at the corner where he occasionally played chess. It was noon, he would only ever be outside, somewhere on his block, I thought. I started to worry. I knocked on his door.

His sister answered. Her gray hair was pulled back into a neat bun, and she was wearing pajamas and a pair of cartoon dog slippers. Anywhere else this would have indicated an illness or crisis of some sort. But this was China, where midday pjs equaled status. Yet, Jie Jie looked pale and distraught instead of angry and irritated, her more common demeanor.

"Ni hao, Mr. Han *zai zhe li ma?*" Hello, is Mr. Han here?

"*Bù zài! Bù zài!*" Not here! Not here!

"*Ta qu na li?*" Where did he go?

"*Tā qù guìlín sǎomù! Dànshì tā bú shūfú. Wǒ jiào tā bié qù, dànshì tā bù tīng! Tā cóng bù tīng wǒ dehuà! Wǒ dānxīn tā niánjì dàle, yīgè rén bùnéng zǒu tài yuǎn.*" He went to Guilin! To sweep the graves of our ancestors. But he's sick and I told him not to go. But he didn't listen! He never listens to me! And now I'm scared. He's too old to go so far alone.

"*Ta shenme shihou qu?*" When did he go?

"*Jīn tiān zǎo shang, zhēn zǎo. Tài zhǎo lè! Tài lěng le!*" This morning very early. He took the 7:18 a.m. train. Too early! Too cold!

I turned and ran.

55.

Twenty-five minutes later, I materialized in front of Daniel's desk like a transported Star Trek character except red-faced, sweaty, and with lungs on fire. The traffic was horrendous, and my bike had a flat, so I'd chosen to sprint there instead of taxi.

Daniel was on the phone, as was Cinderella and his new assistant Clyde. All three of them looked alarmed. I bent over and grabbed my thighs, trying to get my breath back and quell the red balls that were bouncing in my vision.

"I'll call you back," Daniel said and hung up.

"I'm leaving," I said before he could speak, looking at him between the undersides of my eyebrows, barely able to get the words out between gasps.

"Tina." he stood up and frowned at me. "I thought——"

"No, I'm not, leaving you, I'm taking, the train, to Guilin, to find, Mr. Han."

"You're what?"

"I'm going to find, Mr. Han—you can't, talk me out of it. I just wanted, to tell you, so you didn't think, I disappeared again. I'll be back."

"But Guilin is a big city, how do you think you can find him there?"

"I have a plan."

He looked at me like he was deciding what to say next. Then he sighed. "When are you going?"

"Now," I huffed.

"Do you need money?"

"Yes," I puffed.

He pulled out his wallet and slapped a fat wad of red and white Chairman Mao decorated bills on his desk. "You're in luck, I just went to the bank," he said. "Rent's due."

"Thanks." I smiled.

"Do you want me to come with you?" He looked worried.

"No, you stay with the kids. I'll be fine."

He nodded slowly. "Do you need a ride to the train station?"

"How'd you guess?"

"Cinderella can take you. He bought a new electric bike last week. Didn't you, Cindy?" He leaned back and looked at the man sitting at the desk next to him.

Cinderella nodded happily. "It has pedals plus battery, great for hills!"

I stood and dropped my hands onto my hips. "We need to go fast, does your new bike go fast?"

"Very fast, very fast," he said, nodding enthusiastically.

Fast is a relative term, of course, but considering the traffic and coupled with the fact that he seemed to prefer driving on sidewalks, it was by far the quickest mode of travel at that juncture. As soon as he pulled up to the train station, I kissed him on the cheek and said, "You've always been my favorite princess." Then I hopped off and ran toward the entrance.

56.

"*Qǐng gěi wǒ yī zhāng Yī diǎn wǔshí fēn de guǎngzhōu gāotiě chēpiào.*"
One ticket to Guangzhou, 1:50 bullet train, please.

"*Tóu děng, èr děng háishì sān děng?*" First, second, or third class?

I did a quick calculation, then patted the lump in my pocket.
"Tou deng," I said, feeling energized. My plan was unfolding
perfectly.

Because without even looking at the type of train that left at
7:18 a.m., I knew Mr. Han hadn't taken a bullet train. The cost
differential would have been too much for him. Mr. Han may have
been wealthy—I didn't have a clue, and I didn't care—but like
most Chinese people from his generation, regardless of his bank
balance, he was frugal, frugal being a nice way to say excruciat-
ingly tight.

I also knew, from my transportation lesson with Katie, that the
best way from Shanghai to Guilin was through Guangzhou, and the
bullet train from Shanghai to Guangzhou took nine hours. The slow
train, on the other hand, took twenty-five hours, with no heat or
AC, sometimes no seats, and shared space with livestock. But that
wouldn't have deterred Mr. Han. He would be sitting in the least
expensive seat available, no matter how terrible. I would beat him to
Guangzhou with time to spare, maybe even enough time for a foot
massage near the train station. I figured there had to be a massage

parlor near there, and my poor feet had just been pummeled by my speedy cross-town dash in knock-off Ugg boots.

I would meet Mr. Han as he disembarked in Guangzhou with a pack of wet wipes, a steamy dumpling, and a ticket back to Shanghai. This would not be his season to pull a vanishing act.

57.

Twenty hours later in Guangzhou, Mr. Han walked toward me on the train platform looking disoriented, which was understandable considering his likely horrendous journey and minimal, if any, sleep. But still, my chest tightened with fret when I saw him.

He looked even more ancient than usual and extremely feeble. He didn't seem to recognize me, and I wasn't sure if he even knew where he was. He looked downward and leaned heavily on his cane, clutching a beat-up leather satchel with his other hand. His clothes looked like they'd been pulled from either side in an extended tug-of-war match that ended in a draw.

I ran up to him and took his hand. He didn't stop. "Mr. Han, it's me." I squeezed his hand. No acknowledgment. "Mr. Han, It's Tina." Nothing. "Mr. Han, can you see me?" I waved my hand in front of his eyes. No response. "MR. HAN!" I finally yelled into his face. He turned to smile at me but kept shuffling.

"Ting Ting, Nǐ hǎo ma?" he asked casually, like he'd just stepped off a luxury sleeper train from Monaco.

"Mr. Han, are you okay? I'm worried about you; you don't look well."

"I'm a little bit sick," he admitted. "*Yǒu yīdiǎn bú shūfú.*"

"What kind of sick?"

"*Lādùzi*," he grunted. "Diarrhea, from eating too many cold foods and not wearing socks."

I grimaced. "Sometimes, when I have diarrhea, I just tell people I have a stomachache."

"Eh?" He said.

"Never mind."

"I ran out of tea in Fujian Province; I'm very thirsty."

"I have—"

"Good thing there is free water on the next train for Guilin. It leaves soon, I need to get to platform three. Are you coming with me?" he asked.

"No, Mr. Han. I came to collect you and bring you home."

He patted my arm. "Thank you for coming to see me, Ting Ting." He planted his cane to indicate further onward motion.

"MR. HAN!" I yelled again. He kept walking until I stood in his path. "LOOK!" I held up two bags. He stopped to survey my offerings. "I brought tea for you. And baozi. They even had carrot and leek."

He stopped as he reached me. "That is very kind of—"

"I don't want you to die," I blurted. "Please, don't go to Guilin. It's not your season! I need you to come home with me."

He shook his head.

"Even your miserable sister wants you home!" I begged.

He smiled and cocked his head. "I can't go home until I visit my ancestors."

"Please," I pleaded. "Just sit and talk with me for a few minutes and drink your tea."

"*Méiyǒu kòng*." He moved to step around me and continue to shuffle forward.

"Don't you want your baozi?" I hollered after him.

He didn't turn.

"Fine, be stubborn! But you won't win today, Mr. Han; I'm not following you!"

He didn't make it very far until I bounded several steps in his direction and turned to walk backward next to him.

"Never mind, you win, I'm coming, okay?"

He turned his head and twinkled his eyes at me like a naughty little kid. "You will love my village," he said, and bowed his head, as though he knew I would be joining him all along.

After an extended debate, he finally caved and allowed me to upgrade his ticket from Guangzhou to Guilin from the car boasting the worst possible conditions in the history of locomotives, to the class I'll call not-great-but-also-not-terrible. The fare difference? Seventeen dollars per ticket. The cheap and atrocious car was packed wall-to-wall with people and who knows what else. Our car was empty except for us. This allowed him the space to lie down, across three hard plastic seats, using his bag as a pillow on the seat closest to the aisle. I did the same, dropping my head onto my balled-up sweatshirt on the aisle seat across from him.

I was about to launch into my story, how Daniel and I had decided to move home because life was too hard here, but part of me didn't want to admit it because it felt like I was giving up. I wanted to tell him that I was sorry to disappoint him, that I'd miss our times at Mt. Trashmore, but who knows, maybe I'd continue my tai chi practice back home in between the frenetic juggle of work and family. But before I could begin, his soft snores reached my ears. I glanced over at him. His lips fluttered with each exhale. I sighed and sat up, unwinding my sweatshirt and laying it carefully over his torso. Then I scooted over to look out the window. In a few short hours, we'd be in Guilin.

The burial ground of Mr. Han's ancestors was about fifty miles south of Guilin, near Yang Shuo. Mr. Han insisted we complete the final leg of our journey by boat. I didn't question him. After watching him sleep for the entirety of the last train trip and then snort awake with a clear sense of purpose, I resigned myself to the fact that this was his journey, and I was along for the ride until I could turn him around and guide him safely home. I would soak in my time with him, watch him execute his pilgrimage, and only step in when it was imperative for me to do so. I would be the sweeper to his curling stone, mostly gliding alongside, only skating in to madly wield my broom when I needed to alter the course, speed things up, or head off disaster.

Before leaving the train station, we stopped at the minimart near the exit. The lights were off, so I wasn't sure if it was open, but once my eyes adjusted, I saw a woman in a red jumper that matched the sign out front slumping behind the counter. Mr. Han approached her. After a heated negotiation, he pulled a few rumpled bills from his pocket and she reached into the glass counter to grab a single stick of incense, three mandarin oranges, and a rubber-banded two-inch stack of square yellow paper, each piece the thickness of a phone book page. She put these items into a small plastic bag which he stuffed into his satchel.

"Donuts!" I exclaimed, pointing at a package of six round, powdered pastries. "Are we going to eat soon?"

"Maybe on raft there will be food."

"Raft? What raft?"

He grunted as he wrestled with the zipper on his bag. I quickly bought the donuts and two bottles of water, unsure of the food prospects on the adventure awaiting us.

I slept for the entire four-hour raft segment of our journey. Whether it was the sound of the river lapping against the bamboo planks, the tap and squeak of the planks as they rubbed against each other, the chatter of our captain with the other fishermen, or the aroma of petroleum as it overpowered my oxygen supply, as soon as my head hit the armrest, I fell into a heavy slumber that could have gone on for days but came to an abrupt end when the boat captain kicked my lawn chair and yelled, "*Dào le!*" I stood in a daze, pulled my sweatshirt down from my ribs, and wiped the wetness from the left side of my face.

Mr. Han looked at me and smiled as the captain helped him onto the dock. "Nice sleeping," he said once he found his footing on land.

"Thank you." I rubbed my eyes and cleared my throat as I stepped next to him. "I'm not sure I've ever been complimented on my sleep before."

Then I looked up and stopped in my tracks. "*Wo cao!*" F-ing awesome! I said as I took in the spectacular scenery surrounding me: the dramatic Karst mountains surrounded by low subtropical greenery punctuated by the glowing verdancy of newly sprouted rice paddies. The peaceful, majestic Li River flowed to our left, a small dirt path leading to a quaint village to our right. Even without the lovely light of dusk, this would have been a stunning view. This was what I'd wished China had looked like when I'd dreamed my best dreams before arriving. This was a distant cry from Shanghai.

Mr. Han watched me crane my neck like an owl sitting front row at an Imax movie. "I told you you would like my village," he said and then tapped his cane. "Now we walk."

"Can't it wait?" I cried. "I mean, don't you want to rest here for a minute? Maybe we can eat something? Doesn't your bag feel heavy? I think you should put your bag down for a short while. Seriously."

"My bag not heavy. No more rest, we both sleep on raft. Hotels this time of year too expensive. We visit ancestors, then eat traditional food. Get on 10 p.m. bus to go back to train station. Go home. *Huí jiā*."

"Okay," I grumbled like a spoiled child. Although I'd just heard him acknowledge his intention to return home from this trip, which was a huge relief, I wanted to extend our stay for a while. This place was too beautiful to rush out of. But since this was not my trip, I made a mental note to come back here before leaving China with Daniel and the girls. Then I bowed and said, "Whatever you say; I'm following you."

Forty minutes later, we arrived at the burial ground. It was lovely and green, tucked into the base of the sheer sided mountains. The air smelled faintly of incense. Low trees were interspersed with blocks of marble covered in chiseled characters and patches of moss.

Mr. Han knew exactly where to go. He wove in between stones, finally stopping in front of a carved block of marble that stood about four feet high and eight feet long. He brushed two leaves from the top of the slab and then slid off his satchel and placed it where the leaves had been. He pulled out the plastic bag from the train station, and arranged the three oranges and the stick of incense a few feet away from his bag with the tip of the incense hanging over the edge, which he lit. Next, he took out the stack of rubber-banded papers and set them at the base of the stone. He fished a tiny firecracker and a lighter out of his front pocket. He squatted and set the firecracker in front of the paper and then lit it. *Snap!* It flamed out immediately. Then he lit the bottom of the stack of paper. He remained squatting for a while, watching the paper as it burned, then he reached out for the wall to help him slowly return to standing. He turned to look at me.

"*Hǎo le*." He nodded. "Looks good."

"Yes," I said, not sure what "good" meant in this situation.

"We can go now," he said.

"Seriously?" I looked around. "That's it? After we came all this way?"

He nodded.

"Don't you at least want to sing your ancestor's favorite song? Or make a speech? Or cry?"

He looked at his watch, then shook his head. "No, now we eat. Must be on bus before 10!"

He turned to walk back toward the entrance. I grumbled and rubbed my fingers through my knotted hair and followed him.

It was already 8:30 p.m. when we walked into a box-shaped, non-descript restaurant. Only one table had patrons.

"Why don't we go to a restaurant down the street that looks busier? Empty restaurants make me nervous."

"Not enough time," he said. "And this place has dinner special."

"Oh. What's the special?"

He shrugged. "Local food."

"I saw a bucket of snails in the window," I said.

"Maybe snails then."

I admitted to myself that if there was ever a time that I would eat something that pushed the boundaries of my comfort zone, this would be that time. The three donuts on the train were ghosts of distant past and my stomach was making noises loud enough to be mistaken for a rabid animal under the table. But I also didn't want to be sick for our long journey home. This was the fine line I considered as our snails were served. I took a quick, tiny bite of a (snotty, salty) snail and then sucked down two bowls of rice followed by two scoops of green tea ice cream.

"Mr. Han, I want to tell you something," I said once the ice cream was demolished.

"Mm," he said. "Hurry, must leave soon."

"That's exactly what I wanted to tell you. I'm leaving soon. But not from this restaurant. From China."

He looked at me, confused, and said nothing.

"In three months or so, we're moving back home."

"You have more work," he said.

"I know. I'm not leaving tomorrow."

"You've only just started to improve."

I laughed. "It's a stretch to believe I've made any improvement."

He scowled at me, like he was trying to figure something out. Then he slowly stood. "*Jiǔ diǎn bàn. Xiànzài wǒmen xūyào qù gōng gòng qì chē zhàn.*" It's 9:30. Now we must go to the bus station.

It was time to commence the first leg of our restful journey home. Or so we thought.

59.

The two-hour bus ride back to Guilin City was crowded and smelly but otherwise a non-event. The train ride, however, was another story.

"*Gù zhàng le*," Mr. Han said after consulting with several uniformed people at the train station.

"'Gu zhang le' meaning what? Is something broken?"

"The train is broken." He shrugged. He didn't look ruffled by this breaking news.

My good sportsmanship, on the other hand, had soured. My jovial, I'm-just-along-for-the-ride attitude had clocked out for the night. "Shit!" I cried. "What time does the next train leave?"

"No more trains tonight," he said, scratching his chin.

"What do you mean, no more trains? That can't be right."

"Can be right. Next train 7 a.m."

"Will they put us in a hotel until then?" I sputtered.

"No, too late. Hotels all closed for night."

"Then what do we do?"

"We wait," he said.

"Where?" I looked around. "There are no benches at this station."

He followed my gaze, nodding, saying nothing.

"Don't you have any friends or relatives around here?"

He shook his head. "All dead," he said. "That's why I must come."

"That would be the reason I wouldn't come," I mumbled.

"Eh?"

"Never mind. What do we do? I'm tired, I'm filthy, and what am I even saying? You need to rest. You've been sick! We can't stand here all night, and we can't rest sitting against a wall—we'll catch hepatitis! I've only been vaccinated against the first two letters of the alphabet, Mr. Han! There could be Hep L, M, N, O, and P out here!" I shrieked, clutching each side of my head.

He paused for a long while, which I took to mean he wasn't going to answer. Until he did. "We will walk to the park," he said calmly and planted his cane.

"But why? What's at the park?" I asked as he led us down the first of several dark streets. "And what do we do when we get there? What purpose does this serve?" I cried into the night.

He ignored me, and I stumbled after him.

"We're absolutely lost. We walked by that gray building before—I recognize the rust pattern on the blue gate in front of it."

"The park is still this way," he insisted. "*Yi zhe zou.*"

I shook my head and marched up to a policeman on the opposite corner. "Why won't men admit it when they're lost?" I asked him in English.

"*Shénme?*" he said. What?

I sighed. "*Bu hao yì si, gong yuan zai na li?*" Excuse me, where is the park?

"*Nǎge gōng yuán?*" What park?

"*Zuijin de yige!*" The closest one!

"*Zuìjìn de ma? Nà dàgài shì qīxīng gōng yuán. Jìxù wǎng nà'er zǒu.*" The closest one? That's probably Seven Stars Park. Continue that way. She pointed in the direction Mr. Han was walking.

I stepped next to him and said nothing. He didn't rub it in.

Then it started to rain, and I burst into a fit of laughter.

"It's good to laugh," he said.

"I'm laughing because this situation has become comical! You can't tell me that walking in the rain—away from our destination—is a good idea."

"It's a very good idea, Tina."

"But why? How are you so certain this is right? The right path, the right way, the right time to be moving this direction, when every indication says otherwise?"

"I know this is the right path because this is the path we're on. I know it's the right time because the time is now. I know this is the right direction because I am listening."

I stopped and threw up my hands. "Listening to what?"

"To the truth," he said, rubbing a small circle on his chest with two fingers.

"To the truth," I repeated with raised eyebrows.

"Mm. And if you can be still in your body long enough, you will hear it, too."

I paused for a moment, then started walking again. "All I hear is the slap of raindrops hitting sidewalk turds," I muttered.

"Eh?"

"Nothing. Look! A grocery store."

"Eh?"

"There aren't too many grocery stores above ground in Shanghai. And this one's even open twenty-four hours. That's not so common there, either. It's an observation, Mr. Han. See? I must be somewhat still in my body or I wouldn't be paying attention enough to notice that." I made a mental note to stop at that store for train snacks on the way back. Anything I bought at this point would get soggy, and I was looking forward to biting into something crisp when I finally arrived in the sleeper car I was splurging for, for the two of us on both legs of our homebound journey. Mr. Han didn't know it yet, but our ride home would be a welcome, sleep-filled break after this wet all-nighter.

I just hoped he had the stamina to make it until morning. Because while I wanted to protest our ridiculous walk-about in the rain for obvious reasons, there was a reason I hadn't wanted to hammer on and on about it, because drawing attention to it might make it worse. Mr. Han had slowed down significantly, and I was worried; he was looking weaker and paler as the night dragged on.

"Shouldn't we take a break in this doorway for a bit, just until the rain slows down?"

He looked at me and, for a moment, I thought he might agree. But then his vision focused on something beyond me. "There it is," he said softly. "I recognize the large rock."

Sure enough, the park was there, straight ahead of us.

60.

Qixin Gong Yuan was huge and surrounded by a tall gate that appeared locked, but when Mr Han pushed on the turnstile, it spun with little resistance. Although the rain had stopped, I could see a few awnings, trees and other areas with coverage inside the gate, so I didn't question him about entering a place that appeared to be closed for the night.

A woman in a thin brown sweater stepped through the turnstile behind us and scurried down a smaller side path into the darkness. *She must know a good place to stay dry*, I thought. I considered suggesting to Mr. Han that we follow her, but as we walked into the first clearing, I heard myself exclaim, "Wow!" instead. Because even in the rainy dark, I could see this place was enchanting.

"This is way more than a park, Mr. Han."

"Yes," he cleared his throat. "It was deemed by the government to also be a scenic area."

"Psh," I scoffed. "That makes it sound like a place where you'd stop to use the restroom. This is more like a nature preserve. It's so beautiful. Did you come here when you were young?"

He nodded. "This is where my grandfather taught me tai chi, the first place I felt its power."

He closed his eyes and took a deep breath.

"That's nice," I said, smiling, feeling happy for him to be in a

292

place with such memories. "I take back what I said before, I'm glad you brought me here."

He continued to breathe deeply.

"Do you think there's a bench under a tree where we can sit?"

His eyes flipped open. "First I must show you Flower Bridge."

"Sure, okay," I said, scrunching up my face. "But I think you should rest soon." Even though it seemed highly unlikely that he was stalling for any particular reason, I couldn't help wondering, *what is he up to?* But then I decided that was ridiculous. Mr. Han was simply trying to maximize his time at home and see his favorite places. That made more sense than some conspiracy theory I was concocting because I was wet and tired, and my brain was overloaded and glitching.

Be still in this moment, Tina, I scolded myself. *Let him enjoy his time, we'll be home soon enough.*

"Look. Over the edge, into the water," he said once we arrived on the bridge.

I leaned over the side, not sure what I was looking for.

"Do you see the reflection of the arches?"

"I do."

"See how reflection looks like full moon?"

"Yes."

"Tonight is a full moon. But even when it isn't, the reflection of the arches always shows us a full moon."

I stood up, suddenly curious. "Did you know it would be a full moon tonight?"

"Of course," he said. "Now walk with me across to the other side of the bridge."

"Okay, but—"

"There are many places to rest where we're going," he said.

"Now you're talking," I said.

As we reached the far side of the bridge, I pointed at the pagoda straight ahead of us. "The moon makes that pagoda look like it's glowing."

"Mm," he said. "This is pagoda where my grandfather would meet his many warrior friends for tai chi. Here is where they practiced to become strong, focused, and aware."

"I see."

"It is also where I discovered my rooting."

"That's amazing."

Then he stepped away and turned to face me. "Go through the sequence with me, Ting Ting. Show me what you've learned. I want to see if I have been an adequate teacher."

"Mr. Han, my tai chi practice is not a reflection of your teaching ability."

"Shh, Ting Ting. Be quiet now. You must be still. Listen."

"Alright, but as you know I have a hard time quieting my mind and—"

"I know, Ting Ting. Now stop talking and listen."

"But I want you to know that I sincerely appreciate all of your efforts, and I hope—"

"Ting-ah Mah-ting! Your grandfather says BE SILENT!" He said gruffly and then cleared his throat again.

I was so surprised by his attempt at my American name, and also by his tone, that I didn't push back. Instead I did what he directed: I shut my mouth and began my tai chi sequence. I continued to think about the myriad things I wanted to share with him but said nothing. And as a result, I heard many things: the river under the bridge softly lapping on the sandy banks and back on itself. The rushing of the central flow and the bubbling of the water that circled the pillars. Frogs called, insects buzzed, and leaves rustled as the breeze gently blew between them.

The temperature was perfect against my skin as I dipped and turned and shifted my balance. I felt less jerky than usual, more peaceful somehow. I was less aware of how my clothes pulled as I moved, unbothered by the squeak of my wet shoes as I turned. The various itches and areas of bodily soreness weren't presenting themselves, and I wasn't sure why. Maybe it was the beautiful setting, or the numbing effect of our long journey. Maybe it was the rawness of my recent loss, or the softer sadness I felt for our upcoming departure from China. My sequence felt different at that moment. I moved with a level of calmness that I'd never felt before. Instead of feeling stiff and unnatural, I was light and smooth, as though the sequence was moving through me instead of the opposite.

Then I heard it—a small sound so clear, so unmistakable that I immediately jumped out of my stance and sprinted back across the bridge toward it.

61.

She was crying like the days-old infant she was, tucked into a basket under a willow tree by the beginning rise of the bridge, near where I'd leaned over to admire the false moon reflection. Swaddled tightly in a purple and green checkered blanket, she wore a hand-knit, pale-pink cap pulled low over her ears and brow.

An unexpected wave of calm washed over me as I crouched down next to her. "Well, who do we have here?" I said in the soft, high voice I adopted whenever I spoke to babies. I leaned over to pull her carefully out of the basket and cradle her in my arms. She quieted down immediately. "Where'd your mama go?"

I peered into the basket to see if it held any clues. There was a full bottle of milk and a note in characters that I couldn't read. I closed my eyes and held her closer, because I could guess what it said.

"Mr. Han?" I turned to look and see if he'd followed me, but instead of my friend I saw a different figure approaching. A policeman. The same one who'd directed me to the park earlier.

My internal frenzy immediately returned.

"Ohshitohshitohshitohshitbecalmbecalmbecalmbecalm," I muttered under my breath. "Whatever you do, don't act like you've just stolen a baby. Be natural, Tina, be still. Breathe."

As the officer stepped off the path and walked toward us with a purposeful stride, I had the wherewithal to reach into the basket, crumple the note, and jam it into the back pocket of my jeans.

His frown reached me first. It spoke volumes. I don't remember the actual words we exchanged—it was all such a panicky blur! But I remember thinking I needed to get us out of there as he bent down to inspect the basket. He held up the bottle of milk and looked at me. Then he stood again and, with increased volume to his commentary, reached for her.

I turned to run, even though I knew I couldn't get away from him and protect her at the same time. I paused, briefly considering kicking him in the shins to get a head start but decided I couldn't risk the potential (likely) loss of balance. So instead I turned back and faced him straight on, frozen. Inside my head I vowed to bite him hard if he reached for her again, hard enough to leave teeth behind if I had to. They were my only feasible weapon and, at this juncture, expendable. He would regret not donning his white uniform gloves today.

Then I heard another noise, this one harder to decipher.

It was faint—a high pitched ringing, almost like I was eavesdropping on someone else's tinnitus. Then the policeman waved his arms spastically and stumbled away from me.

I turned toward the ringing sound, and there, in the center of the bridge, stood Mr. Han. He looked so strong then, so powerful, with his back straight, his chin high and legs planted, I wouldn't have recognized him if I hadn't known it was him. His arms were pushing as they would in our tai chi sequence, but this time they were also slowly pulsating as though they were shifting energy. And every time Mr. Han pushed at the air, the policeman staggered away from us, from me and the baby. The officer tried again and again to advance, to no avail. He continued lurching backward.

"Come toward me, Tina," Mr. Han commanded in English, in a voice deeper and louder than usual. I snatched the bottle from the ground where the officer had dropped it and crammed it into my sweatshirt pocket. I cradled the baby against my chest and quickly walked to the bridge. Once I reached Mr. Han, his voice switched back to soft and low. "Now, go to the train station. Be sure to walk on the side of the street without lights."

"But—"

"I'll be right behind you, don't worry. I'll meet you there. Hurry!" I nodded and walked at a clip toward the park exit. I didn't turn back.

I didn't dare look left or right until I got to the grocery store, and once there I bee-lined around back to the delivery entrance which was steeped in darkness. I walked up the short, steep ramp and backed into a corner of the entryway. I waited there several minutes to see if anyone had followed me. The coast appeared clear.

I looked down and whispered, "I'm so glad you're sleeping, Baby. I know you'll want your bottle soon, but I need to make a quick phone call so keep your peepers closed for a few more minutes okay?"

I wasn't expecting a response, but I still felt like she deserved an update. I sat down cross-legged, grabbed my phone from my pocket, and dialed Katie.

After four rings, her voicemail picked up.

"Katie! It's me, Tina. I need your help, it's urgent! Please call me back."

I immediately redialed and left that same message again. And again. And again. Finally, she picked up.

"Why must you torture me?" she moaned groggily.

"Katie! I found a baby."

She groaned. "Today's my day off."

"Sorry about the timing, I wasn't looking for her, I just—"

"Ugh. Where are you?"

"In Guilin."

"Mm. Lovely mountains there."

"Katie! What the heck do I do now?"

"About what?"

"About this baby! I can't leave her here; I don't know what will happen to her!"

"Well, you can't bring her out of Guilin," she scolded. "We don't have a license to operate in that province. If you take her, it's highly illegal. You could be—"

"Katie, listen to me—there's an angry police officer out there who's onto me, and I can't hand her over to him. I'm not leaving her, I've already decided."

"And you're sure she was abandoned?"

"Yes. I'm ninety-eight percent sure."

She sighed. "First thing is to clear up the other two percent."

"And I will do that." I felt in my back pocket to make sure the note was still there.

"Okay, good. Now then, is the baby defective?"

"What?"

"Because even if we could assume a license to operate in that province, we don't have the type of license that allows us to assume control of abandoned children without deformities."

"I can't even believe you're saying this."

"If she has no health issues whatsoever you need to turn her over to authorities, Tina. There is a process—"

"But that's ridiculous when I'm here right now and I can help her! I'm supposed to help her, Katie. Her mama must have seen me. She put her in a place where I would find her first, I just know it. She could have put her in the path of the policeman. She could have left her at the door of the hospital. Or dropped her into the river! But she didn't. She put her right where I would find her, so I'm in charge of her well-being now."

Katie paused. "Well you should look closer then," she said quietly.

"Excuse me?"

LINDSEY SALATKA

"For deformities."

"What is wrong with you?"

"It's the only way. Start with her feet."

I wanted to reach through the phone and strangle her.

"Fine, I'll count her toes," I grumbled. I carefully unswaddled her on my lap. She whimpered and turned her head a couple times, then fell back asleep. She was wearing tiny pink snap-front pjs that ended at the ankle and white socks, which I slowly peeled off. Ten shiny little piggies stared back at me.

"Do you see any problems?"

I didn't answer as I tried to think of what to do next.

"Is there a club foot?"

"Uh—"

"Tina, you need to give her over to—"

Then I noticed a faint scratch on the inside of her right ankle, about a centimeter long, probably caused by the sheer, tiny toenail tip I could see dangling from the big toe of her other foot.

"Oh. Uh oh," I said, inhaling sharply through my teeth.

"What? What is it?"

"I found something pretty serious."

"You did? What?"

"I can't really describe—eek. It's—I think you're gonna need to see it."

"Is it an open wound?"

"Uh-huh—it looks bad."

"How bad?"

"Very bad."

Right then the baby started to cry. I nearly squeezed her with pride. *Thank you, Baby!* I wanted to say. *Such a team player!* Then I picked her up and rocked her to quiet down again.

"Very well then, the procedure is for you to wait at the abandonment location for two hours, in case the mom has a change of heart."

"Unfortunately, I can't wait. This injury is far too serious."

"But——"

"I'll wait at the train station; the mom can look for me there," I said.

She sighed. "When will you arrive back in Shanghai?"

"I'm one day out. Hopefully."

"Okay. Call me when you're close. I'll send the van to the train station to collect you."

"Thanks, Katie."

"Of course, no problem. Are you at the station now?"

"Not yet, I'm waiting for someone, then I'll go directly there," I said.

"Alright. Hey, nice job."

"With what?"

"You're already good at your position. No training even!"

"But I'm . . ." I started and then stopped.

"What?"

"Never mind. See you soon."

62.

I found Mr. Han curled in a ball on the bank of the river, near the trunk of an Evergreen tree. He was snoring so loud I couldn't have missed him. I could hear both his inflow and outflow from the middle of the bridge.

I squatted down and touched his head. It was cold. "Mr. Han, are you okay? Mr. Han, wake up."

He blinked his eyes open and smiled at me. "Oh, hi Ting Ting. Where is your baby?"

"Not *my* baby, this baby, who I'm taking care of until I can get her to a safe, loving, long-term solution, is in here, sleeping." I pointed to the sling across my chest which I'd fashioned out of a long off-white cotton tablecloth I'd just bought at the grocery store.

"Mm. *Hen guāi bǎobǎo,*" he said and closed his eyes again.

"Mr. Han, why didn't you go to the train station? I've been so worried, I—"

"I needed to rest."

"But we have to leave soon. You could have taken a taxi and rested on the train."

"Mm. Always so logical. Very practical. Quite efficient! But sometimes sleep must come first. Not optional. Not logical."

I sighed and tapped his forearm. "Come on, I'll help you up. Our train is leaving soon. I have a taxi waiting out front."

He didn't move. "You could have left without me. I can get home."

"Don't be silly! I would never leave without you. You saved me! And you saved her." I pointed at the lump in the sling. "She says thank you, by the way."

He still didn't move.

"Come on, now it's my turn to save you," I said softly, poking his shoulder with my index finger.

"But I don't need saving. I am home here and in Shanghai. It doesn't matter where I am, Ting Ting. I am always home."

I sighed and looked at the river. I noticed the slow swirls close to the bank were dotted with tadpoles. Small pools were forming and then running together as the water ebbed and flowed, continuously changing the pattern of the swirls while the frogs-to-be swam furiously, trying to anchor themselves to anything that wasn't moving, which was nothing.

"I'm such a tadpole," I muttered to myself.

"Eh?"

"Mr. Han, would you translate something for me?" I asked as I pulled the rumpled note out of my back pocket and held it out to him.

He took it and unfolded it. "It says, 'Love her like your own.'"

I dropped my head into my hands. I felt happy and sad, full and empty. Brave and terrified, overwhelmed and yet still searching for more, more, more. I stayed like that for a while, letting the feelings wash over me, noticing when they came and when they left, only to be replaced by more thoughts, added fears, and my typical corresponding emotions. I recognized that this was probably much like any minute in any other day, but also that this moment was unique because, for what felt like the first time, I was sitting with my thoughts and feelings in observation. They were not large, heavy rocks tied to my ankles as I tried to forge a river much deeper and wider than the one in front of me. I raised my head and looked at him.

"Three questions," I said.

"*Wèn ba*," he said and nodded.

"What if the policeman comes back?"

He shook his head. "He poses no threat."

I paused. "Why? Did you hurt him? That is part two of the first question, by the way."

"No, no, he is too full of fear to advance on us again." He chuckled.

"Question two: Why didn't you tell me you had superpowers? That would have been useful information a long time ago."

"I don't have superpower, I can harness energy. This I already told you many times. But only here was there an opportunity to demonstrate."

I paused for a moment to consider this and decided to temporarily withhold comment. "Question three: Is it too late for me to change my mind and stay? I don't want to go home anymore. I want to stay in China for ten thousand reasons that weren't clear until this moment." I looked up at him.

He shrugged. "You and your family have the answer to this question. I know just this simple answer." He struggled to sit up and then he grabbed both of my hot, sweaty hands in his dry, cold, and shaky ones. He carefully placed my hands on the center of my chest one on top of the other. "Can you feel this? Do you hear it? This is your home. Not this," he said, tapping on my forehead. "You have lived here long enough. It is time to move home, Ting Ting. But it doesn't matter whether you stay in China or you move to the US. *Méi guānxì.* In either place your home will be with you."

I closed my eyes and remained still until I could detect my heartbeat. Then I blinked my eyes back open and smiled. "Okay," I whispered.

He chuckled. "Now help me up. We don't want to miss the train. Since I've been away for more than one day, my sister will make me something delicious for dinner. This answer, I know."

I stood up and he raised his hands to mine. I pulled him gently, letting him do most of the work. Once he was standing on his own,

I let go of his hands and walked around him, combing his hair down with my fingers, sweeping the dirt from his shirt and pants, and then holding my hands away from him and clapping, forming dust clouds.

Then I stood next to him and held out my hand for him to grab so we could walk side by side together, out of the park and back to our lives.

"I wish I had superpowers," I mumbled as I pulled open the fold of the tablecloth to make sure Baby's position had not shifted. She was sleeping peacefully. I sighed and smiled as Mr. Han took my other hand in his and squeezed it.

"You do, Ting Ting," he said. "You already do."

ACKNOWLEDGMENTS

This book would not exist without the help of many, many people—some of whom lived the stories with me, some of whom supported my efforts to create them out of thin air, and others of whom weren't part of my life in Shanghai or my life as a writer but had everything to do with hoisting me off the ground and propping me up so I could bring this book to life. To all of you listed below and to those I have missed but who know you belong here, I humbly bow in gratitude.

I'll start with my Shanghai friends. I heap many apologies for all I've left out. It's been a few years, and my memory—it's an issue. Suzanne Freeman and Rick Cooper, you saved our lives countless times and brought much-needed perspective. Bart and Nora Salatka, we're so lucky to call you both family and friends and for our Shanghai stories, such as the OG Mr. Tinsey, Mutton Roganjosh, the silver outfits (and matching eyebrows!), the pig face, and *Wo zhu ni la du zi*. Andy Tainton and Fiona Hewitt—our kid put your kid in a headlock. Then they switched places. Sonya and Stuart MacAusland—your hospitality held no bounds and you kicked my ass in squash. Josefin and Adam Ashe, Emma Longworth and Jonathan Herron, Gabi and Chantal Kool, Andrea Kennedy and Dane Chomorrow, Melanie and Lee Brantingham, Angela and Jeff MacDonald, Kathryn Ferb and William Silsby, Heidi Berry and

Scott Shimizu—freaking hilarious doesn't begin. Aisling and Geoff and your three amazing offspring—we've no doubt been friends for many lives. Katie Liu, best tutor EVER. Mr. Han and all ayis, WE MISS YOU. To all at Tiny Tots, Victoria Kindergarten, Mother Goose, and YCIS staff—thank you for a mostly wonderful and definitely unforgettable educational experience.

To my writing community: Marni Freedman, where do I even begin? Writing coach and savant extraordinaire, talent like yours is rare indeed. Feisty Writers—at this point you are more family than writing group, yet your input is how most things I create move forward (I'll go in room order-ish at Barb's): Marni Freedman, Nancy Villalobos, Nicola Ranson, Suzanne Spector, Barbara Thompson, Anastasia Zadeik, Phyllis Olins, Kimberly Joy, Donna Brown Agins, Tanya Pryputniewicz, Jen Laffler, Gina Simmons Schneider, KM McNeel, Elizabeth Eshoo, and Andrea Moser. To Marcy Mills, Janis Tan, Nancy Johnson, and Tracy Jean Jones, I can't thank you and your wise editing eyes enough. To beta-readers Marijke McCandless, Becca Karpinski, Tomira Baca-Craig, Phyllis Olins, and Anastasia Zadeik, I am forever indebted. I am in awe of my She Writes publishing team, especially Brooke Warner, Shannon Green, Elisabeth Kauffman, Katherine Lloyd, and Rebecca Lown. Thank you to Andrea Kiliany Thatcher, Marissa Eigenbrood, and the team at Smith Publicity. Thank you to Hannah Baker for your voice (literally) and Emily Powers, Becky Parker Geist, and the team at Pro Audio Voices. Thank you to Bruce Fehlan at Barefoot Story for your tech help and website expertise.

To those on the inside: my husband Ed goes first. Thank you for giving me the time to write when we had three small humans at home. I don't know how you did it, but you believed in me and supported this dream no matter what. Our kids, of course, were co-conspirators and thankfully only exhibited their best behavior when they were home with their dad. BAHAHA! But really, our kids are wonderful, and I am so delighted by these humans we created who seem, at this point, to have inherited only the best genes from us and none of the jacked up stuff. Well done, smalls! Thanks to Jay Jones, too, for being amazing and being you.

To Paul Chen, Tiffany Kao, and Ed Franqui for your guidance and help. To Francine Hardaway, who was with me at the start of this journey and has supported me all along. To my lifelong BFFs, Staci Stompoly, Wendy Mulvihill, Jen Sayre, and Lori Logan—I love you. Period, end of story.

Now to my family. Thank you, Dad and Kathy, I love you both and am so glad you found each other. Thank you to Aunt Susan and Uncle Jim for housing me and feeding me and gently calling me on my teenage angsty stuff, and to all of my wonderful aunts and uncles and cousins, whom I feel so lucky to have. Thank you especially to my brother, Tommy, who has always been by my side and is the best human I know.

Finally, thank you to my mom, Lucie, who left far too early and, in that, set my writing back in motion. When I was a young adult and just out of college, I would often call my mom to unload about some drama or another and she would say, "This sounds like great fodder!" At the time, this response didn't always soothe me, but it's possible that I now channel this sentiment more often than I should. *This is all fodder* somehow helps me see that life, in all of its wacky turns and occasional dark twists, is actually mostly good and often quite funny.

ABOUT THE AUTHOR

Lindsey Salatka is an author, ghostwriter, and editor. Her writing has been featured at BlogHer and in *Shanghai Family Magazine, Urbanatomy Shanghai,* and *Shaking the Tree: Brazen. Short. Memoir.* She is on the Advisory Board of the San Diego Writers Festival and serves as a judge for the Kids-Write! Children's Writing Contest. Most nights you can find her curled up with her family or musing about life, love, and culture on her blog, *fishheadology,* or on Instagram (@mywhatlovelygillsyouhave). Lindsey lives in San Diego with her family.

SELECTED TITLES FROM SHE WRITES PRESS

She Writes Press is an independent publishing company
founded to serve women writers everywhere.
Visit us at www.shewritespress.com.

This is Mexico: Tales of Culture and Other Complications by Carol M. Merchasin. $16.95, 978-1-63152-962-7. Merchasin chronicles her attempts to understand Mexico, her adopted country, through improbable situations and small moments that keep the reader moving between laughter and tears.

Notes from the Bottom of the World by Suzanne Adam. $16.95, 978-1-63152-415-8. In this heartfelt collection of sixty-three personal essays, Adam considers how her American past and move to Chile have shaped her life and enriched her worldview, and explores with insight questions on aging, women's roles, spiritual life, friendship, love, and writers who inspire.

Accidental Soldier: A Memoir of Service and Sacrifice in the Israel Defense Forces by Dorit Sasson. $17.95, 978-1-63152-035-8. When nineteen-year-old Dorit Sasson realized she had no choice but to distance herself from her neurotic, worrywart of a mother in order to become her own person, she volunteered for the Israel Defense Forces—and found her path to freedom.

Learning to Eat Along the Way by Margaret Bendet. $16.95, 978-1-63152-997-9. After interviewing an Indian holy man, newspaper reporter Margaret Bendet follows him in pursuit of enlightenment and ends up facing demons that were inside her all along.

Nothing But Blue by Diane Lowman. $16.95, 978-1-63152-402-8. In the summer of 1979, Diane Meyer Lowman, a nineteen-year-old Middlebury College student, embarked on a ten-week working trip aboard a German container ship with a mostly male crew. The voyage would forever change her perspective on the world—and her place in it.

Gap Year Girl by Marianne Bohr. $16.95, 978-1-63152-820-0. Thirty-plus years after first backpacking through Europe, Marianne Bohr and her husband leave their lives behind and take off on a yearlong quest for adventure.